FOR THEIR OWN GOOD

Bradette Michel

Harvard Square Editions

New York

2015

Published in the United States by

Harvard Square Editions

www.HarvardSquareEditions.org

ISBN: 978-1-941861-04-2

For Mike

CHAPTER ONE

Dr. McFarland told us we were the only ones who could cure the unfortunates under our care. Our benevolent kindness would lead them to sanity. Our Christian love would break through their irrational actions.

At first I believed him, but it was not long before I learned of unspeakable acts committed on those lost souls. Many nights I returned to my quarters shaking, my skin covered in sweat at the evil I had witnessed in the name of treatment. My time in the asylum overflowed with events I could not have foreseen, events so momentous I was changed forever.

It was 1857—a time when most Americans believed fortune, recognition, and even divine purpose were attainable for young men willing to uproot themselves and travel across the frontier. I was no different from others of my generation, but I did not seek a new life without direction or purpose. I left the home I shared with my sister Sarah in Seneca Falls, New York to accept the position of medical doctor at the Illinois State Hospital for the Insane in Jacksonville, Illinois.

Perhaps my willingness to travel a thousand miles from all I knew was a consequence of my dissatisfaction with a rural physician's life. My duties as Dr. Adam Fletcher offered little fulfillment to me and even less financial security. The practice I shared with my mentor, Dr. Cyrus Peterson never filled my working hours, and I was seldom paid with money. Most of my patients considered vegetables or small game adequate compensation for my services. When they finally did come to me in distress, I knew they had first consulted a grandmother, a midwife, or a peddler for a cure. A doctor was their reluctant last resort.

I understood why they viewed me and those of my profession with suspicion. After all, I did not have much more to offer them than the old remedies they knew so well and yet my methods were decidedly more uncomfortable, if not worse.

Dr. Peterson recognized my ambivalent feelings and advised me not to be timorous. I was to administer our cures no matter how destructive they were to our patients.

Sarah was well-aware of my dissatisfaction with the practice of medicine. She, too, blanched at the practices we doctors used, but she believed my innate concern for humanity was well-served by my role as a physician.

More and more I felt dread when called to remove the body's impurities by slicing a patient's vein to allow blood to drip into a pan, or induce violent vomiting with calomel, or hold heated glass cups at the nape of the neck to raise huge blisters allowing the blood to come to the skin. It was not squeamishness that created my trepidation, but my increasing conviction that these remedies did more harm than good.

Like some physicians of the time I began to experiment with methods many saw as new, but in truth were among the most ancient of remedies. The healing powers of fresh air, proper diet, and public hygiene appealed to me. Even if the effectiveness of these approaches could not be proven, our traditional methods did not lead to recovery with any more certainty.

Dr. Peterson discouraged me from using anything but the most traditional treatments. He believed physicians who used homeopathic techniques were dangerous. "Such witch doctors are not to be trusted. Our patients put their lives in our hands. Would you have them go to someone who refuses to use the most powerful methods available?"

I remained unconvinced.

Perhaps Dr. Peterson's waning patience with my skepticism motivated him to tell me of the need for a physician in the Jacksonville hospital. The superintendent of the asylum, Dr. Andrew McFarland was a member of a progressive group of doctors who specialized in moral treatment, a new remedy for lunacy. Proponents of this approach believed insanity was a result of unbalanced living conditions. Those afflicted with the disease could be cured if they were removed from the unhealthy atmosphere that had created their symptoms and committed to an asylum offering proper nutrition, fresh air, and meaningful work opportunities. All these therapies were to be delivered under the kind treatment of a Christian staff.

I had not been particularly interested in patients who lost their sensibilities, let alone the establishments that housed them, but moral treatment espoused ideas and approaches I found most appealing. The possibility of serving mankind and remaining a doctor changed my initial hesitation about accepting the position into excitement.

In spite of my eagerness to start a new life, my stomach tensed when I boarded the west-bound train that October. I told myself I could disembark at the next station and return, but as the distance from my home grew, my apprehension lessened. I cannot say I pursued the journey with joy; nonetheless, I began to imagine an uncertain future as more heartening than the dissatisfaction that lay behind.

The first day of my trip the well-tilled land outside the train window differed little from the fields surrounding Seneca Falls. Even the passengers who entered and disembarked the car were dressed like those I saw daily, their speech much like mine. We entered Ohio, and I began to see a change in the aspects of many travelers. Their clothes were decidedly rougher, ready for an untamed terrain.

The change in the passengers' appearance was not the only transformation I observed as we moved toward the western horizon. The land flattened and provided never-ending views of an azure sky dotted with huge white clouds. The disconcerting prairie grass grew well over the height of an average man. I found it impossible to imagine how settlers drove their wagons, with livestock and families, through such an unfathomable wasteland.

Occasionally there was a break in the sea of grass and a small group of buildings pushed their roofs above the grain. A hut, dubbed a train station undoubtedly stood at the edge of these structures. Had I been foraging on foot through the ever-present grasses, I might have thought the settlements were mirages, but the outposts were real, usually built near a stand of timber and a stream.

On the third day of travel I spotted an immense cloud on the horizon containing slashes of white light that appeared to emanate from the ground. We drew nearer and saw fires linked to each other, forming a wall of flames. The smoke from the blaze created the rolling darkness I had thought contained a thunderstorm.

A stink assaulted my nose, reminding me of the acrid smell that emanated from the skin of patients I had blistered. I could not imagine how the same odor reached me out here in the prairie until I spotted its source.

Charred, black dirt surrounded the remains of a lonely wagon. The spokes of its wheels lay on the ground next to their axles, attached to nothing. The skeleton of a horse, reeking of flesh and smoke, lay on its side. A metal bit rested inside its jawbones.

The conductor instructed us to keep our windows closed and, if we had kerchiefs, to prepare to put them over our mouths and noses. "Completely safe, ladies and gentlemen. We'll be through it in no time. Prairie fires pretty common this time of year. Besides, the wind's coming from the north. Fire's on the south side of the track. Might be a little uncomfortable with that smell and all."

The whipping wind's ominous growl accompanied a sudden blackness that surrounded us. No sunset could have come so quickly. The line of fires south of the train was the lone break in the gloom. I considered the scene outside the opposite windows. The conductor was right. No flames broke the murky cloud of smoke on the north side of the car.

I pulled the kerchief from my pocket and wiped the beads of sweat from my forehead. My fellow passengers leaned away from their seats, their eyes wide. I was sure the fear I saw in their faces was reflected in my own. How could our train even attempt to forge what looked like one of Dante's circles of Hell?

A glowing ember of grass flew out of the blackness and skimmed the window next to me. I jerked away from the glass and caught my breath. I was sure a mere change in the direction of the wind would put us in harm's way.

We came alongside a log cabin on the edge of the inferno. Men and boys dragged full buckets of water to soak the dwelling, in an attempt to stand up to the mocking blaze. Two small girls and an older woman beat the flames with wet, ragged blankets.

All of us stretched our necks as the train carried us farther from the family's torment. The pursed lips of the men sitting near me and the moist eyes of the female passengers across the aisle revealed that the pioneers' bravery had touched us all.

We stared at the abyss outside our windows until the sky lightened and the odor of burning prairie grass diminished. The dark cloud behind us was barely visible when we slowed to a stop at the Long Point, Illinois station.

The train did not remain long at these depots. Mail was dropped, produce picked up, passengers strolled outside for a short time, just long enough to eat something at the small eateries often located in the buildings. The conductor recommended we close our windows at these locations to keep the horseflies at bay. The swarms were so numerous none of us went outside for very long. Even so, nearly everyone experienced their painful bites at least once.

I looked out my window to see several wagons pulled close to the freight cars in the rear of the train. The browned arms of men dressed in the roughest clothing threw bushels of soybeans into the cars as if they were potatoes being tossed into a stewpot. As a boy I had loved jumping into cut hay on the back of our neighbor's wagon at harvest time. Perhaps this strange breed of farmers was closer to my experience than I expected.

Trees shaded sporadic log cabins with gardens and livestock pens nearby. I was viewing first-hand the settlement of the West, but I still did not grasp the motives behind the pioneers' willingness—no, it must be their compulsion—to put themselves and their dear ones in that pitiless world.

The conductor approached a man and woman sitting in silence on the platform's single bench. He gestured in the train's direction. The couple did not touch or look at each other, but they moved in perfect symmetry to our car.

The woman's dress was clearly homespun. I guessed her traveling attire was her best. A rope inside belt loops held up the man's threadbare pants. Perspiration stains streaked his broad-billed hat just above its rim.

They were not young, yet not of an age at which climbing the train steps was burdensome. The woman took the conductor's extended hand and they boarded, hesitating inside the door to survey the passengers. She shifted her head from side to side to peek out of the edges of her gray bonnet.

The conductor came up behind them. "Take a seat, folks. Gotta keep on schedule."

The man's rail-thin body moved easily between the woman's full skirt and the seats in the first rows. He appraised everyone until his head bent slightly in my direction. His gaze fell on my shoes, rose to my suit and tie, and ended on the black hat I held in my lap. He pointed to the seat facing me. His mouth opened just enough to get his words out, though his voice was easily understood. "This here seat taken?"

I found myself unable to move my stare from his austere face. "No, sir."

The woman glanced over his shoulder in my direction while the man continued his assessment. "You a man of the cloth?"

My collar tightened. "No, sir."

The conductor stood behind the woman. "I have to ask you to take your seats. We need to get movin'."

The man did not seem to notice the increasing interest of the other passengers. "Undertaker?"

"No. I am a medical doctor traveling to take a position in Jacksonville, Illinois." I thought better about bringing up the word insane, to say nothing of the word asylum. I had no idea what the terms would mean to him.

The woman put her hand lightly on his arm. "It's all right, Jacob. Never was a complaint about Doc Wilson."

The man stood next to the empty seat. "Wife's goin' down the line to get to her dyin' sister. Train's lot faster than my wagon. Much obliged if you'd give her any help she might need."

I rose as his spouse sat down across from me, placing a covered basket at her feet. "I will do my best."

He stood up straight and turned to his wife. "I be comin' to pick you up the end of the week. Got a little more corn to get in. Hope your sister's as good as can be expected."

He tipped his hat in my direction. "'Preciate it."

In one motion he headed toward the end of the car and exited the train. He stood on the platform and watched our window until we began to move. Only then did he nod in response to his wife's wave.

The woman peered out the window. "Never seen things from this side before."

My new traveling companion appeared to be of European stock, but her skin was darker than I would have expected from her heritage. She had a worn appearance that made it impossible for me to judge her age or status. Her face exuded an exhausted wariness, as if she knew she could lose everything dear to her at the whim of weather, sickness, or accidental death. I assumed she met the onslaught of such forces with the never-ending work necessary for survival. Her dull eyes showed no curiosity about her surroundings, merely a blank acceptance of whatever befell her.

Her skin appeared unhealthy to me. She moved deliberately, straining to lift her mending as if it were a far heavier burden. I recognized her symptoms and suspected she suffered the fever and chills associated with malaria. I could not help asking about her condition. "How is your health?"

"Feel poorly in the summer. Better in the fall. Ever'body feels that way out here. After you been here a while you git used to the pioneer shakes."

"My patients with your symptoms have been diagnosed with malaria. Is that what pioneer shakes refer to?"

"'Spect so."

"Have you been treated with quinine?"

A slow smile snaked across her face. "You mean Queen Ann?"

"I have heard the treatment called that."

"Doc Wilson's been usin' it on some. My ma don't like it though. She wants us to use snakeroot and yellow birch tea. She learnt her healin' ways from her ma."

I understood her mother's hesitation to consult one of us *regulars*, as we physicians liked to call ourselves. To tell the truth, before we began to give prolonged doses of quinine, we didn't have much to offer for malaria. Our usual therapies seemed to increase our patients' misery. The old-time remedies didn't cure either, but at least they did no harm. Either way, not all died of malaria, but the long-lasting symptoms made the hard work necessary to survive in the plains almost impossible.

Her hands, dotted with corns, reached inside the basket to pull out a needle, thread, and a work shirt with a large tear in the sleeve. "I better commence to patchin' this shirt. Won't have no time for mendin' at my sister's. I'll be busy nursin' her if she survives 'til I git there."

Her complete acceptance of the probability of her sister's death and the necessity of completing her work took me aback. She was traveling to be by her sister's side, expecting little reward for the trip. I needed to know more. "What is your sister's condition?"

"Just delivered another young'un. It weren't turned right an' near tore her apart. She's a might younger than me—ten years. Her oldest rode over to tell me she's been callin' for me and I better git there quick."

"Has she received medical care?"

The ends of her mouth rose slightly. "Not sure you'd call it medical. Had her husband's ma when it was time. Her boy told me his granny said weren't much she could do for her after the babe came out, 'cept give her a cup of whiskey now and then."

I could not have done much more. "Is the baby healthy?"

She kept her eyes downcast. "Heard so. My sister's boy said she's a tough little one."

The rocking of the train made me sleepy and I nodded off until a bump on the track awakened me. The woman's head remained drooped, her chin touching her chest. The forgotten mending rested on her lap.

Around noon we slowed to a stop in front of the Jamestown depot. The woman's even breathing was uninterrupted. I cautiously touched the sleeve of her dress. "Madam, I believe we have arrived at your stop."

She raised her head slowly as if pulled from an exhausted dream.

I smiled in her direction. "We are in Jamestown."

She put the shirt in the basket and picked up her bonnet. The conductor came down the aisle and paused next to her seat before he headed to the front of the car. "This is where you get off, ma'am."

She rose and picked up her basket.

I stood. "May I assist you?"

"Mighty kinda you, but no need."

"A pleasure to meet you. My best wishes for your sister's health."

"Thank ya. It's in God's hands now."

She walked slowly down the aisle. Right before she reached the door, she grasped the back of a seat and steadied her course. I moved toward her, but before I stepped into the aisle she straightened and turned to go down the steps.

I had never seen someone so narrowly focused. She was fully committed to the survival of her family in a perilous land, even though her role challenged her strength and, I suspect, her soul. All her characteristics had been honed to the bone, yet she was completely sure of her position in the world. Her sacrifice stunned me, but I was envious of her certainty of her life's purpose. Would I ever feel such clear direction?

I glanced at the seat she had inhabited and saw a thimble made out of cheap metal lying in its crease. It had probably fallen from the folds of her skirt. I started to call the conductor to see if he could somehow get it back to her. I knew she would hold dear an object that made her life easier, but any attempt to return it to her after she disembarked was futile. I put my smallest finger in its tiny opening before I stored it in my breast pocket.

Later in the afternoon the train slowed again. The conductor walked down the aisle, calling "Jacksonville,

Illinois." He hesitated a moment in front of my seat. "Next stop's yours, sir. A pleasure havin' a gentleman like you on the train. Best a' luck to ya. Bag'll be on the platform."

A flicker of regret crossed my chest. The train's sway and the reassuring conductor I had met only days before were about to become memories.

I left the train, picked up my bag, and headed inside the depot. The station master agreed to send a message to the asylum to announce my arrival.

I stood outside on the platform. The dust from the dirt roads surrounding the station had replaced the soot of the train's smoky engine in my nostrils. The scent of horse dung on the street and in the livery across from the track added to the general stink.

Wagons and carriages headed to and from what I assumed to be the grassy lawn of a town square about a block away. I glimpsed the fronts of structures on the other side of the square with business signs above their doors. I began to wander in that direction, but the constant movement of the train made my balance precarious.

As I leaned against the side of the depot to get my bearings a young girl approached me. She stood so close I felt her slight body shiver. Her flimsy dress revealed she was barely in her teens. Strands of matted hair covered her lowered head. She held her open hand in front of me. "Got a penny for a lost girl?"

The open buttons at the top of her shift exposed sallow skin that reminded me of the farm woman on the train. I felt sympathy for her and began to search in my pockets for a coin. Before I could meet her request or even inquire about her welfare, an arm came from behind me and slapped her outstretched hand. The arm hovered above the girl's head as if ready to strike again. "You git outta here, Bessie. I told ya not to bother the train passengers."

She tilted her head to the side until one ear touched her shoulder. Her arm covered her forehead. "I ain't doin' nothing, Sheriff."

"Sure you ain't. Git, now."

The girl tightened her shawl, whirled around, and ran through the loose dust she kicked up from the road.

Her attacker's face showed satisfaction in his ability to rescue me from the threat of a scrawny child. "Sorry that was your greetin' to Jacksonville, mister. I try to keep an eye on the station, but those girls can't resist an easy mark. Beg your pardon, mister. Not that you're an easy mark."

"She looked destitute to me."

A grin slipped out from underneath his full mustache. "I suppose you could say that. She used to stay in Miss Maude's down the street before she got put out. Got to hittin' the whiskey pretty hard. Ain't no good to Maude or any of the men she caters to now."

His rough handshake made it difficult for me to maintain my wobbly stance. The six-pointed star with the word SHERIFF gleamed on the lapel of the black coat stretched over his large frame. "Name's Sheriff Paxson. Welcome to Jacksonville."

I backed away from his hard eyes. "Thank you."

He rested both hands on his gun belt. "Plan on stayin' here?"

Something I couldn't define rose from my gut to my throat and I swallowed. "Why, yes. My name is Adam Fletcher, new medical doctor at the asylum."

The sheriff leaned back on the heels of his boots. "I don't know what they think they're doin' out there. Don't matter, though. If'n I catch those crazies in town they'll get some real treatment in my jail. We won't worry 'bout curin' 'em, neither."

Sheriff Paxson took a step toward me. The reek of stale tobacco added to the odors that assaulted my nostrils since I had gotten off the train. "You have any trouble out there, you let me know. Don't go that way 'less I have to. Nice to meet ya." He tipped his hat and swaggered down the same road Bessie had run down.

The walk I had anticipated no longer appealed to me, and I stood next to the platform, unsure of what to do. I had been in Jacksonville less than an hour, and I realized my physical being and my spirit were no longer in their usual safe harbor. I had entered a foreign world.

An open carriage pulled up to the depot. A short, wiry man dressed much like the farmer I had met on the train threw the horse's reins over a hitching post and walked to me. "You Doc Fletcher?"

"How did you recognize me?"

A wide grin covered his weathered face. "Only fella all in black wanderin' around lookin' lost."

I could not help smiling at his observation. "Wanderin' around lookin' lost," described me perfectly. "And you are?"

"Name's Henry Taylor. Hired hand out at the asylum; sort of a jack-of-all-trades, you might say. Matron Ritter sent me to town to fetch you. We best git goin'. Like to pull in before the sun goes down."

Henry jumped up on the platform and threw my bag in the carriage. "You want to sit in the back or next to me? The view's a sight better up here, and you're welcome."

Eager to see my new surroundings, I did not hesitate to sit next to Henry. He flipped the reins on the horse's rump as soon as I had taken my seat. "Looks like you're used to this kinda travel, easy as you climb up."

"I have traveled many miles to see patients in a similar rig."

Henry held the leather straps between his fingers and guided the horse into a comfortable gait. He waved to a man walking on the wooden sidewalk. "That's one of the preachers comes out to the home once in a while. Doc McFarland likes to call the asylum home. I guess that's what it is to the patients. 'Course, most of us workin' at the hospital feel like it's our home, too."

He peered over the horse's head, the slight remains of a sneer on his face. Even though he was most accommodating, his one expression told me his friendliness did not come from any sympathy for me. I was sure he was judging my trustworthiness.

The horse moved down a shady street with two-story residences surrounded by wide yards. The size of some of the dwellings implied many people were doing fine in Jacksonville. Interspersed between the larger homes were smaller, more modest abodes. Apparently not all of Jacksonville's residents were equally well off.

We turned a corner and came to a halt. A carriage coming from the other direction had a wheel stuck in a track of mud. Henry braked and got down. "Just sit still, Doc. I won't be long."

"But I can help."

"Naw, two of us is all it'll take. The driver and I can manage it." Henry aimed his grin toward me. "Besides, won't do for you to show up on your first day with mud all over ya."

Two churches sat on corners, across the street from each other. If I had been sound asleep and opened my eyes to find myself riding in Henry's carriage, I might have thought I was home. The men and women were as well-dressed as any in the East, nodding to each other with the manners of the upper class.

One of the houses of God was made of red brick, with white-framed windows. A brass plaque on a brick structure near the road read FIRST PRESBYTERIAN CHURCH, ESTABLISHED 1853. Double bells rang from the white-painted steeple. Parishioners turned away from those entering the church across the street, climbed the stairs, and went into the sanctuary.

Across the street, worshipers clustered around a wooden sign with WESLEY METHODIST CHURCH, ESTABLISHED 1854 painted across the front. They, too, pulled their attention from the neighboring church to enter their own place of worship. No one from either congregation acknowledged anyone of the other faith.

By the time Henry returned to the carriage, the silence outside the churches was broken by the organ coming from the Methodist side of the road.

Henry switched the horse into a trot. "Gittin' late. Yah, Juanita."

I held onto the carriage arm. "Are there many churches in Jacksonville?"

"Sure. They don't always git along, though. Doc McFarland can fill you in on that. He goes to that Presbytery one we just passed. Lots of the ladies from his church volunteer with the female patients. I don't know what they're fussin' about. All pretty much the same, if you ask me."

"Not a church-going man?"

Henry swerved to avoid a muddy rut. "Naw. My wife, God rest her soul, always pestered me to go. I guess you could say it never took."

"Never took with me, either."

The smirk I'd seen before formed over his mouth again, but this time his face didn't show the same menace.

We passed the edge of town. An occasional brown corn stalk stood in an empty row in harvested fields along the road. Log cabins like the ones I had seen from the train sat next to stands of timber. Life in Jacksonville proper was much different from living barely a mile out of town.

A lone boy swatted the back of the last of several cows, steering them to a shed on the other side of a pasture. He looked our way at the sound of our horse's hooves and the squeak of the carriage springs. The wave he and Henry exchanged did nothing to change the boy's vapid expression.

The sun was low in the sky. A sliver of bright sunlight found my eye, and I squinted. "How far is the asylum?"

Henry pulled his hat down over his eyes. "About a mile from the train station. Keep lookin' to your right. The gate'll be comin' up soon."

We came upon an iron gate attached to two brick columns. A small stone ball sat on top of each. An iron fence ran across the front of acreage that connected more columns. The scene reminded me of paintings I had seen of an English manor. I would not have been surprised to see royalty greet us on majestic steps.

The fence circled a large stand of mature elms. They stood so close together I saw only a few sparkles of light coming from what was left of the sunlight.

Henry descended to open the gate. The evening crickets and the creak of the iron gate broke the profound silence. I took the reins and guided the horse just inside the entrance.

"Thanks, Doc. Well, here we are. Nice stand of trees, huh? They didn't have to take 'em down when they built the hospital, almost ten years ago now."

The horse trotted around the curved driveway. Mature trees gave way to smaller young ones, no more than a few years old. Through their tops I glimpsed the roof of a large structure. A five-story edifice with four-story wings on either side rose in splendid isolation. A murder of crows flew from one end of the building to the other as I attempted to grasp the hospital's enormous size.

Grecian columns held a protruding roof at the center building, creating a covered entryway in front of an immense door. A railed balcony with a perfect view of a graceful fountain topped the porch.

Henry stopped the carriage in front of the wide steps leading to the entrance. I lifted my face toward the building. The windows were dark except for flickers of light that disappeared almost as quickly as I saw them.

Henry tipped his hat and bowed slightly. "Nice to meet ya, Doc." He carried my bag up the steps, where two figures dressed in white stood in the shadows.

On his way back to the carriage his walk slowed as he passed me. He spoke close to my ear. "If you're ever in a fix, tell one of the farm workers and I'll find ya."

Before I could respond he drove away, and I stood before the portico, a small speck beside such grandeur. I turned to look behind me. Dark spaces were beginning to fill in between the trees, and I felt uneasy. I viewed the expanse around me, but I saw no one. In spite of the dim statues waiting for me and the glimmers of light inside the walls of the structure, I felt utterly alone.

I approached the entrance and saw that one of the figures was a woman. Her long white dress was covered with an equally bright apron. A man wearing a white shirt and trousers stood slightly behind her.

The woman held herself very straight. Her hands clasped forearms that rested on her stomach. Her black eyes judged my appearance. "Welcome, Dr. Fletcher. I am Matron Ritter."

She did not acknowledge my outstretched hand, merely bowed her dark-haired head. "Dr. McFarland sends his apologies. He had a church meeting he could not miss tonight. I am to show you to your quarters."

She turned her back to me and addressed the muscular man behind her. "Take Dr. Fletcher's bag, Charles."

Charles lifted my bag and silently gestured for me to follow Matron Ritter.

Inside the door, gaslights attached to the walls lit the long hallway. Matron Ritter picked up a lamp from a circular table sitting in the middle of the corridor. "I will show you to your room."

The arc of light from the lamp fell on tasteful settees and small tables as we passed through the corridor. The gilt-framed pictures on the walls were what I envisioned would be hung in a noble manor. The large wooden doors on both sides of the hall were closed.

Our footsteps against the wooden stairs and the rustle of Matron Ritter's skirts were the only sounds as we walked up the curved stairway. I peered over the banister and saw an impenetrable darkness. We entered the landing on the third floor and proceeded half-way down a dim hallway to a small parlor warmed by a lit fireplace. "Charles will put your bag in your bedroom. I'll have one of the girls in the kitchen bring supper up to you. Do you need anything else?"

The room was perfectly comfortable, furnished much more formally than the house I shared with Sarah. "Thank you, no. Everything is more than adequate."

The glow of the fireplace highlighted her pale, pudgy features. "Dr. McFarland expects you to join him for breakfast in the morning. He eats very early. I will have someone wake you."

"I look forward to it. Thank you again."

Matron Ritter and Charles made their way into the hallway soundlessly. If others inhabited the massive building, they were silent.

The quiet was so absolute that a soft tap on my door caught me unawares. A large woman wearing a food-stained apron stood in the doorway. She held a tray covered with a white cloth. "Brought your supper." Her arduous walk betrayed a lifetime of physical work. "Name's Lena, Doc. I'm always 'bout the kitchen. Let me know if you're hankering for somethin'. Lots of the nurses brag about my apple strudel." A weary smile beamed through her wrinkles before she left me alone.

The hot, heavy food renewed my spirits and filled my aching stomach. I finished the last of my meal and extinguished the light.

I had barely put my head on the pillow when the sound of a horse's hooves on the gravel below drew me to the window. The moonlight was enough to see Matron Ritter and Charles walk from the entryway toward a carriage stopped in front of the fountain. A woman, barely visible except for the lighted lamp she held, approached the others from the porch beneath me. The rig's door opened and a man fell into Charles and Matron Ritter's arms. The woman led them toward the front canopy. Muffled voices and vague steps on the landing below my room ceased quickly, and the utter stillness of the institution resumed.

I returned to bed and closed my eyes. Exhaustion overcame me, but visions of my journey and the faces of Matron Ritter and Charles interfered with my rest. Over time, a sweet peace enveloped me, and I slept. In my dreams I heard the soft, high voice of an angel singing the same hymn my mother had hummed to me when I was a mere boy.

Lo, how a Rose e'-er blooming
from tender stem hath sprung!
Of Jesse's lineage coming,
as those of old have sung.
It came, a floweret bright,
amid the cold of winter,
when half spent was the night.

CHAPTER TWO

The next morning a knock on my door awakened me before dawn. My bare feet were greeted by the cold of the uncarpeted floor when I bounded out of bed. I spoke through my door, thanking the unseen messenger in the hallway for waking me, and went back to my parlor to build a fire with the kindling and wood stacked next to the fireplace.

The room warmed quickly against the chill of an early autumn day, but the same unnatural quiet of the night before kept me uneasy. My ears strained for the noise of any kind. I heard nothing.

By the time I finished my toilet, the sun had appeared between the front trees that surrounded the asylum. I was not accustomed to the rich setting outside my window; a landscape I assumed was maintained by the same workers who raked the pea gravel covering the circular drive.

Another rap on the door interrupted my thoughts. A young girl in a long dark dress covered by a white apron stood in the doorway. "Matron Ritter sent me to take you to the superintendent's quarters for breakfast. If you're ready, you can follow me."

We walked down the narrow wood-paneled corridor to the winding staircase I had climbed the night before. The sun's beams falling through the skylight in the roof allowed me to observe what had been too dim to see the night before. Iron doors on each end of the landing were closed. I assumed they led to the wings housing the patients.

My hand skimmed the polished banister as we descended the stairs. I had seen only darkness between the railings the night before. In the morning light, I could see that the stairs went all the way to the bottom floor.

We stopped on the landing below us and entered a lobby identical to the one above. The girl knocked softly on one of the double doors in front of us. Before her hand dropped to her side, another young woman, dressed in the same attire, opened the door.

Inside the apartment the girl led me through a spacious parlor to an adjoining dining room. A bearded man examined me through spectacles that rested on his bulbous nose. "Welcome, Dr. Fletcher. I am Dr. McFarland."

He maneuvered toward me from the head of the table, his hand offered to mine. Though his face showed the lines of middle-age, his movements were those of a man much younger. He had a purposeful, self-assured manner about him, and I found myself hoping to earn his esteem.

"I am so glad you are here. Please forgive us for starting breakfast without you, but the children need to leave."

I scanned the other occupants of the table, but saw no children. A well-dressed woman, her hair neatly styled atop her head, and two others I judged to be young adults, attended to their breakfasts.

Dr. McFarland gestured toward the chair next to him. "Please, please, sit down." He nodded at the girl who had escorted me into the dining room. "Pour Dr. Fletcher some coffee."

The woman stood and walked to a sideboard laden with food. She returned to her seat with a full platter. "Perhaps Dr. Fletcher would like some of our sausage."

I had never seen this woman before, but something in her manner seemed familiar.

She smiled in my direction. "We make the sausage right here at the asylum."

Dr. McFarland dabbed his chin with his napkin. "Oh, I am sorry, Dr. Fletcher. I neglected to introduce you to my wife,

Carlene, and my daughter, Lucy. The young man of the family is my son, Hayes."

I nodded to Mrs. McFarland and bowed my head to the others seated at the table. Neither Hayes nor Lucy acknowledged my presence. Dr. McFarland glared at them. "I apologize for their bad manners. Lucy, Hayes, I have introduced you to Dr. Fletcher."

The girl sought her father's eyes with the expression of a child far younger than her adolescent years. "Sorry, Daddy. I was just going over a recitation in my head. I have to recite part of *The Iliad* for Miss Lewiston today."

Dr. McFarland's severe glance relaxed into a tolerant smile. "I remember reciting that myself. It is difficult. Well, greet Dr. Fletcher properly, Lucy, and you are forgiven."

Lucy faced me. The remainder of a smile, meant for her father, faded from her face. "Nice to meet you, Dr. Fletcher." She picked up her fork and stirred the eggs on her plate.

Like Lucy, I was uninterested in the food before me. The anxiety I felt on the first day of my new position all but eliminated my appetite.

A clang of a utensil falling to a plate came from Hayes's end of the table. Dr. McFarland's unforgiving stare fastened on his son. "Hayes? What are you doing?"

"Oh, sorry, Father, slipped out of my fingers." He turned his head in my direction, but our eyes did not meet. "Welcome to our home, Dr. Fletcher. I hope you are as happy here as the rest of us."

Dr. McFarland leaned forward, his elbows on the table. "Hayes, you—"

Mrs. McFarland addressed me. "Did you rest well last night, Doctor?"

"Yes, thank—"

The swish of Lucy's skirt interrupted my response. "May we be excused, Daddy? Henry'll be waiting to take us to town."

"You are excused. I want—"

Before he finished, they were gone. The ticking clock on the fireplace mantel was all that penetrated the abrupt silence.

"Please excuse my children, Dr. Fletcher. Their generation does not value manners."

"Are they both in school?"

His face softened as he gestured toward Lucy's chair. "Lucy is almost finished with her curriculum. Hayes has apprenticed with a lawyer in town for two years now."

Mrs. McFarland looked up at me. The enthusiasm in her blue eyes made me believe her interest was genuine. "We are happy to have you here, Dr. Fletcher. I understand you are from New York."

"Yes, Seneca Falls."

"We, too, are from the East. Dr. McFarland was superintendent in our native state of New Hampshire's asylum. I'm sure you will like Jacksonville. We are quite proud of our little community's institutions, including our churches. To what denomination do you belong?"

"I was raised a Presbyterian."

"How wonderful. You must make First Presbyterian your church home."

Before I could answer, Dr. McFarland's form straightened. "Now, Mother, there is plenty of time to tell Adam about our church."

He glanced up at the timepiece and pushed his chair back. "Time for rounds, Adam. Shall we?"

I rose and bowed to Mrs. McFarland. "Thank you for your hospitality, madam."

Mrs. McFarland took a sip from her cup. "We will talk again very soon."

Dr. McFarland was already entering the parlor. "Please come with me, Adam."

I walked quickly to keep up with his pace.

Matron Ritter waited in the middle of the lobby outside Dr. McFarland's apartment. A ray of light fell directly through the hall's skylight, resting on her as if she had been anointed by divine providence. She was not tall, nor was she stout, but her physique was solid and square. I could not picture the strongest of winds toppling her.

Charles lingered on the edge of the sun's beam. I was to learn he was never far from her presence. They conversed sparingly in front of others, but their understanding appeared complete.

The matron maintained the same rigid stance as the night before, but her expression had changed. Like a giddy schoolgirl, her sparkling eyes never wavered from the doctor's face.

Dr. McFarland addressed her without returning her intent look. "Good morning, Matron."

She ducked her head and peeked up at the doctor through short eyelashes. "Good morning, sir. I trust you slept well?"

"Yes, yes. You've met Dr. Fletcher?"

As soon as Dr. McFarland turned his back to us, Matron Ritter's lips changed into an expression of contempt. I was surprised to hear the lilt of interest in her voice as she addressed me. "I trust your accommodations are adequate?"

The dissonance between her face and the tone of her simple question disoriented me. I managed a short reply. "Uh, yes, fine. Thank you."

We descended to the first story. Dr. McFarland halted and swept his arm before him as if to encompass everything he saw. "Here at the hospital we implement a method referred to as moral treatment. We provide respite to patients, away from the conditions that created their madness. A sympathetic Christian staff gives them exercise, meaningful work, and good food. Their time in our beautiful rural setting leads them back to sanity."

Matron Ritter stepped in front of Dr. McFarland, pulled a ring of keys from her pocket, and opened the iron door off the side of the lobby.

The abundance of light in Ward One's long corridor surprised me. Two women, dressed like the girl who took me to Dr. McFarland's apartment, came from one of the doorways on either side of the hallway. "Good morning, sir. Everyone is waiting for you in their rooms."

Dr. McFarland planted his feet solidly. "Good morning, Nurse. This is Dr. Fletcher, our new medical doctor. How is everyone today?"

"Had a good night. Josephine gave us a little run for our money at breakfast. Didn't eat a thing. Couldn't even get her to taste her coffee. Said she wanted to talk to you about what's botherin' her. Other than that everybody's good as gold."

"I will talk to Josephine. Get her a tray. She can eat in her room this morning."

The nurse's eyebrows lifted. The matron nodded imperceptibly. "Of course, Doctor."

Dr. McFarland stopped midway down the hall and directed his discourse to me. "One of the cornerstones of our success is my ability to meet with each patient every morning. They are really like children, albeit a bit cleverer in getting what they want. They think of me as their father."

I tried to listen to his every word, but the environment around me drew my attention. Open doors lined both sides of the long hallway. Each room had bare, sash windows, which extended almost to the ceiling. Large patches of light came through each doorway and fell onto the corridor floor.

Dr. McFarland continued to describe his treatment philosophy. "I use my complete authority as parental substitute to guide our unfortunates to sanity. We show our patients that good behavior will lead to rewards. Bad behavior will be punished by the taking away of privileges, not by physical force. You will find we are like a family here, Adam."

Matron Ritter and Charles waited in the doorway as Dr. McFarland and I walked into a nicely furnished parlor. Stuffed chairs sat next to a table holding a tea service and sewing materials.

A woman sat embroidering in one of the chairs. Her long dress was modestly stylish and her hair done up. She sat as a lady, never leaning on the back of her chair. I was sure she was one of the church volunteers Henry had mentioned to me.

Dr. McFarland approached the woman. "Good morning, Mrs. Packard. How are you feeling today?"

Mrs. Packard placed her work in her lap and glanced at me briefly. She tilted her head, and directed an engaging smile toward Dr. McFarland. "How am I feeling? Quite dissatisfied, sir, unless you bring me good news."

I was more than a little surprised at her flirtatious manner.

"Have you contacted my husband about my release?"

Dr. McFarland rested his hand on her arm. "Now, now, Elizabeth, you mustn't think about things that upset you. I have spoken to your husband. He and I decided you need more time in the hospital to regain your strength and reevaluate your opinions."

Every feature on the woman's face tightened into anger. "Reevaluate my opinions? You are joking. My husband says he brought me here because he is concerned about the exposure of my children's souls to my mistaken thinking, but I know his motives come from the embarrassment he suffers as a pastor whose wife dares to question what he teaches his flock. As far as my children are concerned, no one can say I have neglected them. How can following my conscience be insanity?"

Dr. McFarland's serious expression never left hers. "Mrs. Packard, your choice to defy the rule of the head of your household, your husband, shows your susceptibility to religious excitement."

Mrs. Packard winced. She had squeezed her mending so tightly her embroidery hook had pricked her finger. "Religious excitement? What are you talking about?"

"You suffer a condition that is not unusual in our patients."

"Pray tell me the symptoms of my condition."

Dr. McFarland took a deep breath. He lifted his chin. "In your case, the brain is uneasy with thoughts of religion. Your radical views are misguided at best. To continue to affirm such attitudes that reject your husband's authority is blasphemous and a sign of mental disturbance."

She rose and faced Dr. McFarland. "If I agree with the religious views of my husband and accept his authority, I can leave the hospital?"

"I would see such a change as a sign of your return to sanity."

Mrs. Packard threw her needle-work on the table with such force the fabric knocked a candlestick to the floor. "What about my conscience? Will God not punish me for pretending to believe in something simply for expediency's sake?"

The matron stepped through the doorway.

Dr. McFarland reached for Mrs. Packard's arm. "Now, Elizabeth, do not excite yourself. Why don't you rest in your room while I see the other patients?"

"Just what I need, more rest." Mrs. Packard rushed into the hallway, followed by Matron Ritter.

Dr. McFarland held his hands out from his black suit. "Such cases are more common than you might expect. These patients suffer from monomania, sane in every way except one. In Mrs. Packard's case, she is unable to accept the true religious beliefs of her husband. She refuses to acquiesce to his authority. If left untreated, she will fall deeper into lunacy."

I would not have suspected Mrs. Packard to be insane. She showed an intelligence and demeanor that reminded me of my sister. Sarah expressed her independent views often, but she had no husband.

I thought of my own mother, a pastor's wife like Mrs. Packard. I had never heard her disagree with my father's religious pronouncements. My parents had always presented their beliefs to Sarah and me in tandem. I wondered what my father would have done if Mother had challenged his authority.

Next, we entered a room containing four neatly made beds. A different spread covered each cot, ranging from a beautiful damask fabric to a plain wool blanket. All the ladies in Ward One were allowed personal items in their rooms, even their own furniture, including a trunk at the foot of their beds. Books, newspapers, and sewing materials lay on top of a doily-covered table that sat before a window.

Dr. McFarland introduced me to the room's occupants. The ladies greeted me with warm salutations except for one woman sitting in a rocker facing the window. A child of about ten with wild hair sat at her feet. Her face glowed with recognition at the sight of Dr. McFarland. She ran to the doctor and encircled him with her arms. "Doctor, Doctor. I be real good today. I clean up my bed. I use the broom to sweep too."

Matron Ritter advanced toward the child.

Dr. McFarland untangled the girl's embrace. "I'll take care of her, Matron. Now, Georgia, I'll talk to you in a minute. You wait over by your bed."

The child lowered her head. Dragging each foot, she sauntered back to her cot and picked up a rag doll lying on her pillow. Balancing on the edge of the mattress, she swung her foot against the bed's metal frame. A nurse standing nearby grabbed her arm. "You better stop that racket or else."

Dr. McFarland sat next to the child. "Release her, Nurse. I will talk to Georgia first."

"See my doll? Ada put the ribbon on her dress."

"That was lovely of Ada. Have you been minding everyone?"

Georgia's head dropped. Her shoulders touched her ears. "I been good."

The nurse stood in front of the doctor. "She's a liar, Doctor. We found some poop in the clothes closet right after she came outta there. We know it was her that done it but she keeps denyin' it."

The girl's eyes widened. "I didn't do it. I didn't. It was Baby Essy."

"Now, Georgia. We talked about Baby Essy. She isn't a real girl."

"She is, too. I'm the one she ain't afeard of. That's why she don't let nobody see her."

The doctor stiffened. "Look at me, child."

Georgia burrowed her face into her pillow.

"Look at me, child."

The nurse grabbed the girl's shoulders and twisted her limp body toward the doctor. "Sit up."

Dr. McFarland lifted Georgia's chin until her face was directly in front of him. Her eyes remained downcast. "Look at me."

The nurse grabbed the doll out of her hands. "Look at the doctor."

Georgia lunged off the bed. "That's mine. Give it to me."

No one acknowledged the faint voice coming from the window. "Georgie, you be good now."

The doctor stood. "I believe Georgia could benefit from a bath this morning. Please escort her to the bathroom. Will you assist, Charles?"

Charles lifted Georgia easily off the floor, even though she threw her body against his chest. The muscles in his arms tightened, but his passive expression remained unchanged.

Only the woman in the rocker watched Charles remove Georgia from the room.

Dr. McFarland addressed me. "We do have a few children in the facility. Most of the time their nervous temperaments are so unruly their families lose patience with them. We can be somewhat effective with them if we implement strict discipline. Unfortunately, when the onset of their illnesses comes at such a young age, as Georgia's did, the likelihood of a cure is remote."

He directed my attention to the woman in the rocker. She wore a long homespun dress. Her braids fell along her face, as if she did not have the energy or will to pin them up, like most women her age.

"Good morning, Ada. How are you feeling today?"

I recognized her status immediately. She was from the same life as the farm woman I had met on the train. The emptiness in her light eyes revealed the same acceptance of her rough life. Her hands were swollen and scarred, no doubt a result of the long labor necessary for survival. "Some better."

"This is Dr. Fletcher, our new medical doctor. Doctor, this is Mrs. Jenkins."

Dr. McFarland regarded Mrs. Jenkins. "I understand you are eating better and you are joining the ladies in their mending."

"You know little Georgia helped me when I first come."

"Georgia? How could Georgia assist you?"

"She led me around, showed me where to go an' all. She even fed me when I was too tired to pick up a spoon. She ain't nothing but a young'un. Reminds me of one of my own."

"Georgia must follow the rules, Ada. She is likely to be here most of her life, since no one on the outside wants her.

Enough about Georgia. I am very pleased with your progress. I have communicated with your family and they hope you will be able to come home by spring."

Mrs. Jenkins's eyes darted back and forth. "Spring? I don't know."

"If you continue to make progress, I am optimistic you will be home by then."

Mrs. Jenkins's narrowed brows betrayed her distress. "They'll be gittin' ready to plant. Not sure I'd be much good."

Dr. McFarland put his hand on her shoulder. "Why not let me decide if you are strong enough to leave?"

Mrs. Jenkins resumed her rocking. Her stare returned to something outside the window.

Dr. McFarland stood directly in front of Mrs. Jenkins, but his comments were directed to me. "When Ada came to us, she was mute. She had to be led everywhere, even to the water closet. As a farm wife, she already had more than she could handle. After the death of her husband, she became overwhelmed with her own duties as well as her spouse's responsibilities. Her children were too young and the grandparents too old to take over the farming. The rest and good treatment she has received from us is leading her to a full recovery."

I followed Dr. McFarland across the room to a petite white-haired woman sitting in a cushioned chair between two beds. Her black shoes barely touched the floor. Before the doctor spoke, she raised her hand to take his. "Good morning, sir."

Dr. McFarland bowed slightly. "Good morning, Mrs. Sellers. How are you today?"

"Much better, thank you. Well enough to go home. Have you talked to my husband about coming to get me? He said I could come home as soon as my nerves calmed."

She held her arms straight out in front of her. "As you can see, sir, I am steady. My nervous condition has been cured."

"I am happy you are improving, Mae, but don't forget, your actions made it impossible for your family to keep you at home. That is why I agreed to your stay. Remember, you are no longer married to Mr. Sellers. He believed the children's well-being led to his need to divorce you."

Tears fell on Mrs. Sellers's cheeks. "I am his true spouse, the mother of his children."

"The law no longer recognizes you as his wife."

"Divorce is not recognized in the eyes of God." Mrs. Sellers grasped Dr. McFarland's arm. "Can't you do something? If you could ask him to visit me, perhaps I could persuade him to take me home. How about my daughter? Hannah is sixteen, almost an adult. She and I could live together."

"Now, now, how would you support yourselves?"

Mrs. Sellers held her head in her hands. "I don't know. I don't know."

"Why don't you stay in bed this morning and rest? I'll excuse you from your sewing duties."

Mrs. Sellers slumped in her chair and closed her eyes.

In the corridor, Dr. McFarland directed the nurse to give Mrs. Sellers a dose of opium. "She will not trouble you the rest of the day."

I felt the need to ask about the woman. "What is the cause of Mrs. Sellers's condition?"

"Mae is an example of the type of lunacy that often affects women beyond their childbearing years—nervous exhaustion. The female organs do not act in such a way as to maintain the hormones necessary for mental stability. When her husband told her he intended to seek treatment for her, she accused him of infidelity."

"Her husband deserted her?"

Dr. McFarland pointed his index finger upward. "We should not be quick to judge Mr. Sellers. He bore the burden of a disturbed wife for many years. He has been fortunate to find a new mate to help with his children. I understand she is young enough to add to their family."

Once again, Dr. McFarland's diagnosis surprised me. Mrs. Sellers appeared perfectly harmless. I could picture her serving tea to other ladies, exchanging news about their families. Wasn't her desire to live with her child what any mother would want? Of course, Dr. McFarland was right about her inability to live on the outside with no means of support. She and her daughter would be destitute.

We entered a private room that contained a bureau of obvious quality. A bed with a delicately carved headboard lined one wall. A young woman sat in a stuffed chair near a circular table covered by a crocheted cloth.

"Good morning, Miss Larson. I would like you to meet our new medical doctor, Dr. Fletcher."

Miss Larson did not react to my bowed head. "I need to talk to you, Dr. McFarland."

"I hear we had a little trouble at breakfast this morning."

Barely visible underneath the hem of her silk dress, Miss Larson's feet trembled. Her fingers were pale from the pressure of wringing her hands. Her gaze moved to the door, as if she were some kind of prey in the wild, watching for an unseen predator. She gestured for Dr. McFarland to come closer. "I am unable to eat the slop they give us when you are not here."

"Now, Josephine, you have been doing so well since we moved you up here from Ward Two. I would hate to see you go back. I have asked the nurse to bring breakfast to you. Here it is now."

The nurse entered the room with a tray containing steaming cream of wheat, toast, and coffee.

Dr. McFarland glanced at the food. "It looks very appetizing to me."

Miss Larson peeked over his shoulder at the nurse's blank face. "That's not the food they—I mean, I'll try to eat it."

"I am glad you changed your mind. You have to keep your strength up if you are to get well."

Miss Larson picked up the spoon and slowly put cream of wheat into her mouth. Dr. McFarland turned away and smiled at her over his shoulder. "Very good, Josephine."

In the hallway, Matron Ritter drew near. "Excuse me, Doctor. What do you want to do about her?"

"We will give her another couple of days. If there is no improvement, take her back to Ward Two."

I continued my questioning. "What caused Josephine's illness?"

"Josephine arrived at the asylum in an extremely violent state. Her family brought her to us soon after her father's death. She is very wealthy, you know. She believes her siblings tried to steal her inheritance. Her brother and sister came to me, distraught at her accusations. I agreed she needed treatment before she could manage her affairs. She has made great progress, but I sense she is slipping. I am not sure how long she will last on Ward One."

We continued down the corridor. In each private room Dr. McFarland never failed to be kind and supportive for the few minutes he spoke with each of his patients.

Except for the aura of deep despondency surrounding them, I did not find the residents in Ward One any different from the women I knew on the outside. They wore clothes in the style of the day and were allowed to decorate their rooms with their own possessions. If not for its proximity to the rest of the asylum, Ward One could have been mistaken for a retreat with comfortably furnished, sun-drenched rooms.

We headed to the end of the hallway and came upon several rooms sitting perpendicular to the corridor. Each wooden door was open, but a screen secured by double layers of mesh with strips of metal reinforcement between them blocked the doorways. All were empty except for one. Georgia sat shivering on the floor of a cell. Her hair, dress, and stockings were wet. She was singing a lullaby to the rag doll she held close to her chest.

I could no longer remain a silent observer. "What happened to her? Why are her clothes soaked?"

Dr. McFarland blocked my view of Georgia. "Do not concern yourself with her appearance, Adam. Baths are most effective in quieting patients. Georgia's wet clothes remind her why she is in this room. I am sure her actions will improve tomorrow."

A familiar feeling crossed my consciousness. My instincts had railed against the treatments Dr. Peterson expressed an unwavering commitment to. Perhaps my doubts were foolish. Two respected physicians were not bothered by the results of their remedies, even though the uneducated eye viewed those deeds as torture.

I stood motionless in front of the screen. Georgia opened her blank eyes. I gasped at the red puffiness of her face and the sound of her short sobs.

Matron Ritter stood adjacent to the large door leading to the next ward, her scowl focused on me. "Are you coming, Dr. Fletcher?"

My instincts directed me to remove Georgia from her cage, but I did not have the authority or means to do so. Reluctantly, I walked away.

An even heavier gloom clung to the inhabitants of Ward Two. At first glance, all appeared peaceful, as in Ward One. Soon I noticed an undercurrent of sound, as if unseen mice were scurrying about, their small feet scraping the floor, their tiny squeaks audible only to those who paid them heed.

The corridor looked exactly like the one we had left barely a moment before, except the patients sat in front of the closed doors to their rooms. Some of the women stood next to their chairs. If they wandered away from their assigned spaces, the nurse admonished them to take their seats.

The ward's inhabitants appeared to be waiting for something, perhaps for us. Dr. McFarland greeted each patient. "Good morning." Most of the women did not respond.

All the women wore baggy wool shifts that touched the floor. Their lack of corseted dress and their unkempt hair were in stark contrast to the ladies on Ward One.

Dr. McFarland addressed the attendant. "How is everyone today?"

Before she could answer, another nurse approached us, wiping her hands on her apron. "Sorry, Doctor, Sally threw her milk down and I had to make her clean it up. Spilled some on me."

The nurse accompanying us rolled her eyes. "Everybody's the same, Doctor."

Dr. McFarland chuckled and pointed to me. "Our new medical doctor, Dr. Adam Fletcher." Each of the nurses gave me a short nod before their gazes skimmed past Matron Ritter and returned to the doctor.

He walked in the patients' direction. "Shall we?"

We stopped in front of a woman of middle age whose colorless dress covered an emaciated frame. She rocked back and forth, her lips moving. I could not understand her faint mutterings and no one in our party acknowledged her attempts at speech. Dr. McFarland addressed her while raising his eyebrows in the nurse's direction. "Good morning, Bernice. How are you today?"

Neither Bernice's posture nor her attention to the floor in front of her altered.

The nurse sighed. "No change, Doctor. Not that we expect much."

Dr. McFarland turned to me. "Bernice is hopeless, I am afraid. Her family knows of her condition and has accepted our diagnosis that she is chronic. She came to us after her last child, her seventh, was born. She showed no interest in the baby and was unable to nurse. She began to roam through the family home at night fearing someone would break in and kill the family. The rigors of birthing caused her insanity. Not uncommon among those of her sex."

A patient's shout drew our attention to the end of the corridor. "God-damn, bitch, I will not sit down." Matron Ritter, Charles, and the nurses ran toward a young woman who stood next to her chair with her arms raised.

I could not decipher the words Matron Ritter and the others spoke to the woman. Their stances, which I observed from behind, were firm, threatening.

The woman stepped close to the matron. "God-damn it to hell, you she-devil. I'm not a maniac. You're the one who's crazy." She spit in Matron Ritter's face. "You evil whore."

Charles grabbed the woman's wrists, and one of the nurses clutched her loose hair from the back. The other nurse slapped her soundly across the face. "Shut up."

Matron Ritter unlocked the door at the end of the corridor, and held it open. The others hauled the woman into what I assumed was Ward Three. The door closed, and we heard the lock fall into place. The murmuring quiet of Ward Two resumed.

The absence of the staff brought no change in the atmosphere of the ward. Some of the women turned toward the groan of moving metal when the door opened. Just as hastily, they resumed pursuits known only to them. I wondered if such confrontations occurred frequently.

Dr. McFarland stared at the doorway that had swallowed up our colleagues. Rubbing his hands together and shifting his feet, his usual fluency left him. He began to discuss the woman who had been precipitously removed. "The woman you just, eh, observed, Sally, is eh, eh, disturbed. She—"

He had scarcely begun to speak when a patient with uncombed hair and food on her dress approached us so rapidly we both stepped back in retreat. The girl was barely out of her teens, but her strong trajectory toward us was powerful. She did not hesitate to grab Dr. McFarland's lapels and lean against his chest. "Daddy, Daddy, I knew you would come. Can I go home with you?"

Gripping both her hands, Dr. McFarland tried to remove them from his coat. "No, no, you must not touch—" He attempted to push her away from him, but her strength was much greater than her small frame suggested. I was about to intervene when the voice of Matron Ritter bellowed through the hall. "Harriet, sit down."

Harriet drew away from us and ran back to her chair. She held the edges of the seat, swinging her feet like a child. Charles approached the girl and leaned over her, his lips close to her ear.

She twisted her head away and began to cry. "No, no." Her head dropped to her chest and she cringed. "I'll be good. I'll be good."

Tugging on the cuffs of his sleeves and pushing his shoulders back, Dr. McFarland's confident air reappeared. "Everything is fine, Charles. No harm done."

Dr. McFarland smoothed his lapels. "As I was saying, Sally was brought here when her constant use of obscenities became an embarrassment to her family. She was unwilling to control herself, stating outrageous opinions and using such foul language her parents were unable to take her out in public."

"What opinions?"

"She insisted her father, a respected physician, had taken unholy liberties with her. It was impossible for her family to allow her indiscriminate ravings about such sexual fantasies to continue. Sally shows severe signs of lunacy, and since coming here, has sunk into a most incurable state."

The Ward Two nurses adjusted their aprons as they approached us. "We helped the girls in Ward Three get her under control. They'll know how to deal with Sally."

"I will talk to the Ward Three staff about her treatment after we complete our rounds. Good job."

The nurses dipped their heads. "Thank you, sir."

I felt compelled to inquire about Harriet. "Is Harriet incurable? She thinks you are her father."

"Young girls suffering from insanity often attach themselves to a man near their father's age. Harriet knows she is unlikely to leave here, so she seeks approval from a father figure like me. Her father institutionalized her mother several years ago. I'm sure you know heredity is a powerful cause of insanity."

We walked down the hallway and continued our examinations. I spotted a remarkable-looking woman standing next to her chair with one booted foot situated on the seat. Her elbow leaned on her thigh and her other hand rested on her hip. She resembled a rakish male, not a lady. She ogled Matron Ritter from top to bottom. "Hello, sweetie."

Matron Ritter's brows tightened and the lines around her mouth hardened.

The woman addressed Dr. McFarland. "Listen, Doc, when are you gonna let me work out in the fields? I ain't no good at the sewing and cleanin' you make these other gals do.

Although I do enjoy watchin' them hike up their skirts when they scrub the floor doggie style."

I had never seen a woman who resembled and acted so like a man. Her bosom rose and fell when she breathed, like any woman, but her aspect was completely masculine. Unlike the others in the ward, she had obviously spent time arranging her long hair to be as unfeminine as possible. The resulting style did nothing to flatter her. She had loosened the collar of her dress and turned up her long sleeves. She was not particularly tall; nonetheless, she seemed to fill more space than those around her. "When are you gonna let me have some pants? How'd you like to walk around in this gitup? I can't even pee without drippin' on it."

Matron Ritter's face flushed. She pushed the woman's leg off the chair. "Stand up like a lady, Angelique."

Angelique regained her balance, but her grin never left Matron Ritter. "Anything for you, darlin'. You know I can't say no to you."

The matron stepped close to Angelique, her eyes squinting, her mouth tight. "I told you before. Do not speak to me like that."

Charles grabbed Angelique's upper arm.

Falling to her chair, she sat with her legs spread wide. "All right, all right, no need to get huffy. I'll mind my p's and q's."

She leered at Matron Ritter. "You know I have trouble controllin' myself when you're around, honey. Hey, Doc, what about me workin' on the farm?"

Dr. McFarland pulled his watch from his pocket. "I am afraid that is impossible. The men work outside."

"Doc, I'm goin' crazy here. Feel like a caged lion."

"Perhaps a bleeding will get your body's fluids back in balance and calm you."

Angelique sat up straight and pulled her legs together in a most feminine pose. "No, no, I'll settle down. I won't even gawk at any of the ladies."

"I am glad to hear that, Angelique. I think you will feel better if you join the others with today's mending."

Our entourage walked to the end of the hallway. I followed Matron Ritter and Charles, who, as usual, remained slightly behind her. I believe I alone noticed the glimpse of hatred Matron Ritter conveyed to Angelique. I do not suspect even she saw Charles's hand rest fleetingly between Angelique's legs. His touch was so brief, I questioned if it had occurred until I saw Angelique flinch.

Matron Ritter unlocked Ward Three, and Dr. McFarland entered. Screams of desperation, interrupted by muffled sounds, assaulted my ears. I paused as an odor I was not able to identify hit my nostrils.

Matron Ritter shook the circle of keys. "Dr. Fletcher?"

With a vague trepidation, I approached the open door.

CHAPTER THREE

The sound of the lock turning behind us created a desolate entrapment in me I could not readily explain. Perhaps my confused emotions came from the inescapable stink and the horrible screams in Ward Three. I soon learned the stench was a combination of excrement, vomit, and the filth of unclean bodies. The origin of the cries was not as easily accounted for.

The spotlessly clean hallway was bare except for one lone woman scrubbing the floor on her hands and knees. She sang "Three Blind Mice" in rhythm with the back-and-forth motion of her arms that dripped with soapy water.

The scarcity of patients within our sight did not guarantee quiet. The volume of the voices I heard rose now that I stood in the middle of the hall. We were privy to multiple conversations we could not understand. The inmates spoke with invisible beings who did not share their confinement.

As in the other wards, patches of light came from the patients' rooms and fell on the corridor's floor. Instead of a spirit-raising glow from the outside, Ward Three was covered in gloomy dimness. The same screens I had seen in pitiable Georgia's cell secured the patients' doorways.

The nurses' flushed faces and harsh expressions conveyed a readiness to do whatever necessary to maintain order in the ward. I was not sure even I would fail to acquiesce to their demands. I might have interpreted their sternness as cruel were I not in an institution of healing.

The cuffs of the attendants' sleeves were unbuttoned at the wrists, freed to perform their duties. One of the nurses wiped her hands on her stained apron. "Mornin', Dr. McFarland."

Dr. McFarland gestured toward me. "I'd like to introduce you to Dr. Fletcher, our new medical doctor."

The nurse caught the gaze of Matron Ritter before her eyes squinted at me. "Pleased to meet ya."

We began our trek down the center of the hall. "How is everything today?"

I noticed an unoccupied room to our right. Bolted to the ceiling was a metal hook, one that might be used in a slaughter-house to hold up a slab of beef for cutting. A chain dangling from the fastener sparkled in the brilliant sunshine that streamed through the room's window.

One of the nurses observed my hesitation. "Oh, that's where we tie 'em if they refuse to let us clean 'em up. Hang 'em by the wrists and scrub 'em down before a rinse. Can't be too careful about keeping 'em clean. Not with the lice and all."

I had no time to respond to her or to my abhorrence to such forced bathing. The logic in her explanation justified the staff's actions, but devotion to cleanliness at such costs disturbed me.

Dr. McFarland stopped before one of the rooms. "Look, Adam. Here is Sally."

The nurse swung the screen door open. Sally sat upright in a chair that completely restrained her movements. Her chest was held tight against the back with a belt-like strap. Her forearms and hands were tied to each of the chair's arms. Her feet were clamped inside a wooden restraint, reminiscent of the punishment stocks I had seen in drawings of Puritan settlements.

Sally's head was held in a kind of box that slid down to her neck. A hole in front of the apparatus allowed minimal exposure to air and light.

Her body did not move. She showed no awareness of our presence.

Dr. McFarland leaned back on his heels. "We call this the holding chair. When patients become dangerous, the device is used as a restraint, as well as to help them see the errors of their ways. As you observed, Sally was unwilling to control her actions. Time in that apparatus gives her ample opportunity to think about the unpleasant consequences of her behavior. Some physicians assert that over-stimulating blood flow to the brain is reduced as well."

I tried to cover my astonishment. "How long will she be held in the—I mean, here?"

"Sometimes patients like Sally do not respond to the gentle treatment of our better wards. I do have hope for her, though. She is young, and perhaps after spending some time in the holding chair she will be more amenable to treatment."

"But you must release her to take care of her bodily functions."

He smiled beatifically as the nurse reached down and lifted the hem of Sally's dress. "Oh, no, the design of the chair is ingenious. A bucket secured beneath a hole in the seat takes care of that problem. Anything she eliminates will be caught in the pail below and can be removed easily."

I took in a quick breath. Which was worse for Sally—the physical pain or the humiliation of being held in such a position, unable to attend to the most basic human needs?

The group left the room. I could not stop looking at Sally. She made no sound, even though one of her fingers tapped the arm of the chair repeatedly.

Before I could respond, Dr. McFarland called me from the doorway. "Come, Adam. You'll have plenty of time to examine the chair later."

No one bothered to lock the screen after I left the room. Sally's confinement in the holding chair resulted in no need to secure the door.

I became numb to the sights before me. Screened doors held naked patients writing on the walls with their own feces. Some paced in their rooms until Dr. McFarland mercifully ordered one of the nurses to give them the temporary relief of laudanum. Others sat on the edge of their beds, repeating the same phrases over and over. I saw patients tear whatever they could find, including their own hair and skin, while others howled as if calling for some distant salvation.

Standing in the midst of those lost beings, Dr. McFarland never changed his cheerful, confident attitude. He did not converse with any patients on Ward Three, nor did he ask about any particular inmate. He and the nurses, as well as Matron Ritter, saw no need to evaluate anyone's condition.

My orientation continued. "As you can deduce, Adam, these are our incurable patients. All we can do is keep them in custody. Some think we should not even accept them. But where else could they reside? I think our nurses do an exceptional job keeping order here. Good work, ladies."

The two nurses nodded. "Thank ya, sir."

"That is enough for one morning, wouldn't you say Adam?"

A loud pounding delayed my answer. Both of the nurses, Matron Ritter, and Charles rushed to a wooden door at the end of the corridor that led to the outside. I followed Dr. McFarland as he strode after them.

The door opened and I saw a large form I immediately recognized. Sheriff Paxson held a young girl whose dress and demeanor resembled the adolescent he had protected me from at our first meeting. The girl had her hands tied behind her in the leather strap of a whip. The sheriff held the handle in one hand. With the other, he struggled to drag his small captive inside the ward.

In spite of her youth, the girl resisted Sheriff Paxson mightily. Every part of her thin body protested. She kicked the sheriff and used her matted, dirty blond head as a weapon.

He succeeded in holding her at arm's length. She spit in his face. "You son of a bitch, what you done with Ginny? You hurt her, I'll kill ya."

He wiped his flushed face on the sleeve of his shirt. "Now we'll see who's in charge. These folks'll make you act right."

Charles lifted the girl from behind. His arms easily circled her waist. The nurses grabbed her feet and, with the help of the sheriff, they carried her into a nearby room.

I was so absorbed in what was transpiring before me that I was not aware Matron Ritter had left us until she walked from a storage room with a large white shirt. Charles held the girl on the bed while the nurses forced her flailing hands through the straitjacket's long sleeves. Wrapping her arms around her torso, they tied the sleeves' ends behind her and secured her ankles to the bed frame with leather straps. The agility and speed with which the nurses accomplished their task demonstrated skills that could only come from long experience.

Dr. McFarland approached Sheriff Paxson in the hallway. "Who have you brought us today?"

The sheriff wound the end of the strap. "Nothin' but a whore. Been trouble for a long time. Gittin' outta hand lately. Name's Pearl Cooke. One of the girls in Maude's house in town."

The girl began to scream in our direction. "He's lyin'. He wants me outta the way. He stole my baby." She struggled to move her body, wrenching against the bed and her restraints. "I'll kill ya. I'll kill ya. I ain't crazy, you bastard."

Dr. McFarland glanced at the struggling figure behind the screen. "No need to classify her. She is utterly insane."

Sheriff Paxson stepped to the doorway and leered at the squirming figure. "You hear that? Insane. Doc says you're a God-damn maniac."

He shook Dr. McFarland's hand. "Thanks, Doc. Next time you come into town, stop by the jail. I'll buy you a whiskey."

For the first time the sheriff looked my way. "You, too, Doc."

"You've met?"

"Met Doc at the train station. You could say I was part of his welcoming committee."

Dr. McFarland bowed his head to the sheriff. "We would be delighted to join you in a drink. Glad to be of service."

The sheriff sneered at the supine figure. "Don't worry, darlin'. I'll see your baby's taken care of."

The girl thrashed against her shackles and screamed as if her own life had been threatened. "No, no, don't hurt her. Don't hurt her."

Sheriff Paxson grunted and walked through the outside door.

Our newest patient's movements slowed as she scrutinized the room. I was sure my own observations did not elude her. She did not speak, even though her eyes held me in her gaze longer than I expected.

Dr. McFarland addressed the two nurses. "I am sure she will calm down. She cannot keep up that kind of resistance very long."

We walked toward the door which led us back to Ward Two. "Adam, you can see the necessity of Sheriff Paxson bringing this patient in by the back door. It is too unseemly for visitors to the asylum to see our most disturbed patients, not to mention the disruption their behavior may cause on the other wards. Shall we go to luncheon?"

Of course, Dr. McFarland's reasoning was flawless.

I followed Dr. McFarland and Matron Ritter back through the passage we had so recently traversed, even though my mind was not on nourishment. Wards One and Two were empty, except for Georgia, who remained in her screened cell.

Dr. McFarland informed me that the others were outside on the grounds, taking advantage of the temperate autumn day. They would come back to the wards for their midday meal.

I could not let Georgia's presence go unrecognized. "What about the child? Is no one here to see after her?"

"She is fine where she is. As you can see, she is in no position to do any harm."

I paused to peer through the screen across Georgia's door. She did not look up from her doll.

Dr. McFarland called over his shoulder. "Come, Adam. She does not require your attention."

Once again, I unwillingly left Georgia alone.

We passed through the same lobby I had entered the night before. Dr. McFarland's office was beautifully furnished in a style my sister Sarah would have appreciated. A large desk and comfortable horsehair chairs, clearly meant for those seeking Dr. McFarland's counsel, took up most of the space. A fringed cloth covered a circular table that sat before two large windows with views of the fountain in front of the building.

"Please sit down, Adam, next to Matron Ritter."

Three young girls entered the room, each bearing a tray with large servings of pork loin, mashed potatoes, gravy, green beans, apple sauce, and cherry pie.

"A good diet is essential to our patients. Those of us who work here must be well-fed as well."

I had scarcely lifted my fork when I felt Dr. McFarland's stare scrutinizing me. "Well, Adam, what do you think of the wards?"

I was so overwhelmed with the sights of the day and my inability to describe them I did not know where to begin. "I am afraid I am speechless, sir."

"Your first day can be daunting, but you will feel more comfortable when you begin your duties. While you are in training, you are responsible for the physical condition of patients in the wards you visited today—all sixty of them. As you have seen, their classification varies from maniacal to near ready to go home. Of course, as you have probably surmised by the building's size, we are capable of holding up to two hundred fifty male and female patients. You will be asked to care for more residents, but for now, you are assigned to those three wards."

Images of Ward Three fleeted through my mind.

"I want you to document the patients' food intake, output, and daily behavior. Matron Ritter will show you to your office. As you observed today, we sometimes have to use traditional methods with those who are not responding to our innovative practices. Administering those treatments is your responsibility. For instance, I would like you to bleed Angelique in the morning."

I nodded, surprised that my first responsibility would be to bestow a treatment I had always questioned as ineffective. At least I had extensive experience in bleeding patients; I knew how to handle the lancet.

Dr. McFarland took a drink of his coffee. "Angelique's condition is a result of misdirected sexual excitement. She is under the delusion she will be a lady husband. Have you heard the term?"

"No, I have not."

"A lady husband is a woman who takes the role of the male spouse in a marriage between two women. Her desire to assume the man's role confirms her lunatic tendencies. To stop the progression of her disease, Angelique will take a male spouse. Forced coupling with the right partner can alter her disinclination to accept a man as her mate."

"Forced coupling?"

A demeanor of supreme confidence came over Dr. McFarland. "Some might refer to that treatment as rape, but such a harsh term should not be applied to a therapeutic intervention."

I examined my untouched plate. I did not want Dr. McFarland to see the horror his comments generated in me. Encouraging Angelique to find a male mate seemed appropriate to cure her unnatural urges, but the idea of forcing sex with a man upon her created a visceral response from the totality of my being. My lips remained tightly closed as I considered voicing my objection to such "therapy."

I successfully concealed my inner conflict, and Dr. McFarland continued most indifferently to another topic. "I want you to spend your afternoon on the farm. We grow almost everything we need here, including the food in this delicious meal. Oh, Matron, make sure Dr. Fletcher has a set of keys."

Throughout the doctor's lecture, Matron Ritter had eaten noiselessly. Now she concentrated intently on the top of Dr. McFarland's lowered head. "Are you sure Dr. Fletcher should have unaccompanied access to the asylum at such an early date? I fear for his safety."

Dr. McFarland pulled his pie plate closer. "Oh, I am sure Dr. Fletcher will not fail to ask for assistance if he needs help."

Matron Ritter's searing stare moved to me. "I am always available, sir."

I held her fierce view steadily. "So good of you. I shall not hesitate to utilize your expertise."

Dr. McFarland beamed at us both. "Excellent. See, Matron, Adam will consult you if need be. I am sure he can take care of himself."

The matron escorted me to a small office in the rear of the administration building. The sparsely furnished room contained a modest desk, two chairs, and a bookcase filled with leather folders.

Matron Ritter stood in her rigid posture facing me. I did not yet know why I elicited the hatred I saw in her face. "The patient case files are in those folders. Someone will come presently to accompany you to the farm. If you require nothing else, I will take my leave."

I raised my face to hers, catching a flash in her eyes. "Oh, yes, my keys?"

Although I did not discern any visible change in her appearance, I knew my request had not been well-received. She exited the room and returned in seconds with a metal ring holding a set of keys. She dropped them on my desk and, without comment, left me alone.

I closed the door as soon as she left. My brain was full of the events of the morning and the people who had crossed my path. My reaction to the patients was intense, but equally compelling were my feelings about those responsible for their care.

Dr. McFarland had described moral treatment as a positive remedy delivered by a Christian staff. My instincts recoiled at the practices I had observed thus far, practices that undoubtedly countered that philosophy. However, my intellect insisted I withhold judgment.

I had seen the plentiful, nourishing food served to Dr. McFarland, Matron Ritter, and me. What about the emaciated appearances of many of the wards' inhabitants? Their appearance would surely radiate health if they were fed the same.

The baths forced on Georgia were heartless. The justifications given for the bathing hook and Sally's fate in the holding chair were unimaginable to me. Was I the lone observer to see those practices as un-Christian, if not evil?

The hospitalization of so many individuals I would judge sane confused me as well. I wondered if Dr. McFarland's rationalizations for their presence in the asylum justified their placement away from family and home.

After one morning, I found myself full of reservations. I began to question whether the Illinois State Hospital for the Insane was the place of service I had longed to find.

I selected the folder with the names, ages, counties of residence, and causes of insanity for every patient recently admitted to the hospital. *Insanity by unknown causes* was the most common diagnosis. Others included *insanity by hysteria, uterine disease, religious excitement, domestic trouble, popular delusions,* and *intemperance.* Patients were accepted in the asylum after their families brought them to the attention of a doctor, who invariably agreed with their concerns about the abnormal nature of their behavior.

A hard knock on the door interrupted my reading. I was surprised to see Henry, my first guide to the institution, standing in the doorway.

"Glad to see ya, Doc. They said you needed someone to take you out to the farm. Guess I'm the best fella for that."

"I put myself in your hands."

Henry twirled the hat he held in his hands. A wide grin spread across his face. "I'm not sure puttin' yourself in my hands'll do you much good. I ain't nothin' but a farm worker around here."

Farm worker or not, I felt comfortable with Henry. We passed a closed door near my office with the name, MATRON RITTER painted on the frosted glass and walked outside.

My spirit was renewed when the bright sun warmed my face. The corridors I had recently walked through were not lacking in light, but a darkness unrelated to the well-lit halls had weighed upon me.

A small, free standing building near the administration wing's back door summoned us with the smell of baked bread. Henry pointed to outside stairs that led to a second story. "That's where I bunk. Smells like bread up there all the time. Can't say I mind it."

I followed Henry inside, where he introduced me to two women dressed in white. "This here is Doc Fletcher. He's our new medical doctor."

Faint smiles broke through the sheen of sweat on their faces as they kneaded the dough in front of them. One of the bakers looked up at me. "Pleased to meet ya."

Henry pinched her cheek. "Come on, now. How about a little sample?"

The woman grunted and pushed Henry away. Wiping her hands on her apron, she turned to a table behind her, cut two slices from a still-warm loaf, and handed one to each of us.

Although I had been at the dining table twice that day, I had eaten little. I consumed the piece so ravenously I forgot the behavior expected of a medical doctor. In spite of my informality, or perhaps because of my casual behavior, the woman insisted I take another.

Henry leaned his shoulder against the woman, a spatter of flour dust left on his shirt. "Hey, how 'bout me?"

"You ain't deservin' any extras. That's for people who do work round here."

"Aw, come on. Don't I watch out for ya?"

She sliced another piece and held it up as she would for a begging dog.

"Here, take it and stop pesterin' me."

Henry grabbed the bread, leaned in, and kissed her on the check. She tossed a handful of flour in his direction.

I took a step back to avoid getting powder on my black suit. She lowered her head and peeked up at me. "Beg your pardon, sir. Henry acts just like a young'un sometimes."

"I think I might act the same way to get more of your delicious bread."

Her wary face transformed into a bashful grin. "Thank you, sir. Anytime you need something from the bakery, just have Henry fetch it. And you let us know if you want somethin' special."

I walked out of the hot building and regarded the fields behind the asylum. Rays of sun fell on the backs of men I surmised were male patients. They resembled farmers everywhere, steadily moving down the rows. Some sat on horses that pulled plows over the soil. One or two workers herded livestock into the barn.

Henry stood next to me. "Purty, ain't it? Don't care what Doc and Matron Ritter say, some of these folks were real good farmers when they got here. Have a way with the livestock, too. Got a couple of 'em we can't do without on slaughtering days."

He gestured to a small windowless building. "Smokehouse gets a workout that time of year."

We walked along the path to a small stone cottage adjacent to the barn. "Guess I should introduce you to the steward. He's in charge of ever'thing out here."

Henry knocked and pushed the door open at the same time. "You here, Judd?"

The rattle of a bottle hitting the floor was the only response to our entry. I strained to see in the dusky room. I detected the outline of a man lying on a settee underneath a heavily draped window.

"That you, Henry? Just takin' a little nap. Feelin' kinda poorly."

Henry opened the curtain. The sofa creaked as the man sat up and shoved his tangled hair away from his face. "You tryin' to blind me, Henry?"

"Naw; someone you gotta meet, Doc Fletcher, the new medical doctor. Doc, this here's Judd Meyers, our steward."

Judd slowly lifted his head. His watery eyes squinted. I was not sure he saw me. "Who?" Henry gathered up what I could now see was an empty whiskey bottle. "Doc Fletcher, our new medical doctor. I picked him up at the train depot last night."

Judd stood uneasily. His hand stretched toward me. "Nice to meet ya, Doc. Henry takin' good care of you?"

His handshake was weak, but I felt the remnants of energy from the past. "Yes, he is."

Even though I was sure his disease was a result of his own intemperance, I inquired about his health. "Are you unwell? Would you like me to examine you?"

I heard Henry snort behind me.

Judd dropped into a chair next to a table that held a tray of untouched food. "No, no, Doc, I'll be all right. Listen, you need anything out here, you let Henry know. He's my right-hand man."

I bowed my head slightly. "Thank you, sir."

"No need to call me sir, Doc. Judd's good enough."

Henry opened the door. "Come on, Doc. We better git goin'. Lots to show ya."

I had seen several cases like Judd's in New York. Drink was destroying the man's body and mind; nevertheless, for reasons I could not have verbalized, I liked him, and felt compassion for his soul.

Walking out of Judd's abode, the glow of the sun hovering on the horizon blinded me momentarily. I followed the sound of the gravel beneath Henry's feet. We were in front of the barn by the time I regained my vision. Henry slapped the rear of the last of the cattle entering the open door. "Time for the evenin' milkin'."

Once again, my eyes were required to adapt to darkness. The mucked-out barn smelled of hay and the hides of farm animals. The cattle had not had time to add their turds to the odor.

Approaching one of the stalls, I heard the squish of milk being squeezed out of the cow's teats and the splat into the pail underneath. A woman sat on a stool, leaning her shoulder against the cow's rump, milking rhythmically. Her face was turned away from me.

"Henry, I thought only men were allowed to work on the farm."

"That's right, except for milkin'. These fellas might be crazy, but you can't make 'em do anything they think's women's work. 'Round here the women do the milkin'."

Dr. McFarland had lied to Angelique.

I heard the scrape of the bucket being pulled over straw underneath the belly of the cow. I looked in the direction of the woman in the stall and recognized Ada Jenkins from Ward One. Many of the women's names and faces from morning rounds had blurred in my memory, but I clearly remembered Ada and her meek defense of Georgia. Her comment, "She ain't nothin' but a child," had come back to my thoughts when I observed Georgia in the screened room.

I took the heavy pail from her and handed it to Henry. "Nice to see you again, Mrs. Jenkins."

Patting the animal's head, she returned the cow's lazy look before she addressed me. "Thank ya."

I was eager to learn more about her and, hopefully, about Georgia. None of the sights of the morning had disturbed me more than the unfortunate girl's plight. "Could we talk a bit?"

"Got nothin' but time."

"Shall we sit on the bench outside?"

We sat with a perfect view of the sun setting over the fields. "Tell me about your family."

Her body rested as if she were without energy. She raised her narrowed eyes to the sun. "Pretty much like any other family, I guess. I have five young'uns—three boys and two girls. Alec's ma and pa live with us, too. We got eighty acres over by Sugar Creek."

"How old are your children?"

She watched two men unhitch a horse from a plow. "We got a plow like that one on our homestead. Got two more payments on it. My husband, Alec, was hopin' to get it paid off after this year's crops sold. That is, before he went to meet his maker." Her face took on a gray pallor.

"You have my sympathies."

A tear splattered the dirt next to Mrs. Jenkins's foot. I withdrew my handkerchief from my pocket and handed it to her. She wiped her wet cheeks with a delicacy I did not expect. "I'll make sure I wash this real good for you."

"Oh, that's not necessary."

For the first time she raised her wet eyes to mine and I saw appreciation. "Want to, Doc." Her concentration fixed on the dirt in front of her. "My boys are fifteen, thirteen, and almost two. The girls are twelve and six."

"Have you seen them since you have been here?"

"Coupla times. To tell you the truth, when Alec's folks first brought them out, I don't remember talkin' to them. I was pretty bad off."

A dog ran up and stopped at Ada's feet. She patted its head and the mutt settled next to her feet. "My husband was hit by a felled tree last spring; killed him right off. Don't know what happened to me afterwards. Just didn't care about nothin', so my kin thought comin' here might help."

She reached down and stroked the mutt's back. "Neighbors took care of the crop this year. I'm worryin' about next year. My boys are too young to farm it all, and Granny and Grandpa are too old."

"So now you own the land."

I was surprised to see a grin come over her face. "Never been married, huh?"

My face felt hot. "No, I have not."

Her folded hands were still in her lap. "I don't know how it is back East. In Illinois, a widow don't own the land. She can manage a farm until her sons are old enough to take over. If I'm able to do my work and their daddy's at the same time, we might hold on to the farm 'til then."

A bell rang in the administration wing and Ada stood. "I have to go. I'll get your kerchief back to ya as soon as I can." She looked directly into my eyes. "I'm hopin' Georgie's back to the room when I git inside. I don't like what they're doin' to her. Maybe you can keep an eye on her."

I returned her stare, surprised at the determination in her face. "I will. I am concerned about her as well."

"Now's I'm better, I ain't going to let nothin' bad happen to her. Anybody hurts her, I'll make sure they pay."

I could not have said why, but I believed Ada's assertion. Perhaps her quietness on the ward was not indifference to the world around her, but an effort to observe the occupants' treatment, especially Georgia's.

I was so busy talking with Ada I did not notice what was going on around me. The aromas of vegetables, beef, and pie reached me. The kitchen staff had placed silverware, plates, cups, and crocks filled with food on a long table that sat on the edge of the barnyard.

The farm workers formed a line and filled their plates from the array of food. Henry waved me to the table. "Sit next to me, Doc. One of the girls'll take care of you."

The sun was dropping fast. Remnants of golden light surrounded the table. I sat down, and instantly a full plate appeared in front of me. I was hungry, as were the male patients who had worked in the fields all day. We silently consumed the food until every dish was empty.

Henry pulled a toothpick out of his breast pocket. "Mighty good, huh, Doc?"

"Excellent."

Either the heavy meal or the experience of eating outside in the fine autumn weather made me tired. I would have dozed had I not been aware of a man with feverish eyes watching me from across the table. "You the new doc? Heard you got here last night. Took the train from New York."

I could not grasp how a man I had never seen before had obtained such information. "Why, yes. How did you know I was from New York?"

A grin snaked across his face.

Henry looked up from his plate. "Patients always know what's goin' on, sometimes before we do."

The man put his hands on the table and began to tap a slow rhythm with his fingers, rocking back and forth in time to his drumming. "Do you know 'Turkey in the Straw'?" Giving me no time to respond, his ragged tenor flowed down the table.

The man sitting next to him hit the singer's upper arm with his elbow. "Shut up, Levi. We've heard enough of your damn yodelin' all day. And quit hittin' the table."

Levi's singing ended abruptly.

The man next to Levi reached over the table and shook my hand. His grip was firm, his hands rough from hard labor. "Name's Pete. Glad to meet ya. Don't pay any attention to Levi. He's crazy, but he can act right when he wants to."

Pete's clear voice contradicted the fact that he was in an asylum for the insane. "Why are you here, Pete?"

"Too much drink. At least that's what my old lady says. The sheriff got tired of lockin' me up for sleepin' in the street. He had some doc say I was crazy, and here I am."

In the brief examination of the folder in my office, I remembered "insanity by intemperance" as a common diagnosis for men. I wondered what the asylum did for such a person. "How are you getting along?"

Pete held out his hands. "See how steady I am? Been here six months and I'm over the shakes. Three squares and a cot have done me good. I guess I'd have to say Henry's slave drivin' out here on the farm ain't hurt me, neither." Pete glanced at Henry. "Besides, he knows how to reward a fella for a good day's work."

I observed the stare Henry directed toward Pete: a stare that seemed to contain a warning.

Henry put on his hat and swung around to stand behind the long bench. "Better start gittin' these fellers ready to go in for the night. The nurses like to git 'em in bed before sundown. Can't be wanderin' around in the wards after dark."

I felt I should acknowledge the men in some way, even though most of them did not appear to notice my presence. "I enjoyed dining with all of you."

Pete was one of the few who looked up at me. I addressed him directly. "It was a pleasure meeting you, Pete."

"If you say so, Doc."

Such reticence after his unreserved self-introduction took me aback. I was beginning to observe that conversational etiquette on the inside of the asylum was different than what I was accustomed to on the outside. I was not sure if the conditions of the patients or some secret code of behavior produced such bewildering responses.

The patients formed a silent line to deposit their plates and utensils inside a large wheelbarrow. A young girl from the kitchen waited, her head lowered to avoid the gawks of the men as they passed her. When all was loaded she regarded Henry with a quick smile. "See ya tomorrow, you old cuss."

Henry grabbed the handles of the wheelbarrow and began to push the conveyance. "Let me get that for ya, darlin'" He yelled over his shoulder. "Git on back to the wards, boys."

Most of the men moved in self-imposed isolation toward the building. The voices of those who did converse were barely audible.

The shadows covering the barnyard dissolved into the drabness that followed sundown. I began my walk to the administration wing and felt the edge of a chilly autumn night. I looked back at the scene behind me once more. If I had not known better, I would think the farm was an orderly homestead, maintained by a well-to-do owner, not by men judged to be insane.

CHAPTER FOUR

When I returned to my bedroom, the same clear singing I had heard at the end of my first day floated to my ear. Now I knew the voice was not that of an angel calming me into slumber. The sweet melody came from a patient attempting to soothe herself in the throes of her own chaos.

I lay on my bed. A panorama of images filled my mind— Georgia in the screened room, Sally's fingers rapping on the arm of the holding chair, the young prostitute forced into a straitjacket. Each insistent sight intruded on the next picture. Dr. McFarland's voice and the threatening faces of the matron and Charles were interspersed between screams from Ward Three.

At one point, I considered packing my bags intending to leave on foot. Almost immediately, intellect stopped me from abandoning my new position after only one day. Many times thereafter I would question the wisdom of listening to reason when all my emotions pointed to another course of action.

I rose, wrapped the bedspread around my shoulders, and walked into the parlor. Standing before the window, I observed the bright light of the moon as it fell on the gravel surrounding the fountain. The form of a woman ran toward the building. A shawl covered her head and shoulders. Her skirts dragged on the path.

She raised her head to glimpse at the moon, and I recognized the illusive figure. Lucy, Dr. McFarland's daughter disappeared under the canopy of the front porch. I opened my door, allowing a crevice in the doorway. Light footfalls ran through the hallway up the stairs to the level below me. I heard the distinct click of a turning key and the brush of a door opening and closing.

I stretched out on my bed. It seemed everyone in the asylum had secrets, even those in Dr. McFarland's family.

I awakened from my restless sleep to find that everything appeared the same as the morning before. Now I knew the stillness surrounding my rooms was not a result of my residence in a peaceful haven, but due to a labyrinth of secure doors. My new awareness that the workers on the driveway spent the night in locked rooms marred the idyllic view outside the window.

I attempted to regain a sense of well-being by beginning my usual grooming routine. My efforts succeeded, until a knock on the door startled me and I dropped my razor into the bowl.

I recovered my composure enough to open the door.

The woman who had brought my tray when I arrived at the hospital stood in the hallway.

"Mornin', Doc. Got yer breakfast."

She appeared exactly as she had when we first met, except that her apron was a bright white. I assumed she had not yet had time to accumulate stains from a day of preparing and serving food.

I gestured to a table in the parlor. "Please put my breakfast in front of my chair. I'm sorry; I do not remember your name."

"Lena."

She put a small log on the inadequate fire I had hastily started, picked up the poker, and stabbed at the embers. "That should do it. Fire's a little slow this mornin'."

I took a chair in front of my breakfast. Lena handed the napkin to me and adjusted the position of my salt shaker. "You feelin' poorly?"

I leaned against the back of my chair, grateful for her simple inquiry. "Tired, I suppose. I did not sleep well last night."

She held one wrist in front of her with her other hand. "Now, I'm a might older than you, so it won't hurt you to listen to me a spell. Don't care what Doc McFarland says. If you ain't feelin' right, I'll git you somethin' my granny gave me, and you'll be fit as can be."

Her kind interest sliced through my isolation. "Thank you, Lena. I appreciate your concern. I think I will be fine."

She grunted, and I believed she was suspicious of my youthful bravado. "Well, don't forget I'm in the kitchen if you're needin' anything. You can take it easy today. Doc McFarland went to town early. Some kinda emergency, so you won't have him lookin' over your shoulder."

Lena's expression darkened. "'Course Matron Ritter's still here."

Breakfast energized me, and I prepared to face the day. Even though Dr. McFarland had deserted me, a fate I was not altogether unhappy with, I knew he expected me to bleed Angelique. I wanted to be able to inform him I had accomplished the one task he had assigned to me.

I approached my office to see Matron Ritter standing in front of the door. Charles leaned against the door frame.

I bowed my head slightly. "Good morning, Matron."

Matron Ritter continued to ignore the usual amenities of polite society and did not acknowledge my greeting. "Dr. McFarland has been called away. If you need anything, you will consult with me."

The odious look she directed at me was the same as the day before. I wondered if I was the sole cause of her distain or if others had the same effect on her. Despite the alarm she had created in my dreams the previous night, I did not fear her in the light of day. "Thank you, Matron. I am prepared to perform my duties."

I moved in her direction. "If you will excuse me?"

Her backward step was so minuscule I brushed against her shoulder as I unlocked the door and entered my domain. She stepped to my desk. "What do you intend to do today, Doctor?"

I lifted my medical bag from the floor. "Did you forget? I am to bleed Angelique this morning."

"Of course; I will accompany you."

"No need. I have my keys."

I approached the doorway and held the knob. A distinct blush moved from the matron's neck to her forehead. "Excuse me, Matron. I must prepare."

Not until Matron Ritter departed did I notice a white towel sitting on the edge of my desk. I lifted the cover. The aroma of two thick slices of bread and the thoughtfulness of a warm gift from, I suspected, the ladies in the bakery quieted the core of my being. I ate one of the pieces and recalled a verse of a psalm:—it *restoreth my soul.*

Patting my pocket to ensure the presence of my keys, I left my office. I half-expected to see Matron Ritter standing before me, insisting that she escort me to the ward. Instead, the hallway was empty. Matron Ritter's office door was closed.

I pulled the keys from my pocket and fingered through them until I found one with the stamp W-1-1. I was certain the symbols stood for women, first floor, Ward One. The lock turned immediately and the iron door swung open.

A Ward One nurse approached me. "Dr. McFarland cancelled rounds today. We weren't expecting you. Does the matron know you're here?"

"I am merely passing through. A patient in Ward Two needs my attention."

The nurse nodded and stepped aside. I felt her watching me as I continued down the corridor.

I passed several patients engaged in housekeeping, aprons covering their corseted dresses. Most of the women had their long sleeves rolled up as they washed the rooms' windows and scrubbed the floors. I attempted to address all whose eyes met mine. Breeding compelled several of them to stop working and at least greet me with good mornings before returning to their tasks.

Before leaving Ward One, I stopped at a doorway at the end of the hall. The room was similar in size to the parlor where I had met Mrs. Packard the day before. Two long tables sat perpendicular to each other, one underneath two windows, the other's end touching the first, making a corner. Patients were seated on both sides of the tables. Their heads leaned over pieces of handwork taken from piles of clothes in front of them. A nurse sat in the corner with her arms folded across her waist. At my entrance she stood and glanced at me momentarily before she looked around me toward the door.

I recognized several of the patients from rounds the previous day, but I was most relieved to see Ada sitting at one end of the table, Georgia playing with her rag doll at her feet.

"Good morning, ladies."

Some peeked up at me for a second before returning their attention to the mending. Only Ada did not look away. Georgia crooned a barely audible melody to her doll.

I attempted to establish eye contact with the child. She turned her back to me and scooted closer to Ada. Her singing became loud and fast.

Ada touched the girl's head. "Ain't nothing to worry 'bout, Georgie. Doc Fletcher here won't hurt ya."

Georgia's tune slowed and softened.

I stood next to Ada's chair. "I am glad to see her with you."

"Got back here last night. Been stickin' pretty close to me since."

I gestured toward the piles of clothes on the table. "Is that the work you ladies are assigned?"

Several heads inclined in my direction even as their practiced hands never stopped.

No one answered my question except Ada. "Never ends. We clear off the table and next day there's another pile. Guess they figure we ain't got nothing else to do. We purty near make all the clothes they need."

Dr. McFarland insisted sewing was a perfect melding of the women's skills and the needs of the asylum. Meaningful work was a cornerstone of moral treatment. Did he not observe that their bowed heads showed never-ending hopelessness, not enthusiasm to complete their tasks?

Georgia handed me a patch of fabric from the floor.

"Thank you, Georgia. I will keep this cloth with me. I have something for you as well." I did not know what impulse moved me, but I felt in my pocket for the thimble I had found on the train and placed the shiny object in Georgia's hand.

She held it up to show Ada, who raised her face to mine. "You tell the doc 'thank ya,' now."

But Georgia had gone to the window to hold her new toy up to the light.

As soon as I entered Ward Two a nurse approached me. She looked beyond my shoulder. "Matron with you, sir?"

"No. I'm here to treat Angelique. Where is she?"

The nurse gripped the edges of her apron with damp hands. "Matron Ritter won't be coming?"

Her reluctance to answer me turned my question to annoyance. "No need for Matron Ritter to accompany me. Where is Angelique?"

The nurse's eyes darted back and forth. "She's in the sewing room with the rest. I'll show you."

I could see the housekeeping duties in Ward Two were not accomplished as efficiently as in Ward One, where the women worked methodically. The patients in this ward ceased their cleaning duties intermittently to stare at sights only they were privy to. Occasionally, they sang or rocked from side to side, holding their scrub brushes still until the nurse reminded them to keep working.

A flicker of fear in some of the women's eyes made me wonder if the nurse used force to get them to complete their tasks. The fact that I saw no marks of physical harm on any of the women tempered my suspicions.

We entered a large room at the end of the hall, almost identical to the sewing room in Ward One. The same perpendicular tables were laden with clothes, but instead of industrious mending, I observed hesitation from the women. The nurse walked back and forth behind the seated patients to admonish them to hurry their sewing.

"If you don't get finished this morning, you won't go outside today. You know you have to get everything on the table done by dinner time."

The second nurse appeared as shocked as the first to observe my solitary presence. Her arched eyebrows moved away from me to the nurse who had led me to the work-room.

The women lifted the undone work from the center of the table at a snail's pace. Many stitches were interrupted in mid-mending when an unseen purpose took over their actions.

A sly grin came to Angelique's face when she noticed me. "Hey, Doc. Come here to bleed me? I'm ready when you are."

I was surprised at her readiness to succumb to the lancet. On rounds the day before, she had expressed her fervent wish to avoid such treatment.

Before I could answer her, I noticed the nurse was not alone in encouraging the patients to attend to their duties. A familiar form addressed several ladies, sometimes helping them to hold the fabric properly or even pushing the needle through the cloth for them.

I was astounded to see Mrs. Packard was the benevolent presence I observed, no longer attired in a corseted dress adorned with a broach clasping her collar. She, too, wore the same loose shift as the others on Ward Two, but her hair remained in the neat style of the day before. In spite of her dowdy dress, her lady-like manner could not be hidden.

I was sure my astonishment was unconcealed when I addressed her. "Mrs. Packard, why are you here? What has happened?"

Her eyes revealed a desolation I had not perceived from the distance of the doorway. "Good morning, Dr. Fletcher."

I stood close to the table. "Mrs. Packard, why you are here?"

The nurse stood near the door. Her chin tipped upward. "She was transferred last night. Dr. McFarland's orders."

I was determined to know more. "Mrs. Packard, won't you accompany me to the parlor?"

The nurse began to protest. "She needs to complete her sewing. All these gals have to. You said you were here to bleed Angelique."

I pulled Mrs. Packard's chair from the table. "Mrs. Packard and I will be in the parlor. I will attend to Angelique when I am ready."

Angelique's grin grew into an affable smile. "Take yer time, Doc. I don't mind bein' here. This is my last day of needle pushin'. Goin' to work on the farm tomorrow."

I stopped at the door and inquired of Angelique, "How did that come about?"

"Matron came in this morning and said I could help with the afternoon milkin'. Seems the female sex can work out on the farm, as long as they keep their heads under the belly of a cow. Anything's better than this dang sewing." Angelique glanced at the ladies at the table. "No offense."

I wondered what had changed Dr. McFarland's mind. In any event, the inevitability of toiling outside had improved Angelique's attitude, if not her appearance. Her hair and clothes were still arranged to resemble a man's.

When Mrs. Packard and I were seated in the parlor, I implored her to tell me of the events precipitating her move to Ward Two.

She held her folded hands in her lap, in a manner that reminded me of our first meeting in Ward One's parlor. "Did you notice the difference between productivity in Ward One and Ward Two? Ward One ladies are no more committed to asylum sewing than those in Ward Two, although as a sex most of us have been trained to do little else. Ward One ladies realize that if we do not complete our daily quota, we will not be allowed the meager privileges that keep us from going insane."

Her blazing eyes never wavered from mine. "The poor dears in Ward Two have to meet the quota as well, but their inner voices prevent them from caring about the impact of refusal to pick up their needles. Some days they are forced to sit at that table until the evening light is so dim the nurses must put them in their cots. We are treated like slaves. No, we *are* slaves."

"Mrs. Packard, clearly you do not belong in Ward Two."

A sardonic smile crossed her face. "Ah, Dr. McFarland disagrees with you. Be careful, Dr. Fletcher; the good doctor does not like dissent."

Although her warning would come back to me, I was not interested in Dr. McFarland at the moment. "Please tell me what happened."

The habit of maintaining an upright posture did not allow her to lean against the back of the chair, even though I could see her fatigue. She sighed and began to recount the events of the night before.

"I am sure you remember the circumstances of my residence in the asylum. My husband—the same man I trusted with the well-being of myself and my children—determined my sanity in danger because I challenged the beliefs he espoused. He found no difficulty finding allies in our community who agreed with him, and thus approved of his actions. Soon after I made my opinions known to his parishioners, my husband brought me through the asylum's doors. To my surprise, I learned Dr. McFarland was one of his supporters as well."

Mrs. Packard breathed deeply and stared at the wooden floor. "My husband is a Presbyterian minister, a fervent believer that original sin makes all of us inherently evil at birth. I, too, was born of that faith, but the experience of motherhood affected me profoundly. I watched my five children grow in the most wonderful ways and my beliefs changed. I began to read of others who did not believe such beautiful beings were demons when born into this world. When I shared my ideas with my husband, our home became a battle ground. "

Once again, I thought of my own dead parents. I had been raised to have the same views as Pastor Packard. I could not conceive of my gentle mother expressing disagreement with my pious father.

"My husband became absolutely livid when I shared my opinions at church meetings. He warned me of dire consequences if I continued to speak out to his congregation and associate with those who shared my more progressive views. I had no idea what he meant when he spoke of 'dire consequences.' Apparently, he had planned to get rid of me long before I felt the danger of his intentions."

Her story was extraordinary, unbelievable, but I did not doubt the veracity of what she told me.

"I studied my Bible and other writings that interpreted the Word as I did. I admit I expressed myself freely. I was as confident as my husband that God meant for me to follow His teachings as I saw fit. I never dreamed my ideas put me and the very existence of our family in jeopardy. You see, I was under the delusion that I remained under the protection of my husband as long as I performed my duties as wife and mother. Was I not to be respected for my contribution to the health of my children?"

A glimmer of peace softened Mrs. Packard's face. She reached under her apron and pulled out a folded piece of paper containing a childish drawing. "I taught each of my children to draw. This is the work of my youngest, Libby."

Mrs. Packard held the paper in front of me, then quickly shoved it beneath her apron. "I performed my wifely duties out of affection and love. When my husband left our marriage bed, I began to sense my precarious position. I believe that is when he began to devise his evil plan to silence me."

I dropped my gaze to the floor. I had often had access to the secrets of my patients, but for Mrs. Packard to discuss her relations with her husband was very uncomfortable for me. I was relieved when she moved on to the circumstances of her commitment.

"Witnesses, whom I had called friends, betrayed me, documenting my abnormal behavior, which years before they had not noticed. I was forced to meet with two doctors who, without asking a single question of me, pronounced me insane. In spite of the tearful pleadings of my children, I was torn away from their arms. Even then, I believed that in spite of my husband's determination to bring me here, the head of the asylum would not accept me. Would he not confirm my sanity upon my arrival? Would not a physician who worked with maniacs recognize a sane person on sight?"

Mrs. Packard searched my eyes. I knew she was wondering how much of her trust she could give to me. "When I arrived at the hospital, Dr. McFarland treated me with kind understanding. He gave me access to reading materials and writing supplies. We conversed on a wide variety of topics."

Mrs. Packard paused to grasp the kerchief in her lap. "His compassion convinced me that, unlike my husband, he was a man worthy of respect and, I am sorry to say, love. I was sure affection had grown between us."

I could not have been more shocked. I assumed Mrs. Packard had always deemed Dr. McFarland her nemesis.

"I revealed my admiration and love for him in a letter to the dear doctor. I reassured him any union between us must be in the afterlife, since our marriages in this world bound us to our spouses. I was hopeful the expression of my feelings would hasten my release, but I was wrong. The good doctor used my writings to confirm my dementia."

Once again, I was astonished at the complicated nature of her relationship with Dr. McFarland. Her desire for freedom was fueled by a need for self-determination, as well as feelings of rejection from a man she once held in high esteem.

Mrs. Packard twisted the kerchief into a ball. "I soon learned he and my husband had communicated for weeks about my case. My distress at my husband's actions merely confirmed what the good doctor had already decided was my diagnosis. In Dr. McFarland's Presbyterian eyes, I was a perfect example of religious excitement. Despite my protestations, I was admitted to Ward One, where up until now I have resided."

I began to ask once again why she was in Ward Two when a nurse appeared at the parlor door. She stood with her hands on her hips. "How long are you going to be? Elizabeth has sewing to do."

Her impatient stance angered me. "How long we stay here is none of your concern. Leave us."

She stared at me for a second. "But—yes, sir." Evidently, she had reconsidered her challenge of my order and left the doorway.

When I turned back to Mrs. Packard I noticed her smile. "Well, you will hear about that. The nurses don't like to be challenged. Dr. McFarland will soon know of our conversation."

I pulled at my coat's lapels and leaned back in my chair. "I take my orders from Dr. McFarland, not the ward nurses."

"I admire your commitment. I suspect we are lucky to have you here."

I nodded in appreciation of her compliment. "Please continue."

"Since my incarceration I have not received letters from my children, although I know the older ones would have tried to write to me. Nor have I heard from my friends, whom I am sure are concerned about my plight. All of them reside in Farmington, where my husband and I lived for many years. I am not allowed to write to anyone. I have no idea who is taking care of my children. I lay awake wondering if they are fed and clothed properly. I am concerned they are devastated by the sudden loss of a loving mother."

I did not understand why Dr. McFarland deemed it necessary to restrict communication between Mrs. Packard and her children. How could isolation from her family be part of her treatment?

Mrs. Packard raised her eyes to me, and I perceived the depth of her sorrow. "My anguish has led me to desperate measures. In spite of my pleas and my exemplary behavior on the ward, Dr. McFarland will not relent and allow any contact with or information from my family. I decided to take matters into my own hands. I convinced one of the ladies in Ward One to give me some of her writing paper. I hid a letter to my children in the bottom of my trunk. One of the nurses saw me, confiscated my letter, and reported my dangerous infraction of the rules. Moments later, Dr. McFarland ordered my removal to Ward Two."

Dr. McFarland had told me compliance with the asylum rules led to more privileges for his patients and defiance of them to punishment. Did Mrs. Packard's insanity make it impossible for her to submit to the restrictions necessary for her recovery? I wondered if she understood the reason she was prohibited from contact with her children. "Why do you think you are not allowed to write to your children?"

Mrs. Packard's sighed. "I am sure my husband, with the collusion of Dr. McFarland, has told the children something despicable about me. Perhaps they think I am dead. Perhaps they think I deserted them. If they were to receive word from me of my undying love for them, they would begin to doubt their father's lies."

I could not believe a father, with the assistance of Dr. McFarland, would create such torment in the minds of his own children. "You must be mistaken, Mrs. Packard. Such cruelty could not be proper treatment. Another explanation must exist."

Mrs. Packard stood up abruptly. "There is no other explanation. I am not even allowed to correspond with my friends in Farmington. I am to be completely isolated, in the hopes that I will be cured and accept the beliefs of my husband. If not, I am to be kept from everything I hold dear."

I did not know what I could do to allay her fears, but the forcefulness of her argument convinced me I had to take action. "I will speak to Dr. McFarland this afternoon. I will do my best to convince him to move you back to Ward One."

Mrs. Packard lowered her voice. She spoke with a sad intensity. "I am not insane, Dr. Fletcher. Sometimes I wish I *had* lost my mind. If I lived in a dream, like some of the other women in this hospital, I might accept my sentence in this prison, but forces far more powerful than I determine my fate. I trust God has reasons for me to be here. I try to do my Christian duty by helping the unfortunate patients around me. Nothing, other than our common imprisonment, makes me one of them."

I rose and stood next to her. "If I can help, please send for me."

Her eyes revealed doubt, rimmed with the slightest bit of hope. "I will remember your offer."

We returned to the sewing room. I searched the table for my patient. "Where is Angelique?"

The nurse responded without hesitation. "Not here. Charles took her to the farm."

"The afternoon milking is several hours away."

The nurse shrugged her shoulders.

I was uncertain what to do next. My one assignment was to bleed Angelique, and I could not find her. Should I wait for her return? Should I search for her in the barnyard? If Dr. McFarland learned of my failure to complete my first assignment, would he understand my dilemma or see me as unreliable on the second day of my tenure?

I exited the wards and returned to my office. I peered out my open doorway when I heard the creak of a hinge. Charles was closing and locking a narrow, wooden door off the lower landing. Before he crossed the center hallway to Matron Ritter's office, he brushed what resembled dark soil off his white pants.

Charles would not take Angelique from the ward unless Matron Ritter had ordered her removal. I approached the matron's door, knocked, and without waiting for an invitation to enter, strode through the entry.

The size of the office was equal to mine, but even more sparsely furnished. A table with a straight-backed chair sat in the center of the room. One chair, resembling those in Dr. McFarland's office, sat in front of the table. A drape-less window revealed a view of the back of a storage shed. Where the bookcase stood in my office, hooks were attached to the wall that held rings of keys.

The matron stood behind the table. Her voice was calm, measured. "May I be of assistance, Dr. Fletcher?"

Afraid my voice might betray anger, I allowed my breath to slow before I met her stare. "I was to bleed Angelique this morning. When I was ready to begin she was gone. Where is she?"

The edges of Matron Ritter's lips turned up slightly. "I'm sure she's on the grounds somewhere."

I put my hands on the table and scowled directly at her. "The nurse told me Charles took her off the ward."

Her glare moved to the open door, where Charles stood with his arms crossed in front of him. "Charles needed to find someone to assist in the kitchen. Since you were talking with Mrs. Packard, he chose Angelique. I'm sure she was more than willing to get out of her sewing."

I faced Charles. "Where is Angelique?"

Matron Ritter walked around the desk, her apron skimming my pants leg. My skin crawled at her nearness. "I'm sure she is finishing up her chores. Dinner will be served soon."

I straightened my posture. "I want Charles to bring her to Ward Two. I will be waiting for her in Angelique's room."

The matron stepped to the doorway. "You will excuse me. I have duties to attend to before Dr. McFarland returns. I'm sure he will want to know how you performed Angelique's bleeding."

The intensity of their eyes pushed me out of her office. I entered the hallway and turned to catch sight of the mocking smile Matron Ritter gave to Charles as she closed the door.

I walked back to my office. As a country doctor, I had been treated with respect in my patients' homes. In the asylum, I was confronted with forces that challenged my position. The residents' behavior was puzzling, but the forces that controlled their treatment unsettled me more. I wondered if Dr. McFarland was ignorant of those forces, or if he directed their machinations.

A loud rap on my door interrupted my thoughts. Before I could rise, a smiling Dr. McFarland entered. "Good morning, Adam. I am sorry I deserted you today. I was called away for a church emergency. I am one of the deacons at the Presbyterian Church in Jacksonville. Apparently, they cannot make a decision without me. Well, what have you been doing this morning?"

I was relieved to see Dr. McFarland, even though I was reluctant to tell him about my uneasy morning. After some hesitation, I related how I had gone to bleed Angelique, but was surprised to see Mrs. Packard as a resident of Ward Two.

The doctor sat in one of my chairs, one leg draped over the other. "What did she say?"

"She questions her inability to communicate with her family and friends."

"Based on your conversation, I am even more certain I made the right decision   putting her in Ward Two. She continues to refuse to accept authority. Her attempt to sneak a letter out of the institution shows her condition has worsened and confirms an additional diagnosis. I am certain she suffers from moral insanity. In such a case the intellectual functions are not impaired; however, the patient's moral faculties are completely deranged."

Nothing about Mrs. Packard appeared deranged. "What do you mean?"

"She is unable to contain her emotions."

I questioned him further. "Why is she not allowed contact with her family?"

"Her husband has requested the children not be exposed to her religious ranting and I concur. We want to minimize her influence, to lessen the already dangerous likelihood of insanity by inheritance."

"She is suspicious about your complicity with her husband."

Dr. McFarland leaned forward, shaking his head. "I was afraid she was deteriorating. Obviously paranoia is complicating her recovery. I will contemplate stronger treatments, possibly more baths, some bleeding."

I felt compelled to discuss Mrs. Packard with Dr. McFarland, but the tightening in my chest restrained me. My attempts to understand her condition appeared to result in more severe treatments. Perhaps I would not be so forthcoming about my observations of patients in the future. "How long will she stay in Ward Two?"

"I need to see some effort on Mrs. Packard's part to change her inaccurate beliefs. At the moment, I am not optimistic about her cure. Enough about her. How did Angelique take her bleeding?"

My hesitation created a quizzical aspect on Dr. McFarland's face. "Well?"

"I have not bled her yet."

"Why not?"

"While I was talking with Mrs. Packard, Charles came to the ward and took her to work in the kitchen."

Dr. McFarland's eyes narrowed. "Adam, I asked you to do one thing this morning and because of your conversation with Mrs. Packard, you did not complete your assignment. Am I correct?"

"I had no reason to believe Angelique was going to leave the ward. She was in the sewing room when I arrived."

"You would have completed your task had Mrs. Packard not been in Ward Two?"

"Yes, sir."

"I am disappointed in you, Adam. From now on, stick to the task at hand. Do not be distracted by a patient who does not need your attention. Is Angelique on the ward now?"

My shoulders lowered. "I told Charles to go get her. I was preparing to go to Ward Two."

"Good. Complete your assignment."

I felt a great amount of contrition as I grabbed my medical bag and walked in the direction of Ward Two. I had failed to perform my duties, and Dr. McFarland had treated me like a child.

As soon as I entered Ward Two I asked the nurse about Angelique's whereabouts.

"Not back yet, sir."

"Let me know the minute she is brought back. I will wait in the parlor."

The young woman the sheriff had brought in the day before was washing the windows in the sitting room. I recognized her immediately. Yesterday she had been in a straitjacket on Ward Three. How could her situation have changed so quickly?

Her head slightly lowered, she looked up at me through long lashes. "Mornin', Doc."

"I apologize. I do not remember your name."

"Name's Pearl."

"How were you moved up to Ward Two? Yesterday you were in restraints on Ward Three."

Her slight smile bordered on a sneer. "Guess the sheriff's right. I did need some fixin'."

I wondered how someone deemed so insane as to need complete restraint could be calmly washing windows among the other patients.

"What led to this speedy recovery?"

"Can't rightly say. Didn't much like the feelin' of that jacket, so I did what I had to do to get it off me."

"What do you mean?"

"I was in that ward for the real crazies, so I commenced to think of ways to improve my situation. Soon as I stopped jerkin' around, they let me out of that thing."

"Ward Two's a might better. They're lettin' me share a room with a real lady, Mrs. Packard and that gal tryin' to be like a man."

I recalled some of her ravings the previous day had to do with a baby. I wondered if her mention of an infant was a result of her delusions or if the child truly existed. "You talked of a baby girl yesterday. Is she your daughter?"

She spoke so softly I had to strain to hear her words. "I got a young'un.

"How old is she?"

"Ginny's near on to two."

"Where is she?"

She stood a little straighter. "Last I heard she was at Miss Maude's. That son of a bitch sheriff won't tell me fer sure."

The fate of a young child in a brothel was cause for concern. "I know you are worried about her."

Pearl's hands tightened into fists. "If anything's gonna make me crazy, it'll be frettin' 'bout my Ginny."

Before I could respond to Pearl, I heard the laughter of one of the Ward Two nurses and Charles. Perhaps I was too harsh, but their conviviality mocked the pain I observed around me.

Both of them stood in the parlor's doorway. To my surprise, Pearl smiled coquettishly at Charles.

An air of annoyance replaced the nurse's broad smile. "Angelique's in her room. I'll take you."

I stood between Pearl and Charles to interrupt their line of sight. "I am happy you are no longer on Ward Three, Pearl."

Pearl stepped around me, obviously seeking Charles's attention. "Thanks, Doc."

The nurse led me to the room Angelique shared with Pearl and Mrs. Packard. I found Angelique sitting on her cot. Her whole appearance had changed. The buttons at the cuffs of her long sleeves were undone. The neck of her dress was torn.

The nurse leaned against the door-jamb. "Been that way ever since she got back. Guess she don't like kitchen work, either."

I sat on the edge of her bed. "Angelique, what is wrong?"

Her body trembled when I brushed remnants of black dirt from the back of her shift. I grabbed a rough blanket lying on her chair and draped the cover around her shoulders. Crouching down in front of her, I tried to see through the strands of hair covering her face. "Angelique, what happened?"

She raised her head enough for her vacant eyes to meet mine. "He got me." Before I could respond she leaned on her side and reclined on the bed.

My mind agonized over the cause of her condition. Then I was certain I knew what had happened. Angelique had received her first treatment for sexual inversion. Charles had raped her.

CHAPTER FIVE

The autumn sunlight streaming through Angelique's window reached every corner of the room, but the rays did not touch the waves of revulsion in my spirit. Angelique was not a weak woman in need of protection, or even one who would garner sympathy from most, but like all the others in the asylum, she was clearly at the mercy of Charles and his cohorts. I feared she would never recover from his brutal treatment.

I expected Charles to deny his actions. I was equally certain Matron Ritter would protect him. I was not sure of Dr. McFarland's reaction to Angelique's plight, but I intended to find out if he had approved this intervention, which he himself had called therapeutic.

A moan came from Angelique's cot. As she sat up on the bed I attempted to steady her. "Please do not move. You need to rest."

She pushed away the hand I offered her. She put her elbows on her knee and rubbed her forehead. "You here to bleed me, Doc. Let's get it over with."

Angelique's surrender to the assaults from those in charge of her well-being was something I had not seen before. "I am not bleeding you today. You are in no condition for me to do so. Tell me what happened."

She lay down and stared at the ceiling.

I attempted to raise her sleeve. She jerked her arm away.

"I want to make certain you are all right. Will you not let me examine you?"

I touched her shoulder. She kept her back to me, and clung to the other edge of the bed.

I pondered how I might help her when Mrs. Packard and Pearl entered the room.

Mrs. Packard rushed to Angelique's bedside. "What happened? Is she injured?"

I was not sure of my course of action, so I did not reveal my suspicions. "I am afraid Angelique is not well."

Mrs. Packard's eyes blazed. "Did you bleed her too heavily?"

"No, I did not bleed her."

She kneeled next to Angelique and began to stroke her hair. "My dear, what is wrong? Are you ill?"

Pearl's drawn brow showed concern, but not surprise.

At Mrs. Packard's touch Angelique turned from the wall. She kept her eyes closed while Mrs. Packard pushed hair from her face. "Get me a brush, Pearl. She must have been abused in some way. Perhaps if we wash her face. Look, her dress is torn."

Mrs. Packard washed Angelique's face and brushed her hair. The tension in Angelique's body appeared to lessen with the attention. "There now, your hair looks much better."

Mrs. Packard's body stiffened when she began to button Angelique's sleeve. She raised the shift's fabric from her forearm to reveal a discoloring of the skin. "What has happened to you?"

Angelique pushed her sleeve down.

"My dear, if someone has harmed you, we need to tell Dr. Fletcher and Dr. McFarland immediately. Dr. Fletcher, did you see her arm? Will you examine her?"

The bruise on Angelique's arm strengthened my belief that the rape had occurred. I was sure she had been harmed in other ways as well, but forcing an examination would undoubtedly deepen her injuries. "I have tried to examine her. She resisted me. I do not want to harm her further."

Pearl understood the situation immediately. "I seen this kinda thing lots of times at Miss Maude's. Some of the girls got a bad fella now and then. They got beat around pretty good by 'em. Angelique here is actin' like some of those girls. Made a girl want to turn away for a while. I can't say nobody got used to it. A little whiskey made the pain go away faster. Maude did her best to keep those guys from comin' in. Couldn't keep 'em all out."

Mrs. Packard paced in front of the bed. "I had no idea such things went on in those places. Men beat you?"

Pearl nodded, a weak smile on her face. "Some did. Maude's business ain't all roses. Sure ain't for ladies."

"Who would have ra— I can't bring myself to say the word."

My jaw tightened. "I have an idea what happened."

"Tell us, Doctor."

I feared a reaction I could not control. "I need to talk to Dr. McFarland."

Pearl's face was impassive except for one raised eyebrow. "Ain't gonna do no good."

We stood in a circle at the foot of Angelique's bed. Mrs. Packard's face lightened. "I'm sure Dr. McFarland does not want one of his patient's to be willfully abused. Please speak to him."

Pearl snorted. "How long you been here, Lizzie? You sure don't know nothin' about men like him."

"What do you mean? He's a doctor, a man of healing."

"If you say so."

A nurse in the doorway interrupted us. "What's taking so long? You were supposed to get your wraps to go out on the grounds."

"We found Angelique ill. We are attending to her."

The nurse scanned the room. "Dr. Fletcher will take care of her. Let's get going."

A creak came from the bed. Angelique stood, bending over from her waist like a woman of advanced age. "I'm coming."

Mrs. Packard stepped to the cot. "No, you need rest."

Pearl put a wrap around Angelique's shoulders. "Better than bein' in here alone. We'll help ya."

I watched them move slowly into the corridor. I had never seen such courage and compassion in the face of difficulty, or the unhesitating willingness to assist a fellow patient they knew little about.

My anger urged me to confront Charles. I sped through the wards on my way to Matron Ritter's office. By the time I had worked my way to the administration building reason had slowed my emotions. Before I made accusations against Charles, I decided to confirm what I had been told about his actions.

I headed for the kitchen where workers were scraping carrots and peeling potatoes for the evening meal. Lena squinted through steam coming from the contents of a caldron bubbling over the stone fireplace. "Surprised to see you here, Doc. Need somethin'?"

My speech was interrupted by my own gasps for air. "Were you in the kitchen for the preparation of today's dinner?"

Lena's brows met over her intense stare. "Sure; what's wrong, Doc? You look like you been runnin' after a loose colt."

I lowered my voice to a near whisper. "No, no, I am all right. I need to know if Angelique, a patient from Ward Two, helped in the kitchen this morning."

"I ain't met no Angelique. I can answer your question, though. No patients in here this mornin'."

I patted Lena's shoulder. "Thanks, Lena."

"Doc, you okay? Why'd you think she was here?"

"Charles said she was."

Lena's eyes gleamed with a warmness I had often seen from my own mother. "People ain't always where they 'posed to be around here. If I was you, I wouldn't ask too many questions."

"Why not?"

I leaned close to hear her muted voice. "Matron Ritter and Charles run things around here and they don't like no surprises. Myself, I just stay in the kitchen, and when I have to take a tray to somebody, I keep my eyes down and think real hard on somethin' so as I don't see or hear too much."

"But—"

"Why don't you sit down? I'll get you some leftovers from dinner. I bet you ain't even ate."

I could not have possibly remained still enough to sit at the table. "No, no. Thank you, Lena."

I wanted to confirm one more place Angelique could have been taken. I walked out the back door of the administration building to the bakery, where the women I had met the day before were kneading bread in the same manner. Henry leaned against the table munching on a loaf's crust.

Wide smiles greeted me. "Doc, you get our little present?"

"I did. The bread was delicious."

Henry stood away from the table. "What you doin' out here, Doc?"

"I need to know if a patient from Ward Two named Angelique helped in the bakery or out on the farm this morning."

Henry pushed his hat to the back of his gray head. "I don't know about in here. Just the usual milkmaids came out to the farm. None of them's named Angelique."

The two women shook their heads. "We don't let 'em in here. They're so crazy, they can't wait for the bread to rise."

Henry followed me outside. "What's goin' on, Doc?"

"Charles took Angelique out of the ward this morning. He said they needed her to help in the kitchen. None of the kitchen workers saw her and I wanted to make sure she wasn't outside. When Charles brought her back she appeared harmed, violated."

Henry pulled his hat down so far his eyes were almost covered. "You say Charles took her?"

We both stared at the fields. "Doc, you need to drop it. Charles can't be fooled with. Let it go or you could git yourself in lots of trouble."

"As a medical doctor I am responsible for the health of my patients. If he is hurting them I am obligated to tell Dr. McFarland."

Henry leaned back on his heels. "Do what you have to. I'm warnin' you, though, Charles and the matron are not ones you want on your bad side."

"It is too late for that, Henry. I am already on their bad side."

Charles and the matron were lying. Angelique had not been taken to the kitchen or the bakery. I still did not know if Charles's attack had been done on his own accord or by order of Matron Ritter or even Dr. McFarland.

I tried to control my swirling thoughts as I approached Dr. McFarland's office. Maybe the doctor could put my doubts and fears to rest. Perhaps he was unaware of Angelique's brutal abuse. Perhaps he would punish Charles.

Dr. McFarland's assistant informed me the doctor was entertaining an important visitor and could not be disturbed for some time. My restlessness did not allow me to wait outside his office, so I left the administration building to walk on the grounds. Several small groups of patients strolled beneath the brilliant leaves of the trees.

My head down, I became vaguely aware of the gravel shuffling in front of me. My downcast eyes spotted a pair of shoes, but I could not move quickly enough to avoid a collision on the narrow path. I knocked several books out of the arms of the other stroller.

I had run into Hayes, Dr. McFarland's son. He recovered his balance almost immediately and bent over to retrieve his reading material.

"I am so sorry, Hayes. I was deep in thought."

"No need to apologize, Doctor. This institution has a way of disorienting people."

I was impressed by his easy manner as well as his insistence that I had caused him no harm. He was more self-assured and gracious now than in the presence of his father. I thought perhaps a walk with a companion might calm my spirit. "Will you join me? I am trying to clear my mind. Your father mentioned you are studying the law?"

"For the time being, anyway. Father insists I study a profession. For a long time he wanted me to pursue medicine. After some time, even he admitted I did not have the necessary interest or talent to be a doctor. I cannot stand the thought of poking at people, abusing their bodies in the name of a cure."

I raised my head from the path. "I sometimes question our methods myself."

"That's a refreshing comment from a physician. I thought all of you were cocksure of yourselves."

"Oh, many of us doubt the effectiveness, even the morality, of what we do. Most physicians cover up their thoughts better than I do."

Hayes chuckled. "How long will you work at our esteemed establishment?"

"I do not know. How about you? How long do you intend to practice law?"

"Your guess is as good as mine. I am sure of one thing: I need to get away from here."

"Are you not comfortable here?"

"Lucy and I are well taken care of, but our comfort comes with a price. We are to follow Father's direction, no matter how we feel or what we want. Lucy has her own methods for getting what she wants. She charms him. Most of the time, it works. When it doesn't, she sneaks around him. She has become the queen of subterfuge. I, on the other hand, am unable to hide my desires, which means Father and I are often at each other's throat."

"Can you and your father not compromise?"

Hayes kicked a few pieces of gravel. "Compromise is feasible when it is to Father's advantage. I was able to avoid practicing medicine because he feared my ineptitude would embarrass him. He tells his friends I chose law, when in reality he told me I had to study with one of his attorney friends, or be exposed as the failure I am. It's all about appearances. If you have not figured that out yet, you will soon enough."

"What would you do instead?"

"The newspaper is full of stories about the West. Lately, I have dreamed of walking out the front gate and entering the great unknown. Then fear overtakes me and I remain in the security of my cocoon."

"My father recognized my inability to follow him as a minister. I chose medicine as an alternative, because a physician is in a position to be of service to mankind."

"Have you found your calling as a doctor?"

Hayes's directness impressed me. His temperament did not allow him to hide his opinions.

My own answer to his question surprised me. "I am not sure. I do know I have not found joy in my profession, nor have I felt I have helped those in need."

"And you thought you might find your vocation here?"

"I was hoping so."

Hayes and I stopped to allow a group of patients pass in front of us. A nurse led the ladies from Ward Two. At their rear, Angelique walked unsteadily between Pearl and Mrs. Packard, who held both of her arms. Angelique did not acknowledge our presence. Mrs. Packard's defiant stare assailed me. No words were necessary to convey her demand that I take action.

Hayes was accustomed to such processions. "You know, most of these people are not insane. They break the rules and someone puts them away. I know how they feel. They're not the only ones living here who aren't free."

We entered the administration building and I stopped in front of Dr. McFarland's office. Hayes shook my hand. "Talking to the old man? Good luck."

Dr. McFarland's office door opened. "I heard you were waiting to see me, Adam. Please come in."

The beauty of the room, as well as the readily available service of hundreds of staff, must have reinforced Dr. McFarland's impenetrable sense of well-being. "What can I do for you?"

No coherent thoughts came to me. If words had been available, I doubted the ability of my mouth to form them. My silence prompted Dr. McFarland to raise his head from his papers. "Well?"

"I—I want—need to talk to you about Angelique."

"Yes, how did her bleeding go? Was she cooperative?"

"I did not bleed her."

"What? What is the problem this time, Adam?"

The hint of anger in his voice broke my stupor.

"She was in no condition to be bled, sir."

"What are you talking about?"

"She returned to Ward Two with her clothes and hair disheveled. When I questioned her, all she said was, 'He got me.' Charles told the nurses he had taken her to work in the kitchen. I checked with the kitchen, the bakery, and even the farm staff. None of them saw her this morning. I believe Charles raped her."

Dr. McFarland stood and walked to the window. I could only see his back as he faced the fountain in the driveway. "Why do you think Charles forced himself on her?"

My body tensed at his lack of emotion. "He took her from the ward, and I saw him come out of a door, which I presume leads to the basement, brushing dirt from his pants. Angelique had the same dark soil on the back of her dress."

Dr. McFarland returned to his seat. "How did Angelique behave when you saw her?"

At last, I thought, he was showing concern for his patient. "Her entire demeanor had changed. She reacted in a most reluctant manner to my effort to examine her. When Mrs. Packard and another patient, Pearl, came into the room they share with Angelique she allowed them to brush her hair and wash her face. While they were adjusting her dress we saw a deep bruise on her arm. She insisted on joining them on their daily walk. The last I saw her, she was on the grounds."

"She was able to walk? She couldn't be injured too badly."

"Sir, she needed the assistance of two patients to move. I fear her injuries may be serious."

"Now, Adam, we do not want our patients to experience lasting injuries, but sometimes we are forced to break entrenched patterns of behavior with dramatic techniques. After some time, Angelique will begin to tolerate and accept union with a man. Her lunacy is quite severe. And you say her attitude was one of quiet submission? More feminine?"

"Why, yes, but—"

Dr. McFarland leaned back in his chair, his thumb in his watch pocket. "From what you are saying, Angelique's experience, though extreme, is having the proper effect. With repeated treatments, her masculine bravado will be replaced with gentle acquiescence. A decided improvement, don't you think?"

The logic of his response could not be denied, although the immorality of his words shocked me. "I want her sexual inversion to be cured as well. But surely, you do not condone violence against her."

"Of course not, Adam, but when patients resist treatment methods designed to bring lasting sanity, their own actions may result in harm to themselves."

I had entered Dr. McFarland's office sure of my cause. Angelique's condition was a result of her rape. She showed signs of being beaten. The perpetrator was definitely Charles. She was almost unresponsive, physically weak.

Instead of taking action to protect Angelique, Dr. McFarland saw her passive manner as more womanly. Consequently, the treatment's long-term effect was positive, worth the temporary pain inflicted on her. I was no longer sure my impressions were valid. Evidently, I was the single individual concerned about Angelique, except for Mrs. Packard and Pearl, two women who had been diagnosed as maniacs.

Dr. McFarland stood and headed toward the doorway. "I want to observe Angelique myself. Shall we?"

Matron Ritter and Charles met us outside the office. I could not tell if they were waiting to assist Dr. McFarland or to make sure his scrutiny coincided with their own interests. Either way, I knew their presence was not to my benefit.

"Matron, we will be observing Angelique in Ward Two. Will you and Charles accompany us?"

"Certainly, Dr. McFarland."

Charles held the door open. His eyes lowered when Dr. McFarland passed, but his gaze lifted to meet mine. I stumbled on the doorstep, unable to ignore his sinister grimace. He reached toward me, supposedly to steady me. I yanked my arm away.

Most of the ladies in Ward One were in their rooms, mending or writing letters. Some read newspapers or books in the sitting room.

Several women were taking a turn around the hallway as if they were catching a breath of air in a garden. They walked the length of the corridor, crossed the hallway's width, and headed toward the door we had entered. Some conversed with one another, although sparingly, some remained silent, immersed in their own contemplation.

Waiting for the matron to open the door to Ward Two, I glanced into Ward One's parlor. Georgia was in her usual spot next to Ada. I was surprised when she rose from the floor and approached me. She reached the doorway and saw Charles. The pleased look on her face changed to fear, and she scampered to Ada's side. Ada stroked her hair and looked in my direction. "Now, hush, Georgie. Nobody's gonna hurt you. I'm here."

I wanted to reach out to the child, but before I could make an effort to comfort her, the matron opened the door and we entered Ward Two.

The ward nurses joined us in a semi-circle outside Angelique's room. Dr. McFarland addressed the matron and Charles. "Perhaps you two should wait in the hall. Dr. Fletcher and I will examine the patient."

Matron Ritter nodded. "We are here if you need us."

We entered the room to find Angelique lying on her bed with a damp cloth over her forehead. Mrs. Packard and Pearl sat with their chairs facing her. I assumed they had been attending to her and were now keeping watch over her progress.

Mrs. Packard looked up. "At last, Dr. McFarland. I have been asking to see you and have been put off again and again."

Dr. McFarland bowed slightly in Mrs. Packard's direction. "My dear lady, it is always a pleasure to see you. How may I assist you?"

Mrs. Packard approached Dr. McFarland so quickly he took a step backwards. "Do you have any idea what is going on in this so-called hospital? I know you are committed to curing us from our supposed insanity. Are you willing to do so at all costs?"

She gestured toward Angelique. "This innocent lady has been abused in the most horrible way. She has been severely violated, only to be treated as if nothing has happened to her. If she would allow us to show you proof, you would see her injuries yourself. She is in such a state of shock she will let no one but her fellow prisoners help her."

Dr. McFarland approached Angelique's bed. "She does not seem to be suffering too terribly."

Mrs. Packard's body quivered, her face reddened. "She was taken out of her room to a location she will not talk about and ra—oh, I cannot say the word."

Dr. McFarland's eyes showed a glint of anger. "Of course you cannot say the word. A lady like you is too delicate, too refined."

Mrs. Packard held his stare with eyes that challenged his condescension. "Too delicate? Too refined? She was raped. And Charles perpetrated the criminal act."

"Now, now, don't excite yourself. You do not know the whole story. Some treatments we use have to be dramatic to see results. Would you not agree Angelique is quieter, more feminine in her actions?"

"More feminine? She is distraught, not more ladylike."

Pearl touched Mrs. Packard's arm. "The doc knows what he's doin', Lizzie. Angelique'll be all right."

Dr. McFarland acknowledged Pearl for the first time. "Finally, a calm voice. Thank you, young lady."

"What are you saying, Pearl? Can't you see he doesn't care? We have to do something."

"Now, what are you gonna do? The doc'll take care of everything."

"I will not allow the man who did this awful thing to get away with it." She walked over to her chair and sat down. "Until you punish him, I will not leave this room."

"Mrs. Packard, stand up. This is ridiculous."

"You may force me to leave, Doctor, but I will not move by my own volition."

A blush of color rose from Dr. McFarland's collar. "Mrs. Packard, if you do not stand up you will be moved forcibly to Ward Three. Believe me you do not want to reside with the residents of that ward."

Mrs. Packard raised her chin. "I have told you the circumstances under which I will go willingly. The decision is up to you. If you insist on moving me, do not pretend it is for my own well-being. I will be incarcerated in Ward Three because you have failed to protect Angelique."

Pearl leaned over Mrs. Packard, her back to Dr. McFarland and me. I could barely hear her voice. "Lizzie, you're makin' it worse on yourself for nothing."

Mrs. Packard shook her head.

Dr. McFarland turned away. "If you insist, Elizabeth. Charles, we need you."

Charles and Matron Ritter entered the room. "Move Mrs. Packard to Ward Three. I am afraid you must lift and carry her."

Charles reached for Mrs. Packard, and a strange cry resembling the shout of a warrior came from Angelique's bed. As fast and strong as if in battle, Angelique left her cot and pounced on Charles's back. Her weight pulled him away from Mrs. Packard. He raised his arms, throwing Angelique off his body. Crouching, cat-like, Angelique avoided his grasp and scratched his face. Charles paused to touch the blood dripping down his face. Angelique lowered her head, rammed it into his chest, and punched his torso with her fists.

Her attack was short-lived. Charles grabbed her wrists and twisted her arms behind her.

His face showed neither fear nor anger, but those of us who saw him carry Angelique out of the room could not doubt the evil in his eyes.

CHAPTER SIX

A wooden bench under one of the elms bordering the hospital grounds provided the uninterrupted quiet I sought. My habit of resting here after supper distanced me from the activities of the asylum, but the peaceful setting failed to calm my chaotic thoughts.

The whipping wind twirled the loose earth at my feet into tornado-shaped funnels of debris. Even though I was protected by an overcoat and hat, the gusts bit my face and neck. The orange and red leaves that covered the trees when I arrived had turned to a dull brown. In a few short weeks, the warm air of autumn had faded into the sharp chill of winter.

If I had been sitting outside during the day I would have seen crews of male patients raking the leaves into mounds. Attendants were needed to light the bonfires to dispose of the trees' waste since they alone were allowed to handle instruments of fire. Once the flames were doused, no evidence of the leaves remained, another example of the synergy of the hospital's needs and the patients' labor.

I had come to Jacksonville in search of my life's purpose. Instead I felt my intellect, my spirit, my very soul were in jeopardy. In New York, I questioned the medical procedures lauded as cures. To me they were torture, with no guarantee of success. I now knew blistering and calomel were nothing compared to the hospital's forced baths and cleaning hooks. Under the guise of leading patients to sanity, the attendants' actions maintained order at best. At worst, they provided the means for diabolical individuals to satisfy their own sadistic desires.

None of the institution's angels of mercy was more evil than Charles. He performed his duties as enforcer of the rules with cruel efficiency. The few who dared to challenge him paid the price.

Mrs. Packard's passive stance had created one of the few times I observed Dr. McFarland in a state of rage. He paced in front of her with his fists clenched and spoke of her behavior as evidence of her need to be in Ward Three. Although he addressed his remarks to Mrs. Packard, he refused to look in her direction.

Mrs. Packard's loud protests about his abuse of Angelique, as well as her refusal to walk to Ward Three, had resulted in her forced removal from the room. I stood beside Dr. McFarland and watched Charles and another attendant grip the legs of the chair Mrs. Packard refused to leave, and carry her to Ward Three.

I was deeply disturbed by the close proximity of Angelique's violent reaction and Mrs. Packard's passive refusal to leave her room. Nothing they could do would stop the inevitable grind of the machinery of the institution, their fates ruled by an impenetrable system of control.

The quiet that returned to Ward Two after this bizarre scene seemed to restore Dr. McFarland's spirits. He made his way to his office, addressing patients and staff with the same unwavering pleasantries.

In the days to come, the doctor's manners remained correct, but a crevasse of disagreement opened between his conclusions and mine. I hesitated to comment on any discrepancy of opinion, lest I put the patient under discussion in harm's way.

The ever-present audience of Matron Ritter and Charles further limited the expression of my opinion. I did not fear them, but I knew they missed nothing. As a consequence, my interactions with patients in their presence became restricted.

I began to analyze Dr. McFarland's orders and statements through the eyes of the unfortunate recipients of his care. I noticed the doctor responded quickly to the patients' requests that were easily granted. If their concerns were difficult to address, Dr. McFarland simply ignored them. I remembered a discussion between him and Mrs. Sellers, whose husband had committed her to the hospital and re-married a younger woman.

"Doctor, I fear my daughter has been told an untruth about me."

Dr. McFarland sat next to Mrs. Sellers as if he had come for tea. "Mrs. Sellers, how are we today?"

Mrs. Sellers's brows met. "Doctor, could you let me contact my daughter? I am most anxious about her well-being."

I thought her request entirely reasonable. Any mother in her situation would be concerned about her daughter.

Dr. McFarland did not appear to hear her. "I have been told you have not been eating breakfast. If you continue to refuse meals, we may have to bleed you."

Mrs. Sellers took a deep breath. Her body slumped from her lady-like posture, her resolve draining from her voice. "My daughter—"

Dr. McFarland stood and placed a hand on her shoulder for the briefest of moments before moving on to the next patient. "I will have the nurse bring you a tray. I understand the oatmeal is particularly good today."

Mrs. Sellers's chin dropped to the lace on her collar. Her eyes focused on the immaculately clean floor.

In the hallway I inquired about Mrs. Sellers. "Why did you refuse her request to contact her daughter?"

Dr. McFarland's jaw stiffened. "Dr. Fletcher, my interactions with patients are of the highest therapeutic value. I am their father and they are my children. Having never been a father, I suppose you do not understand that a parent does not always acquiesce to a child's requests. I must maintain my authority at all times."

I had heard the doctor espouse his belief in his superior position many times. "How can contact with her daughter hurt her sanity?"

"Mrs. Sellers's former husband insists all contact with the family be severed. Their children have a new mother. Communication from Mrs. Sellers would confuse them."

"I do not understand—"

"Adam, you need to attend to issues you can control, such as making Mrs. Sellers realize she will eat breakfast or face consequences."

I soon realized any question of Dr. McFarland's methods led to his irritation. Though always correct in his dealings with me, he showed impatience when I questioned his orders. I began to make only those inquiries necessary to clarify my duties, and no others.

Dr. McFarland's sense of well-being was based on his belief in an order he considered absolute. He never questioned his ultimate authority, nor did he doubt that his wishes would be carried out. He was sure the smooth functioning of the asylum was a result of his presence as a benevolent authority figure. In reality, others controlled the institution.

Matron Ritter understood Dr. McFarland completely. Her fawning attention and unfailing willingness to please him added to his sense that all was well.

His ability to put events in a unique order within his mind always suited his purposes. I believed he was the most delusional resident of the institution, and thus the most dangerous.

A cold gust of wind interrupted my thoughts. The gray evening had descended on the trees' bare branches.

I knew I could not remain in my role as medical doctor in the hospital much longer. I had arrived with the best motives, but my good intentions were not enough to weave my way through the maze of the institution. Many times, events outside the asylum's walls would have led to a clear course of action; on the inside the same events confused me, the obvious response rarely considered.

I had been convinced Dr. McFarland did not know about Angelique's rape when I told him, nonetheless he recognized the benefits of Charles's actions almost immediately. If Charles took the unpleasant task of forcing Angelique into changing her inversion, Dr. McFarland did not have to devise a plan for such distasteful therapy.

Some residents moved through the demands of confinement in the hospital in such a way that they were released to their homes after a reasonable time. These patients did not balk at the expected quota of work and, as a consequence, were allowed to enjoy the fresh air and the paltry rewards given them. I wondered whether they had been insane at all. Perhaps their intelligence had allowed them to act in such a way as to take advantage of the asylum's benefits and leave as soon as possible.

Patients who were unable to do so haunted me. My yearning to interfere with their fates blocked my desire to flee the asylum, even though I feared for my own spirit.

I walked along the narrow path to the administration building. Animals scurried through the fallen leaves, interrupting the quiet of the grounds. I glanced at the hospital's dark windows where nature's peace did not penetrate the building's walls.

I came to the entranceway and noticed a figure huddled on the top step. I was surprised to see Lucy McFarland.

"Good evening, Miss McFarland."

Lucy pulled her attention away from the dry fountain and stared up at me. The light of the lamp-post next to the steps revealed tears glistening on her cheeks. "Hello, Doctor."

I was not sure if her watery eyes came from sadness or the winter air. "Are you cold sitting here?"

She stood and paced the top step. "Yes, I am cold, but I cannot go inside yet." Her face was shadowy, but I could see a slow smile covered her face.

"But it is getting late, time for you to go in the house."

A bitter laugh slipped from her lips. "House? Yes, this is my house. It has everything a girl of my age could desire—a comfortable room, a more than adequate wardrobe, extensive grounds to wander, a loving family."

My response was cautious. "It appears so."

Lucy focused her intense stare on me. "But it is an asylum. I step outside my room and there are attendants ready to help me with anything I want. The same hands that fold my laundry, cook my breakfast, and clean my room also care for maniacs who live a few doors away from me."

My well-being was ensured by those same workers as well. I had never resented their other duties, but I had not grown up in the hospital. "Have you and your family always lived on the grounds?"

"We have always lived in the superintendent's quarters. My father says we are lucky to have such a lovely apartment. I was eight when we moved here, but Mother says it is no different than the asylum Father ran in New Hampshire. I don't remember much about that place."

Hayes had mentioned his unhappiness with the expectations of his father. I wondered if he felt the same about the institution he called home.

Lucy dropped to the step. "The worst part is that I have no privacy. If we had a real home like my friends, I wouldn't have to worry about some nurse or farm worker watching me come and go."

I knew about her clandestine arrival on my first night in the institution.

"It doesn't end when I go to town, either. I have to watch my behavior so I don't bring shame on the superintendent, even though he—"

I understood her concern. "I was the son of a Presbyterian minister. I was punished many times for mischief that embarrassed my father."

The door opened, and a young girl dressed as an attendant stood in the doorway. "Your mother sent me to get you."

Lucy rose slowly. "I'd better go in. I'm sure I'll see you again, Doctor."

Dr. McFarland might think himself the father of his patients, but I wondered what impact his parental authority had on his own children.

The next morning I entered Ward Three to deliver my medical treatments. I found Mrs. Packard and Angelique sitting in a sparsely furnished parlor, spotless as a result of Mrs. Packard's influence.

Mrs. Packard complained incessantly about Angelique's treatment and her own lack of contact outside the walls. As a result, she remained in Ward Three.   I was impressed with her ability to make the most of her unfortunate placement. She took it upon herself to prod the most recalcitrant inmate into cleaning herself and her surroundings. Some of women in the ward calmly allowed her to wash their faces, even those who had not bathed unless hung from the cleaning hook before Mrs. Packard's arrival. She even induced a few to assist her in scrubbing the floors of their rooms. Though most were not allowed freedom on the grounds, she persuaded some of the women to take daily constitutionals around the corridor.

Mrs. Packard brushed Angelique's dark tresses. "Dr. Fletcher, I am glad to see you. We have much to talk about." In spite of the amiable smile on her face, her dress hung loosely on her frame. I could see she was paying the price for the weeks she had spent in Ward Three.

"Your presence has led to remarkable improvement in Ward Three. How are you surviving?"

Mrs. Packard began to weave the strands of Angelique's hair into a single braid. "If God has decided I am to suffer here, at least I can help these ill-fated ladies. My Christian duty requires me to do everything in my power to improve their unfortunate station. I assure you, my efforts distract me from my thoughts and benefit me more than they do those unfortunate inmates. If only I could devise a plan to squelch my intellect at night. I fear lack of sleep may interfere with my ability to be of service."

"You do appear fatigued."

"Fears for my children and my inability to help them, or to even know of their well-being, are starting to affect my health. If I am unable to continue my activities, I may not be able to keep myself from falling over the edge of sanity."

Mrs. Packard completed Angelique's braid and patted her shoulder. "There, my dear, your hair is so beautiful. Don't you like the braid?"

Reaching up and touching her hair, Angelique rose and walked to a rocker. "Iffin' you say so."

Mrs. Packard pulled her chair close to mine. "Before the horrible abuse occurred against her, the only insanity she showed was her refusal to accept the demeanor of a woman. Her reasoning was as yours or mine. I cannot believe, as Dr. McFarland does, that her longing to live as a man is cause for such cruel treatment. Those of us who have always accepted our plight as women know forced marital relations do not bring about desire for intercourse. In fact, if any woman has reason to hate the masculine sex, it is Angelique."

Angelique's blank eyes focused on nothing. Only the slight movement of the rocking chair interrupted her stillness. She was quiet, her shoulders drooped, and her body was devoid of aggression. Angelique did indeed act more ladylike.

Mrs. Packard followed my gaze. "I have complained continuously to Dr. McFarland. Charles abuses Angelique with regularity. After the lights in the ward are extinguished I see the glow of his candle and hear his boots against the floor. Despite my protests, he takes her whenever he wants. She does not struggle, although I am sure he strikes her if he pleases. She keeps her arms covered and will not let me or anyone else examine her. She sits in the rocker most of the time. She refuses to come to meals unless one of us leads her to the table."

No one could help Angelique if Dr. McFarland allowed the rapes to continue. My own attempts to interfere had been to no avail. I felt as powerless as Mrs. Packard. "Dr. McFarland is the sole individual who can stop Charles's abuse. I am afraid he sees her despondency as improvement."

Mrs. Packard's voice trembled. "I had come to accept that Dr. McFarland and my husband continue to collude to keep me here, but until recently, I never doubted the doctor's good intentions toward his patients. After all, he talks about giving them a healthful existence. The more I observe the results of his misguided—no—evil practices, the more I am sure he is not well-intentioned. He is dangerous."

I could not disagree with her.

Mrs. Packard's words were spoken with speed. "Dr. Fletcher, I have no choice but to put my trust in you."

I leaned away from Mrs. Packard's eyes, but I could not break the tautness of our connection. "What do you mean?"

"I am not sure how much longer I can maintain my sanity in here, especially in Ward Three. I need your help to get out of the asylum."

A patient's scream invaded the parlor, and I rose from my seat. Mrs. Packard's single-minded determination was not interrupted. "I need you to take a letter to a trusted friend."

I had always questioned if Mrs. Packard's isolation from her family was conducive to her recovery. Her conduct did not justify her placement in Ward Three either. Instead, her deeds were those of a saint.

Her request, though forbidden, was simple. I could see no harm in what she asked. Perhaps contact with a trusted friend would bring some peace to her troubled mind, though

I hesitated to conspire against the express orders of Dr. McFarland. To deliver a single letter put me in the position of choosing between loyalty to a patient and to my employer.

A shudder flew through my body. "Yes, I will do as you ask."

"I knowd you'd help, Doc. You ain't like the rest round here." My head wrenched in Angelique's direction. She had been so silent, I had failed to consider her close proximity to our discussion.

Mrs. Packard did not show alarm. "You are right, my dear. I believe Dr. Fletcher can be trusted. We will not talk of this to anyone. Don't you agree?"

Because I watched Angelique with the utmost attention, I saw the infinitesimal up and down motion of her head. She glanced at Mrs. Packard for a brief second before resuming her watch out the window.

I spoke in a rushed whisper. "She must not tell anyone of our plan. Dr. McFarland would surely release me from service if he knew, and I will not be able to help you from the outside."

"Angelique is not a concern. Besides, do you believe all secrets in the asylum are revealed to Dr. McFarland? Since I have been in Ward Three I have gained the trust of the most unyielding patients and have learned of things unknown to the administration. Angelique will not betray us."

I removed a handkerchief from my pocket and wiped my damp palms. I was sure Mrs. Packard believed her statement. I was not convinced.

Mrs. Packard scanned the doorway. "I have no access to paper and pen. Are you able to procure some for me?"

Once again, the simple nature of her request and the ease with which I could fulfill her need astonished me. "I will bring writing materials this evening."

During rounds the next day Mrs. Packard approached Dr. McFarland. "Sir, it is imperative you do something about the care of these patients." Her fiery eyes focused on Charles. Angelique sat in a chair in the hallway, her head downcast. "The very man accompanying you continues to attack Angelique. When I am released I will make sure the deplorable conditions of this ward are made public."

A slight tremor in Dr. McFarland's voice betrayed his annoyance. "Mrs. Packard, your inflamed statements demonstrate the correctness of your assignment to this ward. As for your friend Angelique, her gentle submission to her treatment is a great improvement. I am thinking of moving her to Ward Two."

I glanced at Charles and Matron Ritter. Their mouths remained tightly closed.

Dr. McFarland stepped around Mrs. Packard. "I must attend to the other patients."

Mrs. Packard followed him a few feet before the matron blocked her way and her vision. Mrs. Packard's voice elevated. "You are not the doctor or the man I thought you were. I am most unhappy with my care."

I was the last to pass Mrs. Packard. She caught my eye, a flicker of light in her expression. I was sure I alone heard her murmur, "My letter is ready. Did you find my acting convincing?"

I approached Dr. McFarland after rounds. "Mrs. Packard appears to be deteriorating. Perhaps a bleeding will help her."

Dr. McFarland broke his usual quick pace toward his office, and gazed at me with wide eyes. "Why, Adam, I thought you had lost faith in the traditional methods."

My brows narrowed, attempting to portray serious concern. I, too, showed a certain acting prowess. "I have expressed my doubts, but Mrs. Packard is not responding to the asylum's treatments. Bloodletting may calm her."

"Yes, I have observed her decline. I think you are correct. She is obviously very excitable."

"I will bleed her today after supper, with your permission."

"Of course."

The implementation of my plan was surprisingly uncomplicated. I used subterfuge to mislead—no, to lie to—my superior without hesitation. My one suggestion assured him I had accepted his teachings. In spite of my constant questioning of his decisions in the past, my status as worshipful underling had been renewed.

I completed my duties throughout the day as if in a dream. In spite of my official position as the medical doctor at the Illinois State Hospital for the Insane, I felt more like a spy working for an alien government, bent on the destruction of the existing order.

My day moved slowly. I ate supper outside with the farm workers and enjoyed an appetite I had not had for some time.

I walked through Ward One for my rendezvous with Mrs. Packard and observed Ada wiping the dining table. "Evenin', Doc." Her eyes moved from side to side. "I been feelin' kinda poorly."

"Let me examine you."

I entered the room Ada shared with Georgia and the others. We both sat on the edge of the bed with our backs to the door. Her low voice reached my ears. "I'm not poorly, Doc. That bastard Charles has been hurtin' Georgie. With me out on the farm at milkin' time, I can't always protect her. He takes her out of the ward. I don't know what he does to her. It ain't good, though. She's talkin' less and less. I gotta git her out of here. Lizzie said you was helping her, so I knowd I can trust you."

I felt as if I had been punched in the stomach. I had enjoyed my performance with Dr. McFarland as well as Mrs. Packard's, even felt lighthearted about my act. The knowledge that my disloyalty to the superintendent had spread throughout the wards conveyed the seriousness and perhaps the foolishness of my plan. How did Ada know about my willingness to betray the rules of the institution?

My fear clearly showed. Ada touched my arm so briefly I would not have noticed had we not been sitting so near to each other. "Don't you worry, Doc; none but patients know, and they ain't about to fess up."

The knowledge that I must depend on the good judgment of patients who had been judged mentally disturbed did not reassure me. "My conversation with Mrs. Packard was in the strictest confidence."

A silent chuckle stirred her body. "Nothing's kept close in here, but that ain't what I'm frettin' about. If I say anything about Charles harming Georgie, I'll git moved down for sure. My family's been clammerin' for me to come home, and I'm ready to go."

Ada stood and looked down at me. Her brow was tight and her body rigid. The resolution in her eyes made me believe what she said. "I'm not leaving without Georgie."

"Will Dr. McFarland let her go with you?"

"'Spect so. I heard some of the Jacksonville ladies who come in here for Bible study say they think no child belongs here. Nobody wants her, anyway."

Ada reached under her pillow and handed a letter to me. "One of my girls is learnin' to write. She's nigh on to twelve. I got this from her yesterday. She's scaring me about the baby. He's not yet two."

I unfolded the crumpled note. A dried petal of a black-eyed Susan dropped into my lap. The handwriting of a child filled the page.

Dear Ma,

This is to show you how I can write. Teacher Gerhardt says if I keep goin' to school I'll be readin' with the older kids 'fore long. I been goin' every day like you said.

We got the crops in purty soon after you left. Granny and me got ever'thing canned and Grandpa smoked the meat from the hog we slaughtered.

Granny said I weren't to make you fret with this letter but I'm worryin' about baby Marcus. He's been sick lately and I'm having trouble gittin' him to eat. He's over his fever but ain't got back to his sweet self. Granny's thinkin' about callin' Doc Ash.

Odell's comin' to see you the first Sunday in November. I sure wish you'd come home with him so as I can see you. I try not to but I been cryin' lots in bed 'cause of missin' you.

Your loving daughter,

Jaimie

I understood the concern Jaimie's letter created in Ada. "How can I help?"

"This Sunday's the first in November. My people's comin'. Dr. McFarland says I can go home with 'em if they want me. I need you to make sure Georgie's safe 'til then. I don't want nothin' to happen to her."

I was at a loss. I wanted to keep Georgia safe from Charles as well. We both knew he was capable of the vilest of deeds. How was I to surmount such precarious odds?

"You know I want to protect Georgia. Let me think about what I can do."

"Don't do too much ponderin'. I go out to milk before dawn."

My mind was churning with Ada's request. I, too, had noticed the change in Georgia. Even Ada had difficulty getting her to respond to her affection.

My head lowered in thought, I entered Ward Two. Pearl stepped in front of me and blocked my progress. "Hiya, Doc."

"Pearl, how are you?"

"Purty good. Getting ready to move to Ward One."

"Ward One?"

"Heard it's a might nicer there."

"How did you manage it?"

Pearl's eyes shimmered with humor. "Ain't you heard? I'm near sane."

I could not understand how such a person, without connection, without the manners of a lady, could possibly move up to Ward One.

The nurses at the other end of the hall glanced in our direction. Pearl's voice was barely audible. "Doc, heard you're helpin' Lizzie Packard."

I was appalled at the speed with which information moved through the wards.

"What do you mean?"

"I know you're gittin' a letter out for her."

I shook my head. "Mrs. Packard and I had a strictly private conversation about her need to communicate with her family."

Pearl's desperate attention never left me. "Listen, the sheriff took my baby and carried me here, just because I wanted to git away from him. A few years ago, he set me up in a place on the edge of town. When I had Ginny, I didn't like the way he treated her, like she wasn't his kin. I went back to Maude's a couple of times to make money to get away from him. He caught me and brung me here. Said I'd never see my Ginny again."

My sympathies rushed to her. "Do you think she's still at Maude's?"

Her face brightened at my interest. "I don't think Maude'd put her out. The girls'd want to look after her, but they got their own business to tend to. I'm sick with worry 'bout her."

"Oh, Pearl, I am sorry."

She grabbed the lapel of my coat. "You gotta help me. If I knew she was bein' tended to I wouldn't worry so much. When you take the letter out to Lizzie's family, can you go to town and see if you can find Ginny?"

I covered her hand and put it down to her side. "Shh, Pearl. I do not want you to get in trouble. I will think about what I can do and talk to you in the morning. Do not do anything to keep you from moving to Ward One."

Her body slumped. "Don't worry about that, Doc. I can take care of myself. Ginny's the one needs help."

Unlocking the door to Ward Three, I turned to see Pearl wandering slowly to her room to spend her last night in Ward Two. Although her pleading had been designed to convince me I carried all of her hopes, I had no doubt that if I failed her, she would find another way to see her child.

Mrs. Packard rose from the edge of her bed as I entered her room. Her voice was soft. "Dr. Fletcher, I'm so glad you are here." Angelique was in her usual position in the rocker.

I opened my bag to remove my supplies. "I am afraid I have to bleed you so as not to arouse suspicion."

Mrs. Packard grinned in the direction of my bag and took her position on the cot. "I am sure the lancet will improve my condition."

A nurse entered with a bowl and several towels. "Here, Doc."

"Thank you, Nurse. I have everything I need. You may attend to the other patients."

Mrs. Packard rolled up her sleeve, totally familiar with the process. "I will gladly submit to your procedure, Doctor."

I put the pan under her arm, tied a tourniquet above her elbow, and cut lengthwise into the vein just below it. Drops of blood splattered into the bowl.

She grabbed my other arm when I attempted to return the knife to my bag. "You are not finished." I began to question what she meant when I heard footsteps approach the door.

A nurse stood in the room's doorway. "Time to get Angelique settled."

Angelique rose from her seat, lay on her bed, and covered herself with the thin blanket.

I glowered at the nurse. "As you can see, she does not need any assistance. Do not interrupt us again."

Upon the nurse's exit, Mrs. Packard pointed to the border of her skirt, lying on the edge of the bed. "Touch the hem until you feel a thickness. That will be where you make an opening."

I did as Mrs. Packard instructed and used the knife to rip the thread holding the seam together. As the fabric separated I could see the writing paper I had left with Mrs. Packard the night before. Folded several times, her letter was lengthy.

"Put it in your bag without delay."

Only Angelique and I heard her instructions. "Take this letter to my dear friend, Agnes Wyatt, in Farmington and no one else. I am confident she does not believe whatever lies my husband has told others about my sanity. She and her husband were my strongest defenders when he made false accusations against me. When you arrive in Farmington, ask to be directed to their home on the edge of town. A hitching post resembling a black child holding a lantern stands in front of the house. If you wait for her to write a response I will be forever grateful."

"Of course."

"One more thing. Agnes may misinterpret your presence. She will accept you if you greet her in this fashion: 'Mrs. Packard wished me a safe journey.' If you do not vary from this statement, she will be sure I have sent you. Do not ask me the meaning of those words. I have put my trust in you, and now I ask you to trust me."

Her insistence that I greet her friend in such a manner puzzled me. Why would Mrs. Wyatt be suspicious of me? "I will do as you ask. Would you like me to seek out your children?"

"No. Your presence in town will create enough interest. Agnes will know how to explain you to the others. My husband will not give you any information anyway."

The squeaking of Angelique's bed brought my attention to her. She raised her head above her pillow. "You're doin' good, Doc. Mighty good."

My heart reached out to her. "Can I take a message to anyone for you?"

She stared at the ceiling. "Naw; people who put me in here are long gone or dead. Ain't no one needs word from me."

Placing a bandage on Mrs. Packard's arm, I closed my bag. "I will travel to Farmington on Sunday and report to you on Monday. Now rest. You must be weak from your bleeding."

"I will maintain my position, even though my heart flies. You have given me such hope. The few short days until Sunday will crawl, but my activities will distract me. Ward Three will be immaculate when you return."

"The nurse will be in to take the bleeding pan. Good night, ladies."

Even though the ward's lamps had been lowered, I could still see the serene expressions on the faces of Angelique and Mrs. Packard. Mrs. Packard's voice bid me goodbye. "Good night, Doctor. God bless you."

The idea of bedtime did not occur to most of the patients on Ward Three. I passed through the hallway and observed the restless behavior of those whose inner demons demanded allegiance.

I looked into a room near the end of the corridor. Inside the metal screen covering the doorway, a form inched along the wall. Her hands and her head pushed against the partition separating her room from the others, as if her desperate efforts held the plaster upright. I was certain she recognized me and headed in my direction.

Her frenzied eyes revealed despair, then recognition, and abruptly returned to despair. Behind me stood a nurse, her hands on her hips. "That's Sally, 'member? Brought her to Ward Three when you first came. Had to keep her in the holding chair for nigh on five days. She don't fight us no more, but she ain't no better. Won't never see Ward Two again."

I backed away from the doorway. Sally had deteriorated so greatly, I would agree she was now insane. Had her treatment merely been unsuccessful or were the severe consequences of her rebellion the cause of her behavior?

The longer I remained in Jacksonville the more uncertain I became—uncertain of medicine and uncertain of Dr. McFarland and his underlings. Most disturbingly, I had lost confidence in my own perceptions. I no longer trusted my eyes or even my ears. Perhaps one's mere presence in an asylum created disorder of the senses.

My contemplation of such insecurity allowed me to pass through Ward Two without noticing the activities there. The patients' doors were closed, the lights low. Ward One appeared the same until a nurse greeted me. "Ada wants to see you again, Doctor. She says she's still feelin' bad."

I entered the room and saw Ada with her arm encircling Georgia. They resembled a mother and child in a quiet nighttime scene.

Ada motioned me to come closer. "Georgie ain't been able to git to sleep. I think she's scared Charles is coming for her. I woke up last night, and she was coming back in the room. The nurse wouldn't tell me where she'd gone to, but I knowd Charles took her. I was so tuckered out last night I didn't wake up when he got her. I don't trust myself to watch the child. You gotta do somethin' tonight."

Georgia had become increasingly unresponsive, defecating in her clothes, refusing to eat. Only Ada's efforts allowed her to remain on Ward One.

"What can I do? I am unprepared to help."

Georgia lay still between us. The sound of hard footsteps approached the room. We raised our eyes at the same time to see a male form in the doorway. The light of the hallway shone at his back. From the darkness of our position, we could not see his features, but his outline was easy to identify. It was Charles.

Georgia threw herself into Ada's arm. Her high-pitched wail penetrated the ward.

I stood and stepped toward the door. "What are you doing here?"

At the sound of my voice, Charles backed away and left the ward.

I knew I had to act immediately. "Ada, will Georgia go with me?"

Georgia's sobs slowed as Ada held her close. "Think so. I told her you'd help us."

A plan came to me instantly. "I will tell the nurses a patient needs their attention at the end of the hall. While they go to her, Georgia and I will leave the ward. Can she remain quiet while I take her?"

Georgia reached for my hand and her breathing slowed. Ada smiled. "I think she knows. You do what Doc says, now."

I left the room and walked to the nurses' station. "Mrs. Jenkins is feeling better, but I heard a sound from Mrs. Harrington's room at the end of the hall. I need both of you to check on her. I will be in my quarters if you need me."

The nurses used their aprons to wipe their hands and walked down the hall. They did not see me step into the doorway where Ada and Georgia were waiting. I gently pushed

Georgia in front of me. Covered in the shadows of the dark hallway, we headed for the ward's exit.

Georgia and I entered the administration building's corridor. I believed we had gone undetected until we turned the corner toward my office and collided with a female figure hurrying toward the main staircase. I grabbed the stranger's arm and yanked her to the dimmed gaslight in the hallway. It was Lucy. I pulled her and Georgia into my office.

In the faint light of the lamp on my desk, I could not tell which girl showed more fright, but I knew it was Lucy I had to contain. If she exposed me to her father, all was doomed. I whispered close to her ear. "Where have you been, Lucy?" She tried to pull away from me, but I held her wrist. "Where have you been?"

The terror in her face told me I had nothing to fear. She would not tell her father of our meeting. "Don't tell my father, please."

I gave her my sternest frown. "Can I depend on you not to reveal what you have seen?"

"Oh, yes, yes." I believed her nervous stammer.

I opened the door slowly. "Go to your room."

She scurried out the door. I barely heard the rustle of her dress in the empty hallway.

Georgia remained against the wall, clutching her doll. I crouched down in front of her. "Do not worry, Georgia. Charles will not take you again."

CHAPTER SEVEN

I put my ear to the office door to listen for any sound penetrating the stillness in the corridor. Hearing nothing, Georgia and I entered the hallway and headed toward the back door. I pulled the ring of keys out of my pocket. Their clatter filled the eerie silence, and I feared we would be found out. I released Georgia's hand to silence them inside my other palm. My damp fingers slid across each key until I found the one that unlocked the door.

We stepped outside and a gust of cold hit us. I remembered Georgia wore one of the thin shifts from the women's wards. I covered her frail shoulders with my coat. My skin felt the winter wind through my shirt, and I knew we needed to find shelter.

The outlines of the farm buildings interrupted the night sky. Thankful for the darkness enveloping the path, I stopped to gauge which structure might provide the best hiding place for Georgia.

A single candle behind a gauzy curtain created an uneven brightness in the steward's house. Having only met the steward once, I was unsure he would help us.

The slam of a door at the very residence I scrutinized interrupted my thoughts, and I saw Henry walking away from the building. Hadn't he said I should come to him if I needed help? I needed assistance now.

I directed my hoarse whisper toward him. "Henry, it's Dr. Fletcher."

His head jutted toward me. "Doc?"

I put my arm around Georgia's shoulders and pushed her in Henry's direction. "I need your help."

"What're you doin' out here? Who's this?"

"A child, a victim I must protect. We need a place to hide her. She cannot stay inside."

It was too dark to see Henry's reaction to my request in his face, but he did not step away. "Let me guess who's been hurtin' her. That bastard Charles?"

My arm felt Georgia's muscles tighten at the mention of Charles's name. She buried her face in my shirt. "Yes. We need to conceal her until she can get away."

"Come on. You'll catch your death standin' out here."

Georgia and I followed Henry to the building he had just left. He knocked but did not wait for an answer before he pushed the door open. Inside, the fire blazed and a meal waited on the table. Judd reclined on the settee. The smell of whiskey filled the room.

Henry picked up a half-filled bottle from the floor. "Got company, Judd. Can ya sit up?"

The steward rose half-way, propping himself on his elbow. "Henry? Thought you left. Wha—?"

Judd came to a seated position. His eyes focused on the floor next to his cot. "Who's here, Henry?"

"Doc Fletcher. Needs some help."

He squinted up at me. "Don't know how I can help you, Doc. You can see for yourself, I'm what you call indisposed."

The room was close from the fire's heat. "I apologize for disturbing you. I would not impose, except Henry believes you are our best hope."

"What're you gettin' me mixed up in, Henry? You know I want no part of the house's business. Git the doc outta here." He turned to me. "No offense, Doc."

Georgia had hidden behind me, using my body as a shield from an unknown threat. She clung to the back of my shirt. I pulled her around to my side. "I do not need your assistance. This helpless child does."

Judd leaned against the back of the sofa. His slackened face tightened when he saw Georgia. "What is she doing here?"

"She needs somewhere safe to stay for a few days. One of our patients, Ada Jenkins, is going home on Sunday, and she will take Georgia with her. You know Ada. She is one of your milkers."

Georgia lifted her face to mine. "I'm goin' with Ada?"

"Yes, Georgia. Ada will raise you as her own daughter."

Georgia clutched my shirt. I could feel the tension in her body ease.

Judd leaned forward. "Why does she need to get off the ward?" I guided Georgia to the table. "Henry has something for you to eat, Georgia. I am going to talk to Judd."

She sat at the rough-hewn table and picked at the potatoes on the plate in front of her.

I sat next to Judd, hoping Georgia could not hear my lowered voice. "Charles comes at night and takes Georgia off the ward. I assume the worst. I am sure you know he has the protection of the matron and, therefore, Dr. McFarland. Her distress has led her to retreat from reality. The nurses punish her constantly for her lapses. We have to get her out of here, but we need a little time to do so. Can she stay with you until Sunday?"

"As you can see, Doc, I'm not always in the best of shape."

"Ada does not believe she can protect Georgia from Charles any longer. She fears the child will not be allowed to leave on Sunday if she continues to worsen."

Henry joined us. "You can sober up if you got a reason, Judd. Seen you straighten up last year, when the state inspectors come out."

I kept my eyes on the steward. "I do not know where else to take her. No one wants the poor child."

Judd glanced at Georgia. "I got a bed in the other room, behind those drapes. She'll be safe with me. Henry, you'll need to bring some extra food out."

Henry pushed his hands in his pockets. "Anything you need, boss."

I approached Georgia and her doll. "I am going to leave you with Judd tonight. You will stay with him until you go home with Ada."

Judd crouched down in front of her. The smell of whiskey radiated from his unshaven face. "Won't be but a few hours 'til Ada comes out to milk. Henry'll bring her in to see you. You done eatin'? I'll show you where you're gonna sleep."

Georgia threw her arms around my neck. "Don't leave me."

Judd pulled back the curtain that hid the bed from the room. "You're the one she trusts. Why don't you stay 'til she's asleep?"

I pulled Georgia's arms down. "I will not leave until you are asleep. If you go to bed now, Ada will be here when you wake up."

Georgia climbed on the bed. I covered her with the quilt Judd handed me and sat at her feet. After a time, the rhythm of her breath evened and she slept.

Henry was waiting for me at the fireplace. His voice was hushed. "Have any trouble gettin' her out?"

I thought I should tell Henry about my meeting with Lucy. "I ran into Lucy McFarland in the hallway."

Henry chuckled and shook his head. "Won't have to worry none about her. She don't want to explain what she's doin' out this time of night."

"Where do you think she was?"

"I know where she was. Meets one of the patients out in the barn real regular."

My first instinct was to warn Dr. McFarland of Lucy's association with a maniac. Henry read my face. "Nothing to worry about, Doc. The young fella's just here for drinkin' a little too much. Besides, Lucy's used to that. The doctor ain't no stranger to drink. Comes in pretty late some nights after he's been on a toot."

"Does anyone else know about his drinking?"

Henry's raised his eyebrows. "What do you think? Let's just say it's a good thing he and the sheriff get along."

"How does he get away with it? He never shows the effects of drink, like Judd does."

"Matron and Charles take good care of him, along with the missus."

Henry and I left the cottage. Our heads pushed through an eddy of wind that swirled through the barnyard. I began to doubt the wisdom of hiding Georgia with Judd. "Do you think Judd can stay sober enough to care for Georgia?"

"Think so. Judd's mighty soft hearted when it comes to young'uns. Never knew him to drink much before he lost his family. Wife and daughter, about the age of Georgia, died with the fever. He ain't never been the same. His other kids're grown, moved away before it happened."

"How long ago was that?"

"'Bout two years now. Pretty near drunk himself to death since. Taking care of Georgia'll do him good. Don't worry, I'll go back and see if he needs anything. She'll be all right. He's mighty kindhearted under that whiskey breath."

We stopped next to the dark windows of the bakery. "I have another favor to ask of you."

"What's that, Doc?"

"I need to visit a town called Farmington. I have no idea how to find it. Could you drive me there on Sunday?"

"You mean you ain't goin' to church on Sunday mornin'?"

I remembered our first conversation, when we had both admitted our distain for churchgoing. "Not this Sunday."

"What about Georgia?"

"We won't leave until she's safely on her way."

Henry headed up the outside steps to his room above the bakery and I walked inside the back door of the administration building. Even though shadows filled each floor's landing, the lowered gas lamps provided enough light to navigate the winding staircase that led to my rooms. I had been in the hospital for a short time, but even I knew of the many hiding places in its massive structure. I hoped I had put Georgia where she could not be found.

I awoke well before dawn. As I had never appeared outside my rooms so early, I repressed my urge to check on Georgia and remained in my quarters.

Staring at the flames in the fireplace softened the edges of my perceptions. My eyes were unfocused. Perhaps unknowingly, my brain was preparing for events that would push my senses and intellect to their limits.

I felt I had been sitting in front of the embers for hours before a knock on my door signaled my breakfast tray had arrived. Lena entered with the usual eggs, sausage, and biscuits. Her broad body stood directly in front of the table. "'Mornin', Doc. You been out yet?"

"No. Why do you ask?"

"Lots of hubbub goin' on. One of the patients went missin' last night."

"Who?"

"That little Georgia on Ward One. When the nurses went to wake ever'body she was gone. Ladies in her dorm room said they musta slept through her leavin'."

I showed great interest in my biscuits. "I hope she's safe. In this kind of weather, I don't think she could survive outside."

"Can't see how the little one'd know where to go. Don't belong here anyway. Needs a decent family, if you ask me."

"I know the girl. I believe Mrs. Jenkins planned to take her home on Sunday."

Lena stepped to the door. "Don't look like that's goin' to happen."

I descended the stairs to the main hall, where Matron Ritter and Charles waited to accompany Dr. McFarland on morning rounds. From my perch on the landing above, I could see the matron was unable to maintain her usual frozen stance. She paced back and forth beneath the bottom step, under the observation of the ever-present Charles. I assumed they anticipated Dr. McFarland's angry reaction to the news of a missing patient.

I had just reached the corridor floor when I looked up to see Dr. McFarland descending the stairs. He approached us with his usual excellent humor. "Good morning, everyone. I trust all of you slept well?"

Matron Ritter interrupted her stride directly in front of the doctor. Her unsettled features replaced the mien of blind devotion she usually directed at Dr. McFarland. She inhaled deeply before she spoke. "I have some disturbing news, Doctor. The child on Ward One, Georgia, is missing."

Dr. McFarland searched Matron Ritter's pasty face. "What happened?"

Charles did not move, with the exception of a twitch next to his left eye.

Matron Ritter dropped her head. "She was gone when the patients sharing her room woke up. The nurses have searched each ward. I searched administration myself. She has vanished."

Dr. McFarland stuffed his hands in his pockets and walked briskly to the door to Ward One. "She could not have vanished. If she is seen wandering around the grounds or in town, we will appear incompetent. We need to locate her before the Jacksonville community learns of her disappearance. She has no family. At least we will not have to answer to them."

The matron pulled out her keys and unlocked the door with a façade of calm assurance. "Don't worry, Doctor. We will find her."

We stopped first in Georgia's room. Ada looked up from her sewing. "Find her yet?"

Dr. McFarland began the interrogation. "Are you sure you did not hear the girl leave last night?"

Ada put her work in her lap. "If I heard her, she'd be sittin' right here. I guess I was mighty tuckered out last night."

"We will find her. She will not accompany you home, as we planned. Obviously she is too difficult for you and your family to handle. She needs further treatment."

Ada's eyes bore into mine. We both knew Georgia had to leave directly from the farm.

Every part of the building was scoured for the child. The pursuit came to a halt when the matron and Charles tried to enter the farm. Judd refused to allow them into any of the outside buildings, including his home.

After supper the next evening, I was sitting in my office when a light rap sounded on my open door. Judd entered, his hair combed, his eyes clear.

"Hiya, Doc. Doc McFarland called me in to have a powwow."

I stood and closed the door behind him. "Why?"

"The matron and Charles were a might peeved when I refused to let them search the farm. Ain't the first time we crossed swords. No love lost between us. We tolerate each other, as long as I don't come in here and they don't come out on the farm."

I must have looked distressed. Judd twirled the hat he held in his hands. "Don't matter anyway. They could search high and low on the farm and wouldn't find nothin'. Ain't nothin' to find outside."

I opened my mouth to respond. Judd put a finger in front of his lips. "Had to remind Dr. McFarland how I'm in charge of the farm. We do our own huntin'."

"What did he say?"

"Looked right at the matron and said to take care of her own."

The floor creaked outside my office door. I understood Judd's warning finger.

"Have you searched the farm?"

He walked to the door and grabbed the doorknob. A smirk covered his face. "Soon as the child went missin'. Gotta get back. Just stopped to say howdy."

Judd's sober presence, as well as his ability to take control of the situation, assured me Georgia was in good hands. "I'm glad you did. I guess the child has gotten out somehow. I pray for her safety."

Judd bowed slightly before he opened the door to the empty hallway.

As usual, I left my rooms to roam the grounds after supper. The cold wind had calmed and stillness permeated the paths winding around the grove of trees. I pulled my overcoat's collar up and with my hands in my pockets strode down the front steps, recognizing another solitary figure several yards in front of me. "Hello, Hayes."

"Good evening, Doctor. Out for a stroll?"

"I need to go outside before retiring. Will you join me?"

The whiteness of his smile penetrated the darkness. "Most definitely. I, too, feel compelled to get out of the house. I'm not sure how much longer I can stay here."

"I am beginning to question my own ability to remain in my position."

"Thinking of leaving? Where to?"

"I have made no plans, even though I find myself more troubled every day."

"Why?"

"Let us say my hope to find a calling here has been destroyed. I feel my attempts to improve the conditions of these unfortunate patients are blocked at almost every turn."

Hayes's body contorted in laughter. Almost instantly he regained his composure. "You expected Father's treatments to work? I guess he could fool someone like you for a little while. I hope you can see he is all bluster. He has no idea what he's doing, but he's so confident—no, arrogant—he convinces people he is right. It's the same way he performs his duties as a father."

"I did not mean to speak disparagingly of your father."

"Don't worry. I have come to believe I have to distance myself from Father or I will never become a man."

The silent fountain in front of the main entrance came into our view. "I know what you mean. Although I grieved for my father at his death, it was then I began to grow up."

We were quiet for some minutes before Hayes addressed me again. "I envy the child who ran away this week. What is her name?"

"Georgia."

"If a mere girl has the courage to flee, why can't I find the nerve to leave myself?"

"Do not be too hard on yourself, Hayes. Things are not always as they seem. You will find everything comes together at the right time and you must act."

Hayes stopped and examined my face. "What do you mean?"

I had said too much. "I mean you will know when your course is clear to you."

"I hope you're right. At times, I am so impatient for my life to begin I fear my very soul will burst."

Hayes climbed the steps to the front door, while I remained on the driveway. "Aren't you coming in?"

"No, go ahead. I am not yet ready to retire."

"I'll walk with you."

"No, I need some solitude before I am able to sleep. I will see you tomorrow."

Hayes appeared reluctant to climb the steps. If he had insisted on joining me, I would have been delayed from my actual destination. The moonless sky ensured I was unseen when I approached Judd's door. His rough voice answered my knock. "Who is it?"

"It's me, Dr. Fle—Doc."

Georgia ran to me and threw her arms around my waist. I released her grasp and held her at arm's length. I was pleased to see the change in her appearance. Her braided hair fell on the shoulders of a clean shift, mended with several colorful squares. A broad smile filled her face.

"Hi, Doc."

"Georgia, you look so pretty."

She dropped her head and peeked up at me through light eyelashes. "My baby doll's got a new dress, too. Ada brought it to me."

Henry sat on the other side of the table. "She's getting purty good at checkers, too. Beat me once. You keep practicin' while I talk to Doc."

Georgia ran back to the checkerboard. "I beat him good."

Henry, Judd, and I gathered in front of the door. "Dr. McFarland is angry Georgia has not been found. If she does show up, he will forbid her to go home with Ada. What can we do?"

Georgia's low voice told her doll which checkers to move. Her mumbles and the crackle of the fire's kindling were the solitary sounds in the room.

It was Henry who interrupted the silence. "You still wantin' to go to Farmington Sunday?"

My errand for Mrs. Packard was far from my mind. "Well, yes, I suppose."

"I can make sure the carriage ain't ready so as we have to take the wagon. We can hide Georgia underneath some seed sacks. If we leave early enough, no one will see her get in the wagon bed."

"I will notify Dr. McFarland on Saturday that I am going off grounds Sunday. I am sure he will not want to rise in time to bid me farewell. What do you think, Judd?"

"Could work. What about the ladies milkin', Henry? You'll have to make sure they won't see her. And your gals in the bakery. Can you keep them from seeing anything?"

"Now you're insultin' me. I can always sidetrack those gals."

Judd's expression did not soften. "You'd have to make sure Ada knows where to meet you. Can you talk to her without anybody hearin'?"

"I am sure I can."

Henry gave the final instructions. "You be out here before light on Sunday morning, Doc. We'll take care of the rest. Right now, I gotta get back to that checker game before she wallops me again."

Until Sunday arrived I went through the motions of performing my duties. I acquiesced to Dr. McFarland's absurd pronouncements during rounds and attended to patients' physical complaints. Although I appeared to be practicing medicine, the treatments I administered were mere distractions from my primary purpose.

In hushed conversations with Ada, I told her of Henry's suggestion to smuggle Georgia from the farm. She immediately agreed to the subterfuge and told me her family always arrived around nine in the morning on their visits. I was concerned about waiting on the open road, exposing Georgia to the winter winds. Ada suggested we wait at the train station in Berlin, well away from Jacksonville. Henry said he knew the depot well.

Ada assured me her family was determined to bring her home. She expected no delay. Although I did not understand it at the time, I was impressed by her certainty that Dr. McFarland and his underlings would not interfere with her release.

As a result of Georgia's disappearance, the ladies in Ward One were not allowed their daily stroll on the grounds. Instead, the patients promenaded up and down the hallway. Even so, they were more fortunate than the patients on Wards Two and Three, who were locked inside their rooms all day.

It was Pearl who caused me the most distress before Sunday. She was adamant that I find her daughter. The immediacy of Georgia's peril made it necessary to postpone my inquiries about Ginny. Pearl assumed her child was at Maude's in Jacksonville, in the opposite direction from my meeting place with Ada. The day was simply not long enough to go to both locations.

Pearl's presence on Ward One continued to confound me. "Pearl, how did you move up so quickly?"

"Ain't you figured it out yet?"

"I have no idea."

"Let's jest say I got friends in high places."

Pearl stood so close to me I could smell the soap she had used to clean the hallway floors. Her whisper trembled. "What about my Ginny? You promised you'd watch out for her, and I know you're goin' outside with Henry on Sunday."

I could not guess how she knew I was going out and even with whom. "I will not have time to check on Ginny this trip."

Her face colored and she hit her thighs with her fists. And then, as quickly as her face had tightened with anger, it transformed into a soft, flirty smile. Her one step in my direction was enough for the length of her body to touch mine. "Any way I can git you to change your mind?"

A shiver went through me before I stepped back from her, and the impact of her closeness lessened.

I felt sympathy for Pearl's desperation. I touched her arm. "You do not have to do anything to get me to help you. I cannot search for Ginny on Sunday, but I will go to town one evening next week to find her. Please be patient."

Pearl's body relaxed. She dropped to her knees, took a brush from the soapy pail next to her, and began to scrub the floor. "I believe you, Doc. Just don't know how much longer I can wait. I got this feelin' she ain't all right."

"I will do my best, Pearl. I am your friend. Do not lose hope."

After Saturday's rounds, I spoke to Dr. McFarland about my intention to travel outside the institution on Sunday. "Since I am not on duty tomorrow, Doctor, I will be taking a ride through the country, with your permission."

My renewed support of Dr. McFarland's opinions put me in his good stead. "Why, what a wonderful idea, Adam. Are you sure you will not get lost? Perhaps I should assign someone to accompany you. Charles, are you occupied tomorrow?"

I did not know if his suggestion disturbed Charles or me more. Charles appeared unable to speak. I was the first to respond. "Oh, I do not want to impose on Charles. I have already made arrangements. Henry has agreed to drive me."

Dr. McFarland scurried to the stairway. "Enjoy yourself. I'll see you Monday morning."

I instructed Lena not to deliver my breakfast because I was going out early. She insisted on leaving several slices of bread and a piece of smoked beef with my supper. "So as you won't starve before you find some dinner tomorrow."

Saturday night I lay on my bed, though I did not expect to sleep. My restlessness pushed me to rise many times, until I acknowledged I had nothing left to do but wait until the night passed. It was sometime in the early darkness of morning that I realized my heart was full, not with fear but with excitement.

I dressed well before the sun rose and moved furtively into the hallway. As far as anyone in the hospital was concerned, I had no reason to hide. Even so, my secret motives kept my gait measured as I made my way down the stairs and walked through the central hallway.

Outside, I passed the bakery door. It was shut against the cold of the morning, but I could hear the women chatter as they began their chores. Through the window's shade I saw their tireless forms framed by candlelight.

Henry opened the barn's wide door. Behind me, several women walked from the building to begin the early milking. With their heads lowered and their shawls pulled tightly around them, they resembled a line of students headed to a school-house.

I stood back, thinking I was unnoticed. The last in the row of the milkmaids raised her head and stopped in front of me. I was not surprised to see it was Ada. "Where's Georgia?"

"I have not been to Judd's yet. I am sure she is getting ready."

"Can I go with you?"

"Won't you be missed?"

"Henry's been lettin' me visit Georgia every morning. Nobody else pays any attention."

Henry approached us. "Come on, Ada. Georgia's probably waitin' for you."

The fireplace inside Judd's cottage glowed through the window curtain. We entered to see Georgia sitting on a small stool, staring into the fire. Her trance ended when she felt the chill from the open door. She rushed to us. "I'm ready."

Judd hunched over the table in front of the couch. He too seemed mesmerized by the flames. "She's been up half the night."

Ada held both of Georgia's hands. "Now, Georgie, you know you can't ride with me 'til we get out in the country. Yer goin' with Doc and Henry in the wagon this mornin', and they'll bring you to me later on. Remember, you got to play hide and seek in the wagon. You have to stay down and hush up."

Georgia's eyes never wavered from Ada's. "Why?"

"So Charles won't come and git you." Georgia raised a shoulder to her ear at the hardness in Ada's voice. "If you keep your mouth closed, he won't find you. Tell your doll to be quiet, too."

"I'll make sure she's good." Georgia held up the nickel-plated thimble to my face. "She's always good when she plays with this. She knows you give it to us."

Ada held Georgia close for a second. "I gotta git back to milkin'. You mind Henry and Doc."

It felt like hours until Henry returned from the barn. "Milkin's done. All the gals gone back to the wards. You ready to go, Doc? We better get our load in the wagon before the sun comes up. She's startin' to get light over east already. I got Juanita hitched."

Judd handed me a table cloth wrapped around something lumpy. "Here's some biscuits in case you're on the road at dinnertime." He lifted the quilt off the bed and wrapped it around Georgia's shoulders. "That should keep her warm."

The quilt fell off her shoulders when Georgia put her arms around Judd's waist. He pulled her arms away and wrapped the quilt around her again. "Go on now. Don't cause no trouble."

Henry picked up Georgia and went out the door. I saw tears in Judd's eyes as we shook hands in silence.

I climbed up on the seat. Georgia was already settled in the wagon's bed between the seed sacks, well-covered by her quilt and the wagon's tarp. The squeak of the springs and the crunch of the gravel on the driveway were the only sounds as we passed through the same stone entranceway I had come through upon my arrival. The beauty of this apparent haven had impressed me. Now I was assisting one of its victims to escape its walls.

On the road, our appearance was so benign we could have been mistaken for brothers on a Sunday visit to relatives. My apprehension lessened as we drove farther from the asylum. Henry and I swayed contentedly on the wagon's seat until the sound of hooves told us of the fast approach of an unknown party. Henry pulled up on the reins and brought us to a complete stop. Fear replaced relief.

Four riders, dressed in dust-covered dark clothing, surrounded our wagon. The sun was high enough for us to make out their rough faces and scrawny beards.

One of the riders leaned over to grab Juanita's bit. Another pulled his horse next to the wagon seat. He sat straight in the saddle. His heavy sheepskin jacket and boots were splattered with mud. They had clearly been riding for days.

The man's gray teeth settled into a sneer. "Mornin', gents. Where you two headed?"

Henry's usual banter failed him. "Well—we, uh—"

I forced myself to push words through my tight throat. "We are headed to Springfield."

"Springfield? What you doin' there?"

I looked down at my boots. "Why—we—"

The rider and his horse snorted at the same time. "What you got in the back?"

"We are taking supplies to my family." As I gestured behind me, the wagon's cover moved.

"Mighty lively supplies. You sure you ain't got no niggers hidin' in the back?"

Could these riders be the slave catchers I had heard so much about? I understood they were paid handsomely for any slaves they returned to their southern masters. Their ruthlessness was well-known.

"Why, no, we—"

The two riders at the back of the wagon dismounted and climbed up onto the bed. Without thinking, I turned and started to clamber over the seat. I heard the cock of a gun and faced the sound. The rider next to Henry held a rifle aimed at my head. His voice was directed to me as well. "I'd stay put iffin' I was you."

I sat down.

One of the men pulled the tarp away. He reached down, removed the quilt, and jerked Georgia to a standing position. In spite of the terror in her eyes, the man holding the gun laughed. "Why this ain't no slave. She's as white as you and me."

A snort escaped his smirk. "What you fellers doin' hidin' a white girl? You Yankees think you're so high falutin', railin' 'bout slavery and all. Looks like you got your own uses for young girls, even if they is white."

I started to protest, but I thought better of it.

"Come on, boys. Nothing here worth shit." The man's broad grin remained steady as he tipped his hat to us. "Pleasure meetin' ya, gents."

The dust their horses kicked up flew back on us as they galloped off.

I climbed into the wagon bed. Georgia shivered and clasped her doll to her dress. I wrapped the quilt around her and held my arm around her shoulders. "I think she is all right."

Henry slumped on the bench. "I ain't been that scared fer a long time." He sat up straight and slapped Juanita with the reins. "Let's git outta here."

I sat next to Georgia until we reached the Berlin train station. We were thankful for the wood-burning stove in the center of the waiting room. No train was due until afternoon, so the three of us sat alone in the small room. The stationmaster remained behind the ticket counter.

Close to noon we heard the creak of wheels approach the depot. We walked outside and watched as Ada and a man sat hunched against the wind. He pulled the wagon next to ours. They both climbed down, and I saw Ada's companion was the size of a man, but had the face of a boy.

Ada took Georgia's hand. "Have any trouble?"

Henry handed Judd's quilt to Ada. "Nothin' to speak of. And you?"

"Easy travelin'. This is my oldest, Odell."

I put out my hand. Odell nodded.

Ada was the one who shook my hand. "Mighty grateful, Doc. Georgia is, too, though she's too young to say so."

My entire body filled with warmth—peculiar, since the temperature was so low. The heat emerged from my skin and filled the space between Ada and me. I wasn't sure why, but I, too, was grateful.

Georgia pulled on Ada's arm. "Can we go now, Ada?"

The three walked to the wagon and I heard Ada say, "'Bout time you started calling me Ma."

CHAPTER EIGHT

Ada took the reins and cut east through the expanse of fields. Her two children huddled on the rough seat next to her. Odell bent slightly forward, draping his boot over the metal foot brace while Georgia leaned against Ada's side.

I could not stop watching the trio. I was barely aware of the daunting challenges their mode of travel and the life they headed toward presented to them; nevertheless, an aura of calm surrounded them. The farm woman I had met on the train had showed the same serene acceptance of her fate.

I did not know what the future held for Ada and her family, but I was sure of one thing: Ada would not allow herself or any of her family to be committed to the Illinois State Hospital for the Insane. She had learned far worse things existed behind the asylum's walls than the trials of life on the prairie.

Henry's voice interrupted my thoughts. "If we're goin' to make it to Farmington and back 'fore sundown, we better get a move on."

It would take us most of the afternoon to get to Farmington. Our intention was to arrive, convey Mrs. Packard's message, and get back to Jacksonville before nightfall.

The weather was holding. No clouds signaled impending snow. The temperature had risen as the sun rose, but the cold continued to seep through my overcoat.

Ruts in the dirt interrupted the slow progress of the wagon. I could see why Henry was adamant about getting back before dark. The road wasn't much more than an indistinct trail surrounded by prairie and cultivated fields.

At one of the homesteads we passed, a man carrying a bucket came out of a large shed. He raised his arm and tipped his hat as we passed.

Henry waved at the man. "Pretty rough out here in the winter, huh, Doc? Grew up on a farm. Don't miss it a bit."

I knew very little about Henry's past. "I did not know you farmed."

"Folks lived a few miles out of Beardstown, over on the Illinois River. They came up from Kentucky. Pa never homesteaded before. Pretty near killed all of us. Started with seven young'uns. Just three of us made it out."

I was silent, trying to imagine how it felt to lose so many in your family. I began to understand Ada's fears for her baby.

"Don't think about my kin much anymore. Guess you could say I was meant to leave."

"What do you mean?"

"I didn't mind walking a few miles to the school house. Learned to read usin' the Bible mostly. My favorite parts were about the cities: Jerusalem, Babylon, Damascus." Henry looked sideways at me and laughed. "Hell, I'd like to see Sodom and Gomorrah. Wouldn't you, Doc?"

I contemplated the expanse of prairie and dreamed of what it was like to grow up in such emptiness. The cities in the Bible must have been mysterious, even romantic to Henry. "I am sure you and I could not begin to guess what it was like."

Henry focused on the whitish air hovering below Juanita's nose. "No one in my family paid any attention to those things. Pa read enough of the Bible to try to put the fear of God in us. My brothers and sister were scared to death of him and his belt."

"And you?"

A slow smile came over Henry's face. "Got more beatin's than all of them combined. I can't say I feared him. I just vowed not to let him see me cry and took it. Probably made him hit me harder."

"Somehow I am not surprised."

"I could read and figure well enough. That one-room schoolhouse was what kept me around. I was twelve when Pa said I had to quit school and help farm. After that, I started lookin' for some way to get out."

"Where did you go?"

"I slipped over to Beardstown and got myself a job takin' flat-boats down the Illinois River to St. Louis. I was pretty green, so one of the other guys on the boat took me under his wing. Lent me some of his books. Seen people on that river like I ain't never seen before or since."

Crows skimmed over the road in front of us and landed on what was left of some prairie grass. Their beaks picked at the seeds on the bare ground. At the sound of our wagon, the birds flew up and disappeared in a stand of trees on the edge of the field.

"I worked on the river a couple of years or so. When the water froze I'd get a job at a stable. Always did have a way with horses. Railroads started carryin' most of the crops to St. Louis, so I hit the road and ended up in Jacksonville. Worked at the livery in town by the train station. People'd hire a wagon to get out to the hospital, and I drove a few. That's where I met my wife, Osa. Drove her to her relatives on the edge of Jacksonville. She planned to live with them. Liked her right off and I married her as soon as she'd have me."

"What happened to her?"

Henry's gaze rose to the horizon. "Caught cholera and passed on not long after we tied the knot."

"I'm sorry."

A sad pride covered his face. "Weren't none like her. None will replace her, either. 'Sides I ain't got time for a new wife."

"How did you get to the asylum?"

"Met Judd at one of the watering holes in town. We were having a whiskey one night when he told me he could use a fella like me out at the farm. Been Judd's right hand ever since. Steady pay and I don't really answer to no one 'cept him. Guess you'd say I'm my own boss, the way things is."

Henry slapped the reins against Juanita's rump. "We better git a move on. Old Juanita here'll crawl all the way if I don't keep at her."

We headed east on Jacksonville Road, a route used to traverse the distance between towns across the center of Illinois. I noticed a railroad track next to the road and realized the train to Jacksonville had taken me along this very route.

We continued until we saw a small wooden post with the word FARMINGTON carved on it. Henry guided Juanita onto a path leading north. The horse's hooves cracked the hard soil; we were the first to break the road's dirt for some time. I wondered why settlers had chosen such an isolated spot to farm.

Henry seemed to read my thoughts. "Ain't too much farther. Good soil out here. See how black it is? Mighty pretty too. Out in the sticks, though."

We crossed over a creek bed on what was not much more than an elevated mound of dirt reinforced by wooden planks. I glanced down at the ditch beneath us and imagined the rushing water that surely came in spring. The silence of the dry ground would break as the water filled the gully. I tried to forget the barren cold of our journey and dream of myself inside the warmth of a spring day. I closed my eyes to picture rows of black-eyed Susans lining the gully.

The events of the day distracted my consciousness, but my body was well aware of the little sleep it had had the night before. The rocking of the wagon and the rays of the sun put me in a stupor. A jolt of the wagon as it went over a rut in the road brought me back to wakefulness. "How much farther, Henry?"

"We'll start seein' some Farmington homesteads just over that rise."

Near a stand of trees along the side of the road, I saw movement out of the corner of my eye. A rabbit ran out from the cover of the woods and scurried across the bare field. Its trek was short. As the animal jumped over one of the plow's furrows, a man stepped out of the forest, aimed his rifle, and shot his game.

The loudness of the blast startled Henry and, without warning, he yanked the reins. I grabbed the railing on the side of the wagon seat to keep from plummeting to the ground. The shooter picked up his quarry and walked across the frozen field. His face was amiable enough, yet he approached us with measured caution. Henry laid the leather strap on the seat and we climbed down. "Nice shootin'."

A slight grin crossed the man's face. "Best time of year for rabbit."

He wore a heavy woolen jacket appropriate for winter hunting. The inflections of his speech were different from that of the locals I had met. I suspected he was from the East, perhaps even New York.

"I am Dr. Adam Fletcher and this is Henry Taylor. We are traveling from Jacksonville to Farmington."

"I am Dr. John Wyatt, physician and, at the moment, farmer."

I pulled the letter I carried from my pocket and checked the name written on the back in Mrs. Packard's hand—Agnes Wyatt.

Henry pushed his hands into his pockets. "I'd say crack shot to boot."

Dr. Wyatt smiled. "Thank you, sir."

I had never seen a man of education tramping in the fields. "May I ask why you are farmer as well as a doctor?"

"Since my family and I settled in Farmington over twenty years ago, I have had to learn how to till the land. As you know, Doctor, practicing medicine exclusively is not lucrative enough to support a family in a populated area. In the country, it is impossible."

"Where are you from?"

"Potsdam, New York."

"I am from New York as well. Seneca Falls."

"What are you doing in Illinois?"

"I am the medical director at the Illinois State Hospital for the Insane."

Dr. Wyatt's blue eyes considered me. "One of our community is in the asylum: Elizabeth Packard. Do you know of her?"

Mrs. Packard had told me not all residents of Farmington were to be trusted. Dr. and Mrs. Wyatt were the exceptions. "I do."

"Then your trip to Farmington is no accident."

"I am here to inquire about Mrs. Packard's children. She has asked me to speak to a friend of hers, Agnes Wyatt."

Dr. Wyatt dropped the rabbit's carcass next to his boot. He rubbed his gloved hands together. "I have the good fortune to be married to Agnes. She and Elizabeth are close friends."

"Would you direct us to your home? We would be most glad to offer you a ride."

"Thank you, no. I am afraid our supply of winter meat is a bit low. I need to complete my hunting for the day. Over the hill you will see a church, Farmington Presbyterian. The parsonage sits next to the sanctuary. About a mile past, you will see our brick home on the south side of the road. That's our homestead. Agnes will be delighted to learn of Elizabeth. A hitching post in the form of a black boy holding a lantern sits next to the porch. You cannot miss it."

We lumbered on, sure of our destination. "What did you think of him, Henry?"

"Seemed a decent sort. 'Course, present company excepted, it's damn hard to tell about an easterner."

We came to the top of the hill in full view of a far more substantial church than I had expected. It was of wood-frame construction, painted white. From the outside it appeared to be a one-room structure with windows lining its sides. No steeple topped its roof, but a chimney rising behind the front door gave the illusion that the congregation reached for the heavens. Leafless trees in what surely was a gracious lawn in summer surrounded the building. I had not expected to see such an appealing structure of worship in the country.

The yard surrounding the church joined that of a white two-story home encircled by a wide porch. I assumed the house was the parsonage, Mrs. Packard's home.

Both buildings appeared deserted until a girl, a year or two younger than Georgia, scampered down the front steps and ran to a swing hung from the large limb of a bare tree. A slender, bearded man stood on the porch behind her and stared at us with suspicion. I could not tell if his stiff bearing was due to the cold or to a rigid character.

The man nodded in our direction when we tipped our hats. The girl observed us directly. She clasped a rag doll like Georgia's close to her chest, but she reminded me of Georgia in another way as well. Her eyes showed too much grief for such a tender age.

We continued a short distance and came upon a two-story brick residence on the south side of the road. Henry pulled the wagon into the lane and stopped near the hitching post Dr. Wyatt and Mrs. Packard had described. "Hope they have feed and water for Juanita. She could use a little rest."

The sound of shoes crunching the frozen grass came from the side of the barn. A black man climbed up the hill from the direction of a small shanty in a hollow below. He grabbed Juanita's bridle as if she were his. "Yous here to see the missus?"

We sat silently on the wagon's seat. Although I had heard free blacks lived in Illinois, I had not seen one since I arrived. I climbed down. Henry remained on the wagon seat, addressing the man with suspicion. "She needs feed and water."

A tall woman, dressed like a New England lady, opened the door. "I am Dr. Adam Fletcher from the Illinois State Hospital for the Insane in Jacksonville. Are you Agnes Wyatt?"

"I am Mrs. Wyatt."

"Mrs. Packard wished me a safe journey."

Mrs. Wyatt's face changed from apprehension to eager acceptance as she bid us to enter. "Josiah will take care of the wagon and horse."

Henry and I sat in a semi-circle of chairs in front of the sitting room's fireplace. On the other side of the hallway a door led to the kitchen. A woman tended a pot hanging over the hearth in the adjoining room. Henry gestured toward the door. "If you don't mind, ma'am, I'd be more at ease in the kitchen."

"Oh. My husband's sister, Ethel, will get you whatever you need. She takes care of us."

"Maybe I can help her." Henry left the parlor.

Mrs. Wyatt picked up a piece of needlework from the table. She spoke in a near whisper. "Please do not make me wait any longer. What news do you have from Elizabeth?"

"First of all, she is well. She has not been subjected to serious illness during her stay in Jacksonville; nonetheless, I fear her mental state has begun to deteriorate."

"Her mental state?"

"I do not mean her sanity is in danger. Mrs. Packard's mind is one of the strongest I have ever come in contact with. I mean her worries could lead to a physical breakdown difficult to treat. I fear her concern for the unknown wears on her, much more than her living conditions, which are deplorable."

"Deplorable? Pastor Packard assures me she is kept in a comfortable room. He claims she takes part in activities with other ladies of her kind, and even has privileges to walk on the grounds. He describes her living arrangements as lovely."

"He is no doubt referring to Ward One, where ladies live in relative comfort, as long as they do not express any dissatisfaction or disagreement. Unfortunately, Mrs. Packard has expressed much dissatisfaction and does not hesitate to disagree with her care."

Mrs. Wyatt placed her sewing on the table and stood next to the mantel. "Yes, that does sound like Elizabeth. Many of us believe her outspokenness is the reason she is in Jacksonville."

"She is in Ward Three, with the most disturbed of our patients. Her response to her placement is most disciplined. She keeps a rigid schedule of exercise and personal hygiene. Most impressive is her acceptance of her situation as an opportunity to help those around her. She motivates patients who have been ignored for years to cleanse themselves and their living quarters. I have the upmost respect for her."

Mrs. Wyatt turned her troubled face to me. "Why is she on Ward Three?"

"Her attempt to sneak a letter to her children was the precipitating incident. It is her continued defiance of Dr. McFarland, the superintendent, which keeps her in the asylum. She refuses to accept his demands that she change her beliefs to those of her husband's. Until she acquiesces to his wishes she will be left where she is. I hope the crudeness of her surroundings will not lead to illness."

Mrs. Wyatt returned to her chair and resumed her mending. "She has long been at the mercy of her husband, and now this Dr. McFarland. I do not believe either have her best interests at heart. I know her well. She will not use womanly wiles or modest agreement to improve her position. She demands respect, always, even in situations in which she knows she will not receive it."

The door to the outside opened and Dr. Wyatt entered. He hung his coat on a knob of wood in the hall and joined us before the fire.

I continued to question Mrs. Wyatt. "Why did her husband take her to the asylum?"

Dr. Wyatt held his hands in front of the flames. "He probably got sick and tired of hearing her state her opinions over and over. Elizabeth does not know when to be silent, even if she is threatened."

Mrs. Wyatt turned sharply to her husband. The fierceness of her expression made me think this was not the first time she and her husband had discussed Mrs. Packard. "What do you mean? She is the most generous of souls."

"Of course she is always on the side of right. Her flaw is that she does not know when to be quiet, even if her silence leads to the accomplishment of her goals. I do not agree with Pastor Packard's actions, but Elizabeth would be hard for any man to live with."

Mrs. Wyatt threw her sewing on the table. "I wonder how you would fare if I expressed my true opinions."

The embers of a log fell beneath the iron grate in the fireplace. Dr. Wyatt faced me. "I regret you have heard such inharmonious conversation in our home, Dr. Fletcher."

He met Mrs. Wyatt's stare with equal irritation. "I have more hunting to do. I will return for supper."

The doctor faced me again. "It was a pleasure meeting you, Dr. Fletcher." He grabbed his coat, walked outside, and slammed the front door.

Mrs. Wyatt's angry glower followed her husband as he left the house. "In spite of my husband's ill-chosen words, Elizabeth performed her duties as wife and mother to her husband's satisfaction. He found her unacceptable as a minister's wife. His pride was sorely battered when Elizabeth expressed her views in public. Their union grew more and more contentious. They might have gone on indefinitely if the issue of slavery had not come between them."

"Slavery?"

Before I could inquire further a rail-thin woman entered the parlor carrying a tray of cookies. She set the plate on a table and wiped her hands on her apron. "Thought you'd like a little something to eat, Agnes."

"Dr. Fletcher, this is my sister-in-law, Ethel."

I stood and bowed in her direction. "Thank you for your hospitality."

Henry stood behind Ethel, carrying a tray with a teapot and cups. "You're gonna love those cookies, Doc. Had a few already." He beamed at Ethel.

Ethel's face flushed. "Give me that. I'll put it down."

She swung her skirt around and headed to the kitchen, shaking her head.

Henry trailed behind her. "Yes, ma'am. Best I ever ate."

The smell of the honey-dipped cookies and the warm steam of the tea reminded me of home. After our parents died, Sarah often comforted us with cookies. We had munched the sweets by a winter fireplace, remembering our childhood and how our mother had fixed our favorites. "What does slavery have to do with Mrs. Packard?"

"How long have you been a resident of Illinois, Dr. Fletcher?"

"Not long, I am afraid. This is the first time I have ventured outside the hospital grounds."

"A group of us from Potsdam, New York settled Farmington. Most of our husbands are doctors, ministers, and teachers as well as farmers. Our Eastern sensibilities are very different from the Kentucky hill people who settled central Illinois. We had kept to ourselves as much as possible until forces beyond our control pulled us into controversy."

"Forces beyond your control?"

Mrs. Wyatt watched me through her scrunched brows and I began to squirm in my chair. She held my gaze much longer than I would have expected, as if she were evaluating my worthiness, but worthiness for what?

At long last, she picked up her mending and focused on the button she was attaching to a shirt. "Some of our community members were actively involved in the abolitionist movement in New York. Upon our arrival in Sangamon County we were stunned to find ourselves living among those who would maintain and even expand slavery. For many of us, our close proximity to southerners deepened our commitment to end the bondage of our black brethren."

"What does that have to do with Mrs. Packard?"

"Our community became more and more divided about what we, as Christians, should do to work toward the freedom of the slaves. Pastor Packard thought we should do nothing. Slavery would die on its own. Elizabeth believes in the immediate emancipation of the slaves. She joined those of us who created a new church to pursue that goal. Pastor Packard's fury at his own wife leaving his church became a ridiculous belief that Elizabeth is insane. As you know, if a husband wants to put his wife in an asylum, no one can intervene. The law is clearly on his side."

Mrs. Packard had sent me on a mission more complicated than I could have envisioned. I was so engrossed in Mrs.

Wyatt's story I had forgotten the letter Mrs. Packard had trusted me to deliver. I pulled a piece of paper out of my pocket. "Mrs. Packard asked me to give this to you."

Mrs. Wyatt reached for the letter.

"I will join the others while you read."

Henry and Ethel sat at the kitchen table with their heads close together. At my entry Henry leaned back in his chair and Ethel rose. "Need anything, Doctor?"

"We have eaten all of your wonderful cookies. Do I dare ask for more of your cooking?"

"I have some stew warming over the fire."

My stomach yearned toward the aroma coming from the wrought-iron pot. Ethel scooped up a helping of meat and vegetables.

The meal and the closeness of the fire reminded me that I had not enjoyed the companionship of friends and family for some time. Although my quarters at the hospital were comfortable, I was a resident of an asylum, an unnatural place. Like the patients, I, too, was isolated from the warmth of home.

Ethel was not nearly as prim as her appearance would lead one to believe. She told us she had received offers of marriage, but had never met a man whom she thought deserving of her hand.

At her statement, Henry put his thumbs in his belt, sat up straight, and pushed his chin upward. He locked Ethel in a straightforward stare. "That's 'cause you never met a fella like me."

I expected such an outrageous statement to insult Ethel. Henry was a man of character, but Ethel came from a different class and background. Would she not think his comment disgraceful? I could not have been more surprised when she moved closer to her admirer and responded in a similar tone. "What makes you think you're deserving of my affection?"

Henry stood and turned to her quite deliberately. He raised Ethel's hand to his lips. "If I was courtin' you, you'd have no reason to doubt my qualifications."

"Oh, I wouldn't, would I?"

Ethel broke into a laugh. Henry and I could not help but join her. She cleared the table, picked up a big bowl from the sideboard, and reached for a shawl hanging on the arm of a rocker next to the fireplace. "I need to go to the root cellar to bring in some smoked meat and potatoes for supper. Will you gentlemen be joining us?"

I did not want to leave such an agreeable setting, but if we were to be back in Jacksonville before dark we had to leave within the hour. "Nothing would be more pleasurable, but I'm afraid we have a lengthy trip before nightfall."

Henry pushed the door open, one foot on the back stoop. "I'd be mighty happy to help you bring those things in from the cellar."

A harsh scowl replaced Ethel's pleasant expression. "No, I will get them myself. Stay in the kitchen."

She walked through the doorway and pushed the door closed. Henry retrieved his foot scarcely in time to avoid being crushed.

"What was that about? I was just tryin' to be a gentleman."

"I cannot guess, Henry."

"Women; you never know what's goin' to vex 'em."

Henry and I were pondering over the mystery of the female sex in silence when Mrs. Wyatt entered the kitchen. She clutched a lace handkerchief in one hand and Mrs. Packard's letter in the other. "Dr. Fletcher, won't you come to the parlor with me?"

We sat before the fire in silence until Mrs. Wyatt took a deep breath and addressed me. "Elizabeth's letter has moved me, but I fear the truth about her children may be harder for her to bear than her current state of ignorance."

"I do not feel she will be able to maintain her health without knowledge of her children."

"You will have to decide the wisdom of telling her that except for her youngest daughter the rest of the Packard children have been sent to her husband's relatives in the East. But their departure is not the worst of it. When my husband inquired about their welfare, Pastor Packard stated it was his duty to break all connections between the children and their mother. To ensure they would not contact her, he asserted she was possessed by the devil and no longer claimed them as her own."

"Did they believe him?"

"The pastor told my husband the children did not resist getting on the train. I am not sure if their passivity was due to a belief that their mother had abandoned them or a wish to flee from their father."

Mrs. Packard's worst fears were in fact reality. What sadness had visited those poor children—to lose a mother and then to believe the loss was of her own volition. "This will cause Mrs. Packard the utmost distress."

"Pastor Packard intends to send the youngest, Libby, away next week. His sister from Manteno will be here Sunday to take her to her home. If she cannot be with her mother, living with her aunt is the better alternative. I fear her father is too quick with the rod."

I began to understand the hopelessness I saw in the Packard child's eyes. "We passed the parsonage, and I believe we saw Pastor Packard and Libby. He watched her from the front porch, a most stern expression on his face. Libby's appearance was one I had seen in an unhappy child before, full of loneliness and despondency."

How would I tell Mrs. Packard what I had found? So much bad news at one time might indeed endanger her sanity. "A letter from you would benefit Mrs. Packard greatly. Henry and I must leave soon, so I am afraid I cannot allow you much time to write. If you pen a longer note to her after we leave, mail your letter directly to me. I will make sure she receives your message."

I found Henry and Ethel bantering back and forth as Ethel peeled potatoes in front of the kitchen hearth. Their short scrap seemed to have been forgotten.

Mrs. Wyatt waved tentatively from the porch as we headed toward the barn. Her note to Mrs. Packard was safe in my pocket. I was glad to have a message from a dear friend to give to Mrs. Packard, though I was apprehensive about the impact of the information it contained.

Alert to the activity around the property, Josiah hurried up the hill from the shanty. He hitched Juanita to the wagon, but neither looked our way nor acknowledged our expressions of gratitude. Midway down the lane, I turned to see Josiah open the door to the same root cellar Ethel had forbidden Henry to enter.

We passed the church and the parsonage on our way west. The residence appeared deserted. The hour had arrived when the sun no longer illuminated the inside rooms, and yet the darkness was not deep enough to raise gas lamps or light candles. For many, supper interrupted the gloom of a winter's late afternoon. I wondered if a simple meal could suspend the desolation inside that home.

CHAPTER NINE

A slight wind braced us as we lowered our heads against the sunset. Our conversation was sparse. I could not speak for Henry, but I spent the ride home in contemplation of the events of the day. We had rescued one unfortunate girl and learned of another child in distress.

I pondered the best way to present the news of her children to Mrs. Packard. I shared Mrs. Wyatt's apprehension about her friend's reaction to the fate of her offspring. Mrs. Packard was strong enough to endure the extreme living conditions of the asylum and the outrageous treatment of Dr. McFarland. I was not certain she could maintain her health when she learned of the loss of her children. Since I did not know how I was going to communicate the bad news to her, I was glad I did not have to face her until morning.

On rounds the next day I found Mrs. Packard wiping off the remains of Sally's breakfast from her uplifted face. Sally vacillated between aggressive actions against others in the ward and passive refusal to eat or to attend to any of her bodily functions. She had become one of the asylum's most disturbed patients.

Mrs. Packard approached me as Dr. McFarland and the others walked to the ward's exit. "Dr. Fletcher, might I have a word with you? I fear I am ill."

I called to Dr. McFarland. "I will join you shortly. I need to check on Mrs. Packard."

Matron Ritter and Charles trailed behind Dr. McFarland, who scarcely broke his stride. "Do not spend too much time on Mrs. Packard. I am sure her constitution is strong."

Mrs. Packard scanned the hallway lest we be interrupted. "Do you not have news for me?"

Aware the nurses were nearby, I spoke more loudly than necessary. "Let us go into your room so I may examine you."

As usual, Angelique occupied the rocker next to her cot.

Mrs. Packard wrung her hands. "Did you find Farmington? Did you deliver my letter to Agnes? Did you learn of my children?"

I touched her arm in an effort to quiet its tremors. "I will answer all of your questions. I beg of you to control your emotions and listen to me."

"Of course, of course. I am most anxious. Sleep eluded me last night. Preparing the other patients for breakfast was the only way I kept my mind within the realm of sanity."

I slipped the letter from my pocket into Mrs. Packard's hand. When the sound of footsteps approached the door I grabbed Mrs. Packard's wrist and pulled out my pocket watch. My body blocked the view of the nurse who stood in the doorway. "Need help, Doc?"

"No, thank you, Nurse. Mrs. Packard is a bit faint. She will be fine after she rests."

"She's been hunky-dory all morning. Hard to get her to sit down."

A desperate screech pierced the corridor. "Oh, Sally's at it again. I better make sure she ain't tearin' up her room."

After a few minutes the letter slipped out of Mrs. Packard's hands and fell to the floor.

"Mrs. Packard, what is it? What has Mrs. Wyatt related to you?"

She lay on the bed and stared at the ceiling.

"Mrs. Packard, may I do something for you?"

She rolled over to her side and faced the wall.

I picked up the letter.

My Dearest Elizabeth,

I received Dr. Fletcher today. He appears most congenial and I am comforted you have someone in that wretched place to care for you and with whom you may confide.

I will answer your letter briefly, since Dr. Fletcher must return before dark. I will send a longer reply directly to him. He assures me he will forward my letters to you.

Many truly miss you in Farmington. None as desperately as I. The loneliness of the prairie is most pronounced without my sweet friend. Then again my misfortune at the loss of your company does not compare to the anguish you must feel in your isolation.

Dr. Fletcher tells me of your dedication to the care of those around you. Your goodness has always been in evidence to those of us who know you best. I am not surprised you have bettered the lives of the lost souls around you, in spite of your impossible living conditions.

It is most painful for me to cause you the agony I know you will feel when I inform you of your children's lot. I wish I could tell you all is well and that they are flourishing. Unfortunately, I cannot. I considered deceiving you, but I know you will eventually learn the truth, which would make lies even crueler.

So, the truth it is. Without your sweet influence, Pastor Packard has proved to be as uncompromising a father as he is husband. The children, except for Libby, have been sent by rail to his relatives in New York. You know the nature and circumstance of his kin. I do not.

Libby remains at home, but only for a short while. Pastor Packard's sister from Manteno is to come on Sunday to take her to their home.

You inquire if I have knowledge of what your husband has told your children. Dr. Wyatt had a conversation with your husband about this very theme. Pastor Packard admitted he told the children you had deserted them and were possessed by the devil himself. They have been led to believe you do not want to see them again. Such harshness is beyond understanding. It is clear he is the one possessed by Satan.

If only I were with you to help bear this knowledge. My heart aches for the loss of your children. Their deaths could not be more painful to you, I know.

I implore you to seek comfort from the Lord. Such tragedy is His way of testing our resolve.

Take heart, my cherished friend. I am always here to love and help you.

Dr. Fletcher is preparing to leave and I must close.

May God's grace be with you.

Agnes

I no longer had to be concerned about telling Mrs. Packard what I knew. Mrs. Wyatt had performed that task for me.

Certain Mrs. Packard would be punished if the letter was found in her possession, I put it in my pocket. I did not know how to help her. No medical treatment could assuage the absence of her children or their affection. "You should rest today. I will be back after supper to see how you are feeling."

She did not speak or move. Before I stepped into the hallway, I turned in their direction. Angelique had moved her rocker closer to the bed. She rested one hand on Mrs. Packard's arm, but her eyes continued their vigil of the grounds outside the window.

I had hoped taking a message outside would bring peace to Mrs. Packard. Instead, my efforts caused her more pain. The image of Libby floated through my mind. Could anyone forget the plight of such a helpless child?

My head was lowered as I walked through the wards, barely aware of the greetings of the patients. Pearl blocked my exit from Ward One. "Got some time for me, Doc?"

Her predicament was far from my mind. "I must continue rounds on the other wards. I will speak to you later in the day."

The hem of Pearl's dress hovered over my shoes. "I was expectin' to talk to you about my Ginny."

I took a step back. I knew I would be unsuccessful at putting her off. "Come into the parlor and we will talk."

I followed the sway of Pearl's skirts into the sitting room. She sat next to a round table with her back to the sunlight that flowed into the room. A golden contour of light framed her body. I was unable to make out the expression of her features because of the brightness of the rays. I moved to a chair adjacent to her, where the impact of the glow would not interfere with my concentration. "I know you are anxious about your daughter."

Pearl's manner had changed dramatically in the short time I had known her. At her arrival she had been a wild beast, thrashing against her predator, Sheriff Paxson. I had been convinced Dr. McFarland's diagnosis of insanity was completely correct. Only when she had caught my glance did I see an animal intelligence behind her eyes, coolly assessing her chances of survival.

Pearl sat up straight, her back away from the chair. She was agitated, but her discomfort was completely under her control.

"You want me to find your daughter and make sure her care is adequate?"

"I told you that son of a bitch sheriff prob'ly dropped her at Maude's before carryin' me here."

"Where is this Maude's?"

"In town, near the train depot. Ever'body knows where Maude's is."

"Could you give me a note of introduction? I'm not sure I will be received kindly if I start to ask questions, especially if the sheriff is around."

The corners of Pearl's mouth dropped. Her young face grew much older. "I cain't give you a note."

"Why not?"

"I ain't never learnt my letters."

Another obstacle most would find insurmountable, yet Pearl survived on the outside as well as inside the asylum. I wondered how an illiterate girl had managed to maneuver so smoothly through the maze of the asylum to Ward One. "When did you begin to work at Maude's?"

"Pa and Ma throwd me out right after we come to Illinois from Kentucky. Said I sassed 'em too much. Too many of us to feed anyway. If it weren't winter, I mighta been able to stay in the woods. Too freezin', so I walked into Miss Maude's and did what I had to."

If I had been in similar circumstances I wondered if I would show such canniness. "Don't worry. I will find out about Ginny."

Pearl grasped and dropped my hand in a single gesture. She stood and paced back and forth in front of the window. "I'm frettin' she's so little she can't take care of herself. The girls are well-meanin', but they got their own business to take care of and some of 'em hit the whiskey pretty hard. Maude's too old to take care of a young'un. I just keep picturin' Ginny wanderin' off and nobody knowin'. Hope they remember to feed her. I wonder where she's beddin' down."

I took Pearl's hand. "Shh—one thing at a time. I will ask Henry to take me to town and find Maude's."

Pearl's tight brow relaxed. "Henry knows where Maude's is. He's a regular customer. Can't say he's ever been one of my fellas, but he knows most of the gals."

I was not surprised Henry knew of Maude's. "I will not leave Maude's until I find out about Ginny."

"When? You won't wait long, will ya?"

"We will go tomorrow night."

Pearl threw her arms around my neck. Her lips hovered next to my ear. "Thanks, Doc. If you ever need anythin'—"

I pulled her arms down and backed away, although my body quivered as if forced to move in a direction my senses opposed. "I am happy to help."

Pearl was pretty in a slight, insubstantial way. She had acquired the manners and mien of those in my class, but she was nothing like the women I knew. Her desperation at having no shelter had led to a plan for survival, not defeat: "I walked into Miss Maude's and did what I had to do." Pearl's instincts were her weathervane. She never hesitated to heed the direction to which her heart pointed.

After supper I entered the barn to see Henry supervising the evening milking. The close proximity of the cows and the milk-maids created a warmth that belied the chill outside. Henry's boots scattered straw from his path as he approached me. "Hey, Doc. What are you doin' out here?"

"Looking for you. Do you have time to talk?"

"Always got time for you, Doc."

Henry closed the barn door behind us.

"First, thank you for your help yesterday. Although the news we gained from Farmington gave Mrs. Packard little peace, at least she knows the fate of her children."

"I suspect knowin' is better. Her little one sure was pitiful. You could tell by sight her father's a mean son of a bitch, even if says he's God-fearin'."

"I am afraid I agree with you."

The rattle of a milk bucket and the soft lowing of a cow penetrated the barn door.

"I have another assignment that has to be kept between us, Henry."

"Why, Doc, you're becomin' a regular outlaw. Never knew a doctor so much fun."

I felt a grin cross my face. "I did not know I was so amusing. One of the patients, Pearl, has a young daughter who has been left at Miss Maude's in town. I understand you are familiar with the place."

Henry stomped his boots on the hard ground. "Hell, Doc, how'd you know that?"

I could not resist teasing him. "Rumors around the hospital say you are a well-known customer."

"Aw, Doc, I guess you could say I get around."

"I need you to take me to Maude's. Pearl wants me to find out if her daughter is all right and I have agreed to do so."

"I'll bet you have. Pearl's a mighty persuasive gal."

I was glad the darkness hid any evidence of the heat I felt in my face. "She has always been utterly correct with me. She is most anxious about her little girl."

"Maude's ain't exactly a right spot for a young'un. When you want to go?"

"How about tomorrow, after the patients are put to bed?"

The next evening Henry had Juanita harnessed by the time I came out the back door of the administration building. We followed the circular drive and left through the main gate unnoticed. A short distance on the road to town, a figure stood directly in front of us and waved in our direction. Henry pulled up on the reins.

Hayes McFarland stood next to Juanita. "Hello, Henry. I thought I recognized the wagon. Dr. Fletcher, too? Where are you two off to?"

Neither Henry nor I had a ready response to his inquiry. Before either of us could speak Hayes climbed over the wagon's side and sat in the bed. "Mind if I come along? I cannot return to my cage. You don't mind, do you?"

Henry stared straight ahead and I addressed our unexpected passenger. "Hayes, Henry and I may not be back until very late. Are you sure you won't be missed?"

Hayes leaned his back against the hard side of the wagon. "I don't give a damn if I am."

For Pearl and Henry's sake, as well as mine, I did not want Dr. McFarland to learn of our mission. Now the superintendent's son was accompanying us. I had no choice but to bring him into our confidence. "Hayes, I must ask you to keep our journey secret."

Hayes sat up and leaned over the wagon's seat. "Secret? Where are you going?"

"To Jacksonville to find out about one of the patient's children. She is extremely worried about her."

"Why not contact her family?"

"She has no family."

"If she has no family, where is the child?"

Henry and I exchanged glances. "We suspect she is being kept in a brothel."

Hayes nearly stood up. "A brothel?"

"Yes. You must not tell anyone, especially not your father."

"I will not tell anyone if you take me with you."

I knew we had no choice.

Hayes peppered Henry with questions about Maude's House of Leisure. How many ladies worked there? How much did they charge? Could he borrow some money?

The gaslights in front of the houses on the edge of Jacksonville broke the darkness of the country road. We passed the mercantile establishments around the town square and turned on a road heading north. Several blocks from the train station, Henry slowed in front of a two-story address with a gas lamp on the corner. Candlelight in the windows flickered through transparent curtains.

Henry pulled the wagon over and tied Juanita to a hitching post. Several carriages were parked next to the wooden sidewalks though the street was empty of pedestrians.

Hayes vaulted down. "This can't be it. No one's around."

"Come on, you two. 'Round the corner."

Henry led us to a side door where two girls stood on the stairs. Their provocative stances revealed black stockings and garters under shifts that resembled those worn by the female patients in the lower wards, except the flimsy fabric of theses dresses revealed the outlines of their breasts.

Henry kissed them both on the cheek. "Brought a couple of friends with me tonight, ladies. They're a little shy, so I won't introduce you." The girls laughed and peered at us through long lashes. Henry entered the door, deserting Hayes and me on the steps.

Hayes froze until the brown-haired girl took his arm. "You don't want to tell me your name, sweetie? I'm Maggie. Let's go in and get acquainted." She tugged on Hayes's sleeve and he followed without resistance.

The other girl took my arm. "My name's Dicey. What can I do for you tonight?"

She smelled like rose water. I cannot say her advances did not move me. With some difficulty, I put my unease aside and remembered the task at hand. My voice was not as strong as I would have liked when I spoke of my mission. "I need to ask you about someone."

"What're you talkin' about?"

"I am looking for a child. Her mother has sent me. Do you know Pearl?"

"Pearl still out there with all the lunatics? We all been wonderin' about her."

"She is fine, but she is very anxious about her daughter. I have come to find her and tell Pearl about her condition."

"Ginny's around here somewhere. We can see about her after you and I find a room." Dicey tugged on my sleeve and led me through the door into a softly lit corridor. We went into a room off the hallway. She pointed to a man behind a bar. "Joe'll get you a drink. Whadya have?"

I glanced around at plush chairs and a settee. "I'm here to find Ginny. Where is she?"

"Oh, she's around. You got plenty a' time for her. Why don't me and you go upstairs for a while?" Dicey leaned against me.

I closed my eyes. I could see myself standing on a cliff overlooking a river. A stream below enticed me to take one step. I backed away. "I need to see her now. I will pay you for your help."

Dicey placed her elbow on the bar. "Well, in that case, let's go find the young'un."

Before either of us moved, a gentleman entered and yelled at the bartender. "Hey, Joe, how about a whiskey?"

I recognized the bulky form of Sheriff Paxson.

Aren't you that new doc out at the asylum? Glad to see you patronizing one of our local establishments."

Dicey took a step toward him. "Oh, he ain't—"

I smiled at the sheriff. "This is my first time at Maude's. We were just about to go upstairs."

"Mighty pretty rooms upstairs. Dicey's showed me a few of 'em. She's a good one."

Dicey brushed against him. "I'll be here all night, Sheriff."

I pulled the girl through the doorway and leered in the sheriff's direction. "Dicey may not be available for some time."

The sheriff's voice followed us. "Well, I'll be. Never took him for one of Maude's customers."

We climbed the stairs to another low-lit corridor. I heard moans and grunts coming from the other sides of the thin walls off the hallway, until the sound of footsteps on the front stairs seized my attention. In the faint light I could see the sheriff's hat looming over the curly head of a blonde. I pulled Dicey inside a room before he could see us. My voice was a mere whisper. "I do not want him to know who I am looking for."

A door slammed and Dicey took my arm. "Let's go down the back way to the kitchen. Miss Maude's usually sitting by the fire, figuring. She probably knows where Ginny is."

The narrow staircase led to a large kitchen. A cook was preparing something hanging on the spit over the fireplace. Sitting at the table was a substantial woman, old enough to be the girls' mother. Her head remained bent over what appeared to be a ledger.

Dicey reached around the cook and stuck a finger in the pot. "That tastes good, Josie. Got any for a working girl?"

The woman at the table raised her head. "Get away from those vittles, Dicey. Payin' customers ain't had none yet."

"Miss Maude, this here fella's lookin' for Ginny. Pearl sent him."

Maude's wry stare appraised me. "You from the madhouse?"

"I am."

"Shame puttin' Pearl away. She ain't crazy. Just came up against the wrong man."

"I'm here to inquire about Ginny. Pearl is worried about her."

Maude gestured toward a corner. "She likes to sit under that window. Weren't much trouble at first. Now she's pullin' on the girls' skirts, not wanting them to leave her when they got a customer. Interferin' with business. We can't do right by her anyhow."

Ginny wore a torn dress, stained with food. She held a piece of cloth, which she put into her pocket, simply to take the rag out to refold and return it to its hiding place. Golden hair the color of Pearl's covered her downcast face. She did not acknowledge my presence, as if she were accustomed to the sight of pants legs standing next to her.

"Good thing you came today, though. She's leaving in a couple a days."

"Where is she going?"

"Orphanage in St. Louis. One of them temperance ladies is always stoppin' by to talk my girls into leaving. She don't like the idea of a young'un in this kind of establishment. Taking her on Saturday."

"Saturday?"

"Said she'd pick her up after breakfast and carry Ginny to St. Louis herself. Guess she don't want a child for herself who's the daughter of sinner."

My attention returned to Ginny. How could I ever tell Pearl of her daughter's fate?

I reached into my pocket and handed Dicey the money I had promised her. "Please do not mention my inquiry to Sheriff Paxson."

Maude's shrewd face showed no surprise. "We're used to keepin' our mouths shut. I would say most of our customers don't want people knowin' what they're up to."

My business completed, I waited for Henry and Hayes in one of the front parlors where I heard the repeated ringing of a doorbell followed by the swish of women's skirts and the thud of heavy boots on the carpeted floors. Those who entered the house did not come my way. Other doors on the first floor opened and closed. I assumed sitting rooms similar to the one I occupied lined the central hallway.

I wondered if I had made a mistake in not taking advantage of Dicey's company. I ordered a whiskey, hoping the drink would reduce my agitation. The liquid followed a warm trail from my gullet to my belly. I could not have described the path my second drink took as distinctly since my senses had entered into a pleasant numbness.

I leaned my head against the back of the chair and closed my eyes. Surely Pearl's daughter would have more advantages in the orphanage. What possible life did her mother have to offer her? Pearl was uneducated and a disgraced woman. At least in the orphanage someone with a proper home would likely adopt Ginny.

A thump on the door and the entrance of Henry and Hayes brought my attention back to the room.

Henry glanced at my empty glass and ordered three whiskeys. He offered one to Hayes and set one on the table next to me. "To the three musketeers of Jacksonville. I read in a book somethin' about them Frenchies. Them boys had some times."

We drank.

Hayes threw his head back and asked for another. "Whooeeee!"

In spite of the fuzzy glow surrounding my companions, I could see Hayes's light hair was rumpled as much as his suit jacket. His collar was partially unattached and his shirt tail was not tucked into his half-buttoned pants.

Hayes's breath told me the whiskeys we shared had not been his first of the evening. He fell into the chair across from me, his eyes watery, his complexion flushed. I was not so sure my appearance was any different from his.

Henry stood between our chairs. "I'd say we need one more whiskey before we leave. I'm a little short, Doc. Will you stand for the last round?"

I rose with great effort. My stance was uneven, but I was able to withdraw my wallet from my coat pocket. With a deep bow and a flourish of my arm, I gave the purse to Henry. "Take what you need, sir. I trust you completely. A musketeer's honor is never in doubt."

Henry took out a bill and returned the wallet to my pocket. "One for all and all for one."

Hayes lifted his glass to his lips and bellowed. "Whooeeee!"

Certain details of the night still elude me, but I do recall leaving the parlor with Hayes supported between Henry and me. We staggered to the front door and announced our departure with upraised voices to the unseen guests, busy with pursuits behind closed doors. No one investigated the commotion, except for one person at the back of the hall.

Miss Maude emerged from the kitchen, a smirk on her face. "'Night, gentlemen. Don't be strangers."

We bowed low to our hostess, mumbled unremembered parting words, and entered the chilly darkness of the street.

The cold brought me back from the musketeers' Paris, but the night air did not have the same sobering effect on Hayes. Henry and I lifted him into the bed of the wagon before I took my seat on the bench.

Henry nudged Juanita on with a flip of the reins. "Some night, huh, Doc? Young Hayes was introduced to the pleasures of one of the fair belles. Told me upstairs this was his first time. Maggie figured that when she laid eyes on him. Gave him a couple of drinks to give him courage." Henry chuckled and Juanita brayed. "Hope he remembers his night on the town. You find out what you needed to know?"

Even though a heavy fatigue began to flow through me, my spirit retained the lightness of our camaraderie. "I did. We may have another secret wagon ride in store, my fellow musketeer."

A moan floated up from the back of the wagon. Henry and I grinned at the thought of Hayes's new manly status. I was no longer worried about Dr. McFarland finding out about our mission. Hayes had more to lose than Henry or I if his father learned of our evening at Maude's.

CHAPTER TEN

My arrival in my room was far too late for any lullabies to drift through the walls. The patients had retired hours ago. I strained my ears, but only the brush of wind against the window soothed me into a deep sleep.

I woke with a start well before dawn. No doubt the whiskey, to which I was unaccustomed, had caused the soundness of my sleep and my sudden wakefulness.

A wild premonition drifted through me, making further rest impossible. I was sure something was wrong. Had I known what was to come, I would have heeded my mind's foreboding.

I built a fire and stared into the flames. I knew I could no longer stay in the hospital as a reluctant assistant to the asylum's immoral practices. For the sake of my soul, I had to leave as soon as possible. Escape, I must; to where, I did not know.

My reflections lasted until dawn, at which point I shaved and dressed. I was certain Pearl would demand to know what I had found. I had no letter to inform her of what I had learned on the outside, so I would be the deliverer of bad news.

Dr. McFarland was not his ebullient self when he joined Matron Ritter, Charles, and me in the hallway after breakfast. Before entering Ward One, he stopped and faced me. "Adam, you are a young man. Perhaps I can gain some insight from you."

"Why, if I can be of assistance—"

"Hayes did not rise for breakfast this morning. When I entered his room I had difficulty rousing him. He complained of illness. I have my doubts."

I had some difficulty suppressing a smile. "What else could cause his symptoms, sir?"

"I believe I detected the smell of whiskey coming from him. You and Hayes are near in age. What motive would he have to imbibe spirits? I have raised both my children to know the evils of drink. Of course, Lucy is not at risk for that kind of thing."

I was struck by the hypocrisy of Dr. McFarland's statements. "I am sure you are mistaken. Hayes is probably using a medicine that smells like alcohol."

Dr. McFarland's brow wrinkled. "I hope you are correct. I would be most embarrassed to have my son frequenting the saloons in town. I will not tolerate such disrespect. Would you agree to examine him?"

"I will see him this morning."

Following Dr. McFarland and the others into Ward One, I allowed myself to grin. I knew the true nature of Hayes's illness, but the effect Dr. McFarland's suspicions would have on his son tempered my amusement. Hayes had returned to his cage and his keeper was not happy.

We found Pearl in the sewing room, engaged in organizing the clothes to be mended that day. One of the nurses mentioned that Pearl had volunteered to get the table ready.

Dr. McFarland addressed her brightly. "Good morning, Pearl. I am happy you are keeping yourself useful. The nurses say you are improving every day."

"Thank ya, Doc. Just trying to stay busy."

"Keep it up."

I hesitated as the others walked into the hallway. Pearl touched my arm and I saw her expression contained a threat, not an entreaty.

I raised my palm to delay her advance in my direction. "I will speak to you soon. Be patient." Before she could respond I joined Dr. McFarland's entourage.

We passed through Ward Two uneventfully. When the matron opened the door to Ward Three, the odor of human waste and bodily decay enveloped us. Could one day of Mrs. Packard's inactivity result in such a return to the status quo?

Dr. McFarland asked the nurses if they needed him to examine any Ward Three patients. One of them mentioned Mrs. Packard's altered behavior. We observed her sitting next to Angelique. Now both stared out the window. Dr. McFarland stood next to Mrs. Packard. "I understand your condition has worsened. Perhaps more time on Ward Three will benefit you."

Mrs. Packard did not take her eyes from her view of the grounds. "I am not feeling well."

"I know you are not satisfied with your treatment, Mrs. Packard. I will have Dr. Fletcher bleed you again. A less innovative practice may be more to your liking."

Mrs. Packard's head rose sharply and revealed utmost scorn. "Innovative?"

Dr. McFarland leaned back as if she had assaulted him. Although his tie was meticulously straight, his hand pulled at the knot. "Why—"

Mrs. Packard resumed her examination of the scene outside her window. The movement of her rocker was barely discernible. "Whatever you wish, Doctor."

Dr. McFarland addressed me as he rushed to the door. "Please examine Mrs. Packard. Do whatever you think is appropriate."

He left the room and I leaned over Mrs. Packard. "I am glad to see you have recovered from the news I brought you."

She lifted her head. Her sorrowful eyes dominated her features. "Recovered? No, I have not recovered, although I find in spite of my misery I am regaining my strength. God has given me a constitution that refuses to yield even to the most abhorrent of circumstances. I desire to succumb to lunacy in this horrid prison, but a will I do not understand pulls me from insanity."

"Your inner strength is obvious to all who know you. Mrs. Wyatt spoke of your fortitude at length."

"I wish to take to my bed and enter a dream world known to no one but me, yet I cannot do so. Instead, I sit here devising plots to change my fate and the fate of my children. My schemes are improbable, if not impossible, but I cannot quash them."

"What are you talking about?"

Mrs. Packard stood and faced me. "Perhaps I have lost my older children, but Libby remains within my reach. If I can get out of this cell I am sure Agnes and John Wyatt will help me regain custody of Libby so I will be able to spirit her away to safety. I cannot remain in Farmington or anywhere nearby if I am to be a free woman and live with my youngest child."

"How are you to gain her custody? The laws are clear on this matter. Your husband has legal custody of Libby."

Mrs. Packard raised her clenched hands. "I don't care about the laws of man. God's law demands a mother should be with her children. I will have custody of my daughter, no matter what my husband says or does."

She glared at me, but I knew her avowal was meant for her husband. "I do not have time to work my way into Dr. McFarland's good graces, which is the single way he will allow me to leave. Do you think I could disappear as the child on Ward One did? I find her absence most suspicious. She was never found and Ada was released days later. They were close, were they not?"

I swallowed before I stammered and viewed the scene outside the window myself. "I—I—Yes, Mrs. Jenkins protected Georgia, uh, while she was in the hospital."

"I am confident you helped the child. How did you assist her?"

Mrs. Packard had astutely determined my role in Georgia's exodus. Could I trust her? Were her motives and mine so in tune she would keep my subterranean activities secret? And who would she share them with? Dr. McFarland and his staff were her enemies. Her fellow patients in Ward Three were not able to understand the simplest of statements, or so I thought, until Angelique's sparkling eyes met mine. "You might as well fess up, Doc. Lizzie here's purty good at figurin' things out."

"Angelique—"

"I knowd you thought I was in my own little world in this here rocker. Sometimes you mighta been right. Seemed safer to keep my own company. Lizzie's the one I talk to."

Mrs. Packard crossed in front of me and put her hand on Angelique's shoulder. "Angelique is the one who brought me out of the shock of losing my children. She encouraged me to eat and get out of bed. We are both outcasts."

"You ain't nothin' like me, Lizzie, but I never forget someone who's helped me. Considerin' who I am, I ain't had more than a few on my side."

Angelique fixed her eyes on me. "So, Doc, what are ya gonna do to help Lizzie?"

I began to pace in front of the window. I was not sure I could do anything. The need to remove Georgia from Charles necessitated my immediate rescue of the child. And she had been on Ward One, not the impenetrable Ward Three.

"Don't forget, Doc, you got 'til Sunday, before that young'un is gone."

"I know. I know."

Mrs. Packard touched my arm. "I have known from the beginning you are a man of character. My stay here has convinced me that Dr. McFarland is merely interested in his own stature and power. If he has to deny the freedom of innocents, as many of us here are, to maintain the status quo he will. Your moral duty demands you help me."

At that moment I knew I would help Mrs. Packard. My decision was a righteous one, but I knew morality was not my primary intention. My motives had more to do with the growing thrill in my stomach and the lightness in my mind.

I felt a grin creep over my face. "We need a well-thought-out plan. I will be back late this evening to discuss what we will do."

Angelique slapped the arm of the rocker. "We can count on Doc, Lizzie."

Mrs. Packard kissed my cheek. "I am most grateful."

Helping Mrs. Packard was a hazard to my position in the institution and my status as a law-abiding citizen, but Mrs. Packard was sure certain universal laws superseded the laws of man. My actions could support such a higher force.

I walked up the staircase to evaluate Hayes's strange affliction. I was sure he was suffering from the aftereffects of whiskey, but I was willing to confirm his ruse of illness. The night before, Henry and I had walked Hayes around the barnyard until he regained most of his sobriety. When the hour was late enough for him to enter his parents' apartment without being noticed, he had saluted us, and disappeared into the building.

Hayes's pale complexion added to his sickly appearance. He shook his head at my smug attitude. "Don't say a word, Doctor."

I felt his forehead, pulled out my watch from my pocket, and held his wrist. After determining he had no fever and his pulse was normal, I walked to his desk where a tray of breakfast sat. "Your father asked me to check on you. Have you eaten anything?"

"The thought of food makes me nauseous. The room stopped spinning only within the last hour. Even now, I can make no sudden movements without my stomach's rebellion."

I stepped to the door and spoke to one of the girls waiting in the hall. "May we have a pitcher of water, please?"

I returned to Hayes's bedside. "Drink several glasses of water. I assure you, the liquid will help you recover from this mysterious sickness."

"I will never drink whiskey again."

"Of course not."

"Do you think my father knows what is wrong with me?"

"He suspects. I will tell him the scent of alcohol came from a tincture you used to clean a shaving cut."

The girl came into the room, carrying a platter containing a pitcher of water and a glass. I took the tray from her and set it on the table next to the bed. "Thank you. You may leave."

I poured water into the glass and Hayes gulped it down. "I knew a musketeer would cover for another musketeer."

"So you remember everything about last night?"

"If you're talking about Maggie, I do. She has changed my life."

"Do not forget. Maggie was paid handsomely to change your life."

"Still, I feel I owe her my gratitude."

I pulled a chair next to the bed. "You showed your gratitude by paying her. You owe her nothing, except an excellent recommendation perhaps."

"Perhaps I'll return to Maude's as soon as I feel better."

"You need to rest. Don't you have work to do at the law office?"

"I am finished reading the law. I am ready to practice."

"Congratulations. I hear law is a very useful occupation for a young man in the prairie."

"In spite of the fact that my father procured my apprenticeship, I am looking forward to riding the circuit. I accompanied a judge on the road once. The arguments, the crowd, the camaraderie were so exciting. We were welcomed as if we were famous. Father wants me to practice in Jacksonville. He expects me to live with him and Mother until I marry. But I cannot stay with them any longer."

"Where will you go?"

"The papers are full of news of the California frontier. I believe my prospects are in the West. Would you consider California? You and I would make excellent traveling companions."

I could not help but shake my head. One night with the fair Maggie and Hayes's dreams had taken flight. "Maybe so, but right now you have to recover from your illness and I have to complete rounds."

After rounds I found Pearl in Ward One's parlor. "I'm afeared at what you're gonna tell me."

"I saw Ginny. She's in good health and as safe as her circumstances can permit."

Pearl's damp eyes searched mine. "She's all right?"

"She is fine, and I believe well-fed; however, your fears have been confirmed. Ginny cannot stay at Maude's much longer. She and the girls are unable to take care of her properly. She needs far more than they can offer."

Pearl stood up and circled the table. "I knowd it."

"Pearl, sit down. I have more to tell you. One of the temperance ladies in Jacksonville has learned of Ginny. Like you, she believes Maude's place is unsuitable for a small child. She is picking her up on Saturday to take her to an orphanage in St. Louis."

"An orphanage? If she goes to St. Louis I ain't never gonna see her again."

"Maybe it is for the best. She will have a chance for a good home and—"

Pearl leaned across the table, her face almost touching mine. I backed away from her fierce expression. "Ain't no way I'm losin' my Ginny."

The steel in her voice convinced me she would not let her daughter be taken from her without a battle. Pearl would fight until the end.

"What can you do?"

"I'm gettin' her before Saturday. One thing I gotta know: are you helping me or not?"

I was not sure I could match her strength of conviction. My sensibilities told me to help Pearl, but my mind was full of the obstacles she faced to regain custody of her child.

Pearl judged my hesitation as refusal. "I'll do it without you. I never had nobody help me anyway."

"I did not say I would not help you."

"Well, you're not jumpin' at the chance, that's for sure."

"How can we help Ginny?"

"Don't know. I gotta think on it."

"Okay, I will think about it too."

Throughout the day the challenges of helping Mrs. Packard and Pearl distracted me. Would assisting two mothers to escape from the asylum ensure the rescue of their children? Even though they possessed more personal resources than most women, I could not grasp how Mrs. Packard and Pearl would care for children by themselves, on the run. I began to think my desire to be of service to these unfortunates was unrealistic and perhaps insane.

I could discuss my deliberations with no one. The idea was so outrageous I dared not pull anyone into my plans for fear of the well-being of any confidant.

After supper I decided to seek the comfort of the grounds. My mind was so full I scarcely noticed the cold of the night until I found myself approaching the barnyard.

I was happy to see Henry walking in my direction. "What you doin' out here, Doc?"

"Taking my evening stroll."

"You don't usually come back here, do ya?"

"No. I am restless tonight, I guess."

"What's on your mind?"

Henry had proven himself a hearty ally. Since my plan was vague I was hesitant to share any details. "I was thinking how fortunate we were to assist Mrs. Jenkins and Georgia. Have others tried to leave the asylum?"

"Oh, some of 'em try to run away. Thing is, most of them just walk off and head home. 'Course they don't know which direction to go most times. Some local usually picks 'em up on the road and brings them back. They're pretty easy to spot with their hospital clothes on."

"What happens to them when they're brought back?"

"You know how Doc McFarland don't like nobody breakin' the rules. They get back and spend a lot of time in the baths, or in the holdin' chair. 'Course they're put in the worst wards for a long time. Tell you the truth, most of 'em that run never leave here—alive, that is. They end up in the Diamond Grove Cemetery down the road."

"Cemetery?"

I would never let a family member be buried with fellow inmates for eternity. Who would leave their loved one inside a cemetery where lunatics were buried? Then I recalled the circumstances of many of our patients—no family at all, or a family grateful they were put away.

"Don't ever'body go home. Matron's mother's buried in Diamond Grove. She was crazy as they come. Spent all her time on Ward Three. Not long after she passed, the matron started workin' here."

I had never considered the possibility that Matron Ritter had been related to a patient. "How do you know so much about the matron's family?"

"You're forgettin', Doc, most of the people who work here lived close by for a long time. They know ever'body."

I realized how little I understood about the inmates of the asylum, as well as the employees.

I decided to pursue my initial questioning. "Except for the one we know of, did anyone ever make it out?"

"Well, some of the smarter ones snuck out in the warmer months. Not many though. Pretty hard to manage escapin' with no help. You and I know you that. What you askin' all these questions for?"

I stomped my feet on the frozen ground and put my gloved hands in my pockets. I knew if I needed him to implement a plan he was most valuable, nevertheless I was not yet ready to put him at risk. "I would think many of the patients would want to run away. I merely wondered if any of them had tried."

"If you say so, Doc. You sure you don't have anything on your mind? You're actin' kind of nervous."

"If I need your help I will let you know."

"Now there you go agin. You're up to somethin'."

"Henry, you have a wonderful imagination."

"Um, remember, one for all, and all for one."

I doffed my hat, swung the cap across my coat, and bowed deeply. "You are a man of honor, sir." Before I entered the back door of the administration building I watched Henry head up the outside stairs to his room above the unlit bakery.

It was not yet eight o'clock when I walked down the shadowy staircase to the vacant main corridor, and yet the quiet of night had settled in the asylum. Bedtime descended early in the hospital; patients were led to their cots after an early supper, well before dark. I imagined bodies tossing and turning on their beds, waiting for darkness and a restless sleep.

I had selected the key to Ward One in the light of my room so I was able to place it in the keyhole with little noise. I was prepared to explain my presence in the wards at such a late hour: concern for a patient with a fever. Even so, I felt like an intruder.

I stepped inside Ward One and removed my shoes. The silence was profound. If I had not known beings rested in the rooms lining the corridor, I would have sworn I was alone. The open door of the attendant's room revealed the lone nurse on duty sleeping on her cot. My stocking feet did not betray my presence as I walked the length of the hallway and entered Ward Two.

The ward nurse detected me and pointed to my feet. "Dr. Fletcher, what are you doing here?"

"I was trying not to disturb the patients at such a late hour."

"Oh, they don't care. Most of them can't sleep anyway."

I dropped my shoes to the floor and slipped them on. "I am headed to Ward Three to check on a patient with a fever. I could not sleep, so I thought I might as well see how she is faring."

"Hope it don't spread. Terrible thing when sickness goes through the house."

"I do not think the fever is caused by anything like that. Probably a female problem."

The revolting odor of Ward Three accosted my nostrils as soon as I opened the door. Muted conversations and cries came from the darkness behind the rooms' screens.

I found no one in the attendant's room when I passed. Uncertain of the nurse's location, I decided to go directly to Mrs. Packard's room.

I used my master key to open the screen across her doorway. She sat by the window, as she had that morning. The glow of the moon coming through the panes provided the only light.

She stared outside. "I've been waiting for you."

"I have arrived at this hour to avoid being seen. Just the nurse on Ward Two approached me. I told her I was checking on a feverish patient. If we are asked, *you* are that patient."

"Certainly. I am becoming good at deception. Apparently, trickery is the best way to regain my darling Libby."

"I fear it may be impossible for you to be with your daughter."

"With God's help, nothing is impossible, Doctor, but first, I must get out of here. With your assistance I know I can."

"Escaping is merely the first of many obstacles. If we succeed, where will you go?"

"Agnes and others in our church will help me. I have not informed you of everything about our little community."

"What do you mean?"

"The final straw for my husband was my alliance with our community's abolitionists. We formed our own house of worship, Central Presbyterian. My husband saw separation of the churches, which was a matter of conscience to me, as the ultimate betrayal."

The speeches of my sister Sarah's abolitionist friends had touched her deeply. She had attended several of their meetings and supported their efforts. I agreed with their principles, although I never felt moved to act upon them. Slavery felt far away from Seneca Falls. "Agnes told me some of that."

"As you have seen, if my soul is moved, I do not fail to act. Although patience is valued as a womanly virtue, such tolerance is not a quality I am in possession of, especially if the course of action is clear. My brothers and sisters at Central

Presbyterian believe God demands we help those who are in chains. Have you heard of the Underground Railroad?"

"Yes, but I know little about how such an organization works."

"The railroad offers slaves a way to escape from their owners and make their way to Canada. Depots—homes of sympathetic individuals along the way—provide them with shelter and food. Those of us who are committed to their freedom, provide safe passage from depot to depot."

I remembered the black man at the Wyatt home who came from the shanty, and his entrance into the root cellar. I also recalled Ethel refusing Henry entry into the same cellar. At the time, her actions were merely curious. Now I was sure the Wyatt homestead was part of the Underground Railroad.

"Our participation in this road to freedom is not without risk. The Fugitive Slave Act dictates the arrest of those who help slaves run away from their owners. Even if our own law enforcers look the other way, plantation owners don't. They hire the most nefarious individuals to search for the fugitives who stoop to the vilest of methods to catch and return their employers' property."

Mrs. Packard had no idea of my own terrifying experience with slave catchers. I had made a concerted effort not to think about their confrontation with Henry and me. "What does this have to do with your flight from the asylum?"

"I will be a fugitive. When Dr. McFarland learns I am missing he will contact the sheriff to search for me. My husband will use every means at his disposal to find me and send me back to the asylum. I will lose Libby forever."

"Do you think your friends will hide you and speed you away?"

In the semi-darkness I could not clearly see the features of her face, but her voice brightened with hope. "If you can get me to Agnes's farm, I will find a way to get Libby and be moved to the next depot. And then? God will point me in the right direction."

A sharp cry pierced the room. I leapt from my chair at the shriek's volume and my recognition of a male voice as its source. I had assumed I was the only man in the ward.

I peered into the unlighted corners of the room. "Where is Angelique?"

"Charles took her. I have given up trying to stop him."

"The scream is not Angelique's."

Mrs. Packard and I ran through the door into the darkened hall. All of the screens were closed and locked. We headed down the corridor toward a faint light that spread into the hallway from the dining room's doorway. Mrs. Packard gasped and leaned against the frame of the open door. I remained motionless, sure the scene before me could not be real.

Angelique stood with her back to a gas lamp sitting on a dining table. The light's glow outlined her figure, but I could not see her face clearly. She loomed over a still figure lying on the floor, kicking the unmoving form repeatedly. The glint of a blade shone from her hand.

When I bent over the body she pulled her foot away, and dropped the knife. I recognized the corpse at once. It was Charles.

CHAPTER ELEVEN

Angelique's black eyes glimmered in the semi-darkness. "I done it. I finally done it."

"Finally done it, finally done it, finally done it" echoed from across the hall. Shrill laughter interrupted the refrain. Other noises I would have attributed to animals had I been in a faraway jungle ricocheted down the corridor. Fists banged against screens. A clamor I could not decipher pierced my core and I was frightened. I was in the midst of the devil's minions.

Mrs. Packard was the first to take action. She stood outside the dining-room door. Her voice carried throughout the ward. "Be quiet, my dears. I need you to go back to bed. Say your prayers and God will sustain you."

She turned to the room across from us. "Melinda, be still and lie down. I'll brush your hair in the morning."

The cacophony dropped to the ward's familiar drone. Mrs. Packard closed the dining-room door behind her and guided Angelique to a chair away from Charles.

I felt Charles's neck. I did not feel any pulsing of blood through his artery.

The scene was certainly gruesome, yet I found my own reaction to Charles's death disturbing. I was not in the least bit sorry about his demise. In fact, I felt an inhumane and un-Christian glee. As a physician, I was committed to revering the sanctity of life, even if the existence of such a life meant untold pain to others. I had no such inclination for this particular mortal.

"Doctor, we need to determine our next move. Angelique is not to blame. That fiend violated her repeatedly. She had good reason to kill Charles."

Mrs. Packard's insistence that we take action brought me back from the assessment of my shaky ethics. "I agree, but Dr.

McFarland and the authorities will not. Given their knowledge of Charles's continued abuse of Angelique, I am positive suspicion will land on her."

"We must get her out of here before the morning shift arrives."

"Clearly she is in no condition to proceed out of the hospital alone. I can see she is still in shock. Would you agree to accompany her?"

"Are you sure we can get away unnoticed?"

I glanced at the dumb-waiter in the corner of the dining room. A railroad in the cellar brought the daily meals from the kitchen to the wards in carts. A worker unloaded the food into the dumb-waiters along the track's route. The nurses raised the meals to the dining room. "I believe I know a way."

"Even if we leave the hospital successfully, where will we go? Where will we hide at such an hour?"

The threat of capture and recrimination provoked my brain into quick action. I paced in front of Mrs. Packard and spit out my strategy.

"First, you and Angelique must leave the ward without notice. I don't know if Charles is the sole attendant on duty tonight, or if one of the nurses will come back into the ward. We have to get you out of here now. I will pull up the dumb waiter and lower both of you into the basement. You go first to receive Angelique. The two of you need to follow the tracks leading to the kitchen. This gas lamp will light your way. I will leave the ward as I came so as not to create suspicion. The nurse on Ward Two who saw me enter will see me exit the same way."

"How will we know where the kitchen is? I have heard it is foul in the basement."

"I will wait for you at the bottom of the stairs that lead from the kitchen to the cellar. You will see me by the kitchen lamp I am holding."

"What will we do after we get to the kitchen? The cooks will arrive soon. What about Angelique? Her actions may prove to be unpredictable under such stress. Can we depend on her to be silent?"

The sound of a chair scraping against the floor startled Mrs. Packard and me. Angelique faced us in the dim room. "I know when to keep my mouth shut."

Mrs. Packard wrapped her arm around Angelique's waist. "I know we can depend on you."

Angelique's gaze returned to Charles's body. Her low voice trembled. "I ain't crazy 'cause of what I done. I ain't sorry neither."

"Did you hear how I plan to get you out of here? Do you think you can manage going into the cellar?"

Mrs. Packard pulled Angelique away from the corpse and answered for both of them. "We have no choice. We must leave now. Angelique and I are in your hands, Dr. Fletcher. Pull up the dumb waiter."

Did only western women show such uncanny bravery? As much as I loved and admired my sister Sarah, I could not picture her behaving so courageously.

"I will go as quickly as possible to the kitchen. Expect to pass the dumb-waiter shared by Wards One and Two. The next opening will be the kitchen. Look for my light. Do not call out. We must move as if invisible."

I pulled one of the ropes attached to the dumb-waiter. The empty apparatus lifted easily. I helped Mrs. Packard climb into the space and handed her the lamp. In spite of my utmost care, she arrived at the bottom with a thud, exited the contraption, and tugged the rope. I pulled the dumb-waiter up to the ward. Angelique pushed my hand away and entered the device. "I got it, Doc."

The dining room was so dark I could not see if I had stains from Charles's blood on my suit. I would have to depend on the faint illumination of the corridor's gaslights to avoid the scrutiny of anyone I might meet.

I stepped into the unnatural quiet of the hallway. Although I had no evidence to support my conviction, I believed the patients on Ward Three knew what had transpired in their dining room. My excitement at Charles's murder could not be as deep as the joy the recipients of his many cruelties would feel. Their silence implied they were willing to keep the secret of Charles's death.

Entering Ward Two, I noticed a glow of light on the hall floor that radiated from the attendant's station. The nurse who had greeted me on the way in came from her room. "Patient all right?"

"Much better. Are you well? Is something interfering with your sleep?"

"Oh, nothing's wrong with me. I just got caught up in one of those novels from the library. Keeping me up all night trying to find out what happens."

I did not slow my pace. "Better stop reading. Morning will come too soon."

All was dark in Ward One when I entered. I took my shoes off, not wanting to wake the nurse. I neared Pearl's room and realized she could be the instrument I needed to hide Mrs. Packard and Angelique on the outside. I opened the door to her room. "Pearl, it is Dr. Fletcher."

Pearl sat up in her bed. "Doc? What's wrong?"

"We are going to get Ginny. Grab your shawl, your dress, your shoes."

I knew if I mentioned her daughter, Pearl would not hesitate to come with me. She rose silently, gathered her clothes, and followed me out of the ward.

We ran carrying our shoes through the first floor of the administration building toward the kitchen next to the back door. The creak of the outside door startled me and I pushed

Pearl behind me. Pearl was so shaken she dropped her shoe on the wood floor. The thump echoed off the walls of the corridor.

An indistinct form stepped inside the doorway and halted at the sight of us. The figure's shawl dropped from her downcast head. The intruder was Lucy. Her frightened eyes moved from me to Pearl. She picked up the shoe, handed it to Pearl, and disappeared into the black hallway.

I lit one of the lamps the kitchen workers used to begin the preparation of breakfast and opened the door to the cellar. At the bottom of the stairs we reached the railroad track and I had the chance to explain to Pearl what had happened.

I held up the light and walked around the car sitting on the track in front of me. My eyes searched for Mrs. Packard and Angelique in the gloom that stretched beyond the circle of my lamp's light.

Pearl dressed quickly behind me. "Where are they?"

I put my finger to my lips and whispered. "I don't know. They should have been here by now."

It took all the discipline I had to fight a growing impulse to run up the stairs and flee back into the kitchen. The knowledge that Mrs. Packard and Angelique were navigating through the same horrid space kept me at the foot of the stairs.

"I will follow the tracks to Ward Three. You stay here."

Pearl grabbed the edge of my jacket. "I'm goin' with you."

She followed me as I crept along the track. Entering the darkness, I felt something skim across my stocking feet. My skin prickled at the certainty that rats and snakes inhabited the lower chamber. The pops of steam emanating from large heating pipes attached to the sides of the passageway unsettled my already shaky nerves.

We reached the dumb-waiter for Wards One and Two. "I do not know what could have happened to them. If we don't

find them at Ward Three's waiter, I will have to go upstairs and
go back to the ward that way."

"I ain't goin' back in there. You go back upstairs and I'm
runnin' outside."

A faint rustle came from the track ahead of us. The noise
was so slight I doubted I had heard the sound at all. The
murmur came to us again and we continued our trek, more and
more confident something or someone was in the darkness. I
projected a hoarse whisper. "Mrs. Packard, Angelique, are you
there?"

No immediate response came even though the rustling
noise grew. Pearl grabbed my arm. "Sounds like dresses
scrapin' the dirt."

Before I could answer, a throaty voice muttered, "Over
here, Doc."

I lifted the lamp over my head. The circle of light revealed
Mrs. Packard leaning heavily on Angelique. Her pristine
grooming had succumbed to the dismal passageway. Her hair
was out of her combs, her dress ripped. I handed the lamp to
Pearl to lift Mrs. Packard. "What happened?"

Angelique's eyes were wide. "When I come down the
waiter Lizzie reached to get me out. You know how I am, Doc,
about 'ceptin' help. I pushed her arm away stronger than I
meant. She fell back, broke the lamp, and hit her head on one
of these here pipes. Ain't been herself since. We been makin'
our way close to the tracks. Had to stop a lot along the way.
Ain't used to carryin' a body."

With my assistance, Mrs. Packard stumbled the distance to
the kitchen. By the time we reached the stairs she was able to
speak. "Are we here? I'm so sorry we did not keep to your
plan, Doctor. Unfortunately, I was the one who needed to be
rescued. Why is Pearl here?"

"I will explain later."

I was leading the three women to the top of the stairs, when I heard the sound of boots approaching the kitchen. "Shh." I extinguished the lamp, closed the door to the cellar, and secured the lock.

The kitchen prowler had to be the night watchman checking the security of the building. We heard the rattle of food tins opening. The watchman was having a midnight snack.

Hard steps moved near the cellar door. I do not believe any of us were capable of breathing as the watchman checked the door knob. The lock held. He left the kitchen and we exhaled in unison.

Our lamp remained unlit when we entered the kitchen. My voice never rose above a whisper. "So far we appear to have gone undetected. I must leave you here for a short time. Do not make a sound until I come back."

I stood at the kitchen door, straining to determine if anyone was moving in the hallway before I entered. I heard nothing.

My forehead was wet with perspiration. What had I been thinking to enter into such a scheme? Three fugitives waited for me and I had no idea what I was going to do with them. I needed help, and I knew where to find it.

I went outside and ran through the cold wind up Henry's steps, praying he was in his room. Henry's familiar form opened the door. "What're you doin' out here, Doc?"

"Henry, I need you. Come to the kitchen."

Henry dressed quickly and we entered the administration building. He stood beside me as I closed the kitchen door behind us. "Mrs. Packard, Angelique, Pearl, where are you?"

The moon outlined the three figures as they rose from their crouched positions beneath the window.

Henry's whisper filled the room. "What the hell, Doc?"

"I will explain when I can. As musketeers, we are honor bound to remove these fair damsels from this dungeon. Will you help me?"

I could not see Henry's features, but I heard the wide smile in his muted voice. "One for all. All for one. Ladies, follow me."

Henry led us outside to one of the stalls in the barn, where I told him of the night's events.

"Can't say I'm sorry to see that son of a bitch dead." He looked directly into Angelique's eyes. "You did good, girl. Got rid of one less devil in the world."

Mrs. Packard addressed Henry. "You can see how important it is that we leave the hospital. How can we get out? Where will we go?"

I shared my reasons for asking Pearl to come with us. "Pearl, do you think Maude would let you stay with her?"

"No doubt she'd help us. She's taken in a few strays in her time. Give me a chance to git my Ginny."

Henry examined the straw at his feet. "Maude's about a mile or so down the road. You gals can walk to town easy. Hitchin' up a wagon'll cause too much racket."

Mrs. Packard peered in Henry's direction. "Won't three ladies on the road in the middle of the night create some notice?"

Pearl shook her head. "I know the back roads, but we need to keep an eye out in town. The sheriff'll carry all of us right back if he sees us."

Henry watched the women. "I think you better not go out lookin' like that. I'll get some men's clothes from one of the storage rooms. We always got extras."

The ladies gathered their hair underneath the hats Henry gave them. In their new attire, they assumed the appearance of adolescent boys. No one would question their reasons for making their way to Maude's.

"Henry and I need to maintain our usual schedules. If we leave with you tonight we will not be able to help you get out of Jacksonville. I will assume the best and find you at Maude's tomorrow evening."

Mrs. Packard peeked out from underneath the brim of her hat. "I have to get to Farmington before Sunday. Tomorrow is Wednesday."

"I have not forgotten. We will discuss your trip to Farmington when I get to Maude's."

Henry opened the barn doors. "You better git before the milkin' starts."

Before I could give them any word of encouragement the women followed Pearl outside. The quiet of the farm resumed, except for the crunch of frozen grass beneath their feet.

I pondered the risk of their undertaking after they left. The murder of a hospital attendant and the disappearance of three patients would lead to an investigation. At least one of the escapees was sure to be identified as the killer. The others would be seen as her accomplices. If captured, Mrs. Packard, Pearl, and Angelique would never see freedom again.

Henry and I walked back toward the building. "For a guy with an education, you sure git yourself in lots of hornets' nests."

"I am glad you are around to get me out of them."

I built a fire and changed into night clothes to pass what was left of the night in my room. If anyone did interrupt my privacy I wanted to appear as if I had been asleep.

Watching the glowing cinders, I reviewed the events of the day. I believed Mrs. Packard and I had responded to a law far higher than the ones to which most are bound. We were protecting and hiding a person others would see as the perpetrator of a horrible crime. We saw Angelique's action as a logical, if unfortunate consequence of her persecution. I realized I was directed more and more by my intuition, not by my intellectual assessment of the advantages or disadvantages of any endeavor.

It was still dark when a loud knock pulled me from my chair. I had fallen asleep in front of the dead fire. "Doc, Doc, you decent?"

Lena's red face greeted me in the doorway. "You better get dressed and go down to Ward Three. Somebody's killed Charles." She ran back to the stairs.

Lena had not allowed me to pretend shock in the discovery of Charles's body. I had time to prepare for my portrayal of calmness and appropriate amazement at Charles's unfortunate death. I dressed quickly and went down the stairs.

Matron Ritter stood alone in the center of the hallway. Although wearing her usual white uniform, she appeared undressed. Her indispensable accessory, Charles, no longer complemented her. She did not meet my eyes or greet me but continued to watch the stairs. She held her hands in front of her, squeezing one so sharply it had turned pale. The trembling of her feet caused the hem of her dress to jiggle.

I knew she was waiting for Dr. McFarland to descend, as was I. Presently the sound of running footsteps announced Dr. McFarland's arrival. He stood in front of the door leading to the wards.

He was impeccably dressed, as always. Only an uncombed lock of hair hanging to the side of his forehead betrayed his haste. One swipe of his hand ensured all was in place. Waiting for the matron to open the door, his thumbs pulled the breast pockets in his vest so vigorously they gaped from their stitching.

Matron Ritter fumbled through the ring she held in her shaky hand, unable to locate the correct key. Dr. McFarland stared at her with a hostility I had never seen before. "When may I expect you to open the door?"

The matron's face flushed. "I—I—It's here some—"

Dr. McFarland grabbed the key ring from the matron's hand. "Give them to me. I'll open the door."

I had never seen him unlock a single door in the institution. With deliberate speed and agility, he found the correct key and we entered Ward One.

Dr. McFarland sprinted to the end of the corridor, the jangling key ring in his hand. His gait did not slow when one of the nurses approached him.

"Dr. McFarland, Pearl is—"

I held my breath. My concern was ill-founded. Dr. McFarland did not acknowledge her presence.

She tried again. "Doctor—"

Dr. McFarland's pace was barely interrupted when he stopped to unlock the door to Ward Two.

We sped as quickly through Ward Two to Ward Three. The overpowering stink was exceeded by the noise that assailed our ears. Moans and howls punctuated unearthly cries. The din escalated at our sight. I suspected the source of the uproar was uncurbed merriment at the reason for our visit.

The nurses led us down the hall. "In the dining room. Never seen anything like this before. God save us."

The room was undisturbed from the night before. In the light of day I could study the scene more carefully. Charles lay where we had left him. Blood seeped from his back, spreading out from under his inert body. His accusing eyes seemed to bore into mine. Only I felt the indictment in his gaze.

The matron waited in the hallway, her face ashen and her stance unsteady. I was sure she would faint. "Matron Ritter, do you need assistance?"

She shook her head slightly and breathed deeply.

Dr. McFarland stepped out of the room to address the nurses. "Close this door. Do not let anyone enter. I will send for the sheriff." He did not notice the matron's distress before leaving the ward.

I turned my head to a voice coming from the room directly across the hall. "Finally done it, finally done it, finally done it."

One of the nurses followed the doctor. "That ain't all, Doc."

Dr. McFarland stopped sharply. "What now?"

The nurse pointed to an open door near the dining room. "When we come in this morning, we seen this screen open. This here room is where Mrs. Packard and Angelique stay. They's gone."

The meager possessions of Mrs. Packard and Angelique remained in the empty room, as if they were only gone for an activity or meal. Matron Ritter and I followed as Dr. McFarland studied the space. "Matron, instruct the staff to lock all patients in their rooms. Initiate a search of the house. Tell the steward to speak to me about searching the farm."

I could not determine what Dr. McFarland was thinking. Knowing of his prescribed treatment for Angelique, had he guessed she was responsible for Charles's death? Did he suspect the rationale for Mrs. Packard's absence?

On our way to the administration wing, a nurse on Ward One blocked our path. "Dr. McFarland, Matron said I should not let you leave before I tell you another patient is missing. Pearl's gone, sir."

Dr. McFarland headed toward Pearl's room. "I don't understand. She was responding so well to treatment. When did you discover her absence?"

"Soon as I came in. Can't figure how she got out."

"I will notify the sheriff. Make sure everyone is locked in."

I had been concerned I would not be able to display the expected shock at the appearance of Charles's body or the disappearance of the ladies. I need not have worried; Dr. McFarland did not even glance my way. I merely followed behind, an observer of unfolding events.

All organized patient activity ceased as soon as the order had been given to lock everyone in their rooms. I checked on patients I knew to be ill. The nurses remained in the common rooms, talking or reading.

I decided to go to the farmyard to locate Henry. Not surprisingly, I found him standing outside the bakery.

"Hey, Doc, what're you doin' out here?"

"Just getting some fresh air."

Henry lowered his voice. "Ever'thing go all right on the inside?"

"So far, so good. Dr. McFarland has not looked my way once."

"Don't worry, Doc. They're safe at Maude's."

I returned to my office. I had been sitting at my desk for some time when I heard my name called. Dr. McFarland, Matron Ritter, and the sheriff were standing in the main hall.

"Mornin', Doc. Heard you had a murder here last night." The sheriff's eyes scanned mine and rested on Matron Ritter. "This Charles fella, Matron. Your right-hand man, so to speak. Got any ideas who'd want to kill him?"

The matron's usual steady voice quivered. "A number of patients are violent. Charles was often called to subdue them. Ward Three is full of those who are the most dangerous."

"What do you know, Doc?" The sheriff's small eyes sought mine.

My skin bristled. "Nothing. I was awakened early this morning and told Charles had been found dead."

Sheriff Paxson's bushy brow narrowed over a slight sneer. He held my gaze for a moment too long before he gave his attention to Dr. McFarland. "Any of them dangerous ones able to do this, Doc?"

The matron and the doctor exchanged glances.

"Two of the women on Ward Three are missing."

"Missing?"

"When the nurses came in this morning, their room was found unlocked and they were gone. We have done a thorough search. They are not in the house or on the grounds."

"The other maniacs accounted for?"

Dr. McFarland straightened his posture. "One other patient is missing. She resided in one of our best wards. In fact, you know her. She's the girl you brought in recently. Remember Pearl? She was making tremendous progress. I do not understand why she would escape."

At the mention of Pearl's name the sheriff's face darkened. He gripped the butt of his holstered pistol. "How'd that little bitch get out?"

"I do not believe she had anything to do with Charles's death. She was responding so well to our treatment."

"If she's anywhere near Jacksonville I'll find her and bring her back."

"Let us go to Ward Three, Sheriff. We were waiting for you to view the scene before we removed the body."

I had been called upon to lie once and that was to the sheriff. His reaction to my denial made me uneasy.

After the sheriff inspected Ward Three we headed for Dr. McFarland's office. Dr. McFarland stopped in the corridor and addressed Matron Ritter. "Inform the kitchen and the nurses immediately that only soup and bread will be served to the patients while the hospital is locked down."

I could not let his instructions go unchallenged. "Why soup and bread?"

Sheriff Paxson and I followed Dr. McFarland into his office. "These events have excited the patients. Restraining their diets will calm them."

"But—"

Dr. McFarland's assistant brought us a tray with coffee and rolls. I had no appetite, but the sheriff ate with enthusiasm.

"Well, as I see it Dr. McFarland, ya got a couple a things to worry about. First thing is a dead worker. It'd be different if one of the crazies killed another one—people'd understand. You can't have a lunatic gettin' away with killin' an attendant. That could get outta hand."

Sheriff Paxson took another roll from the tray. "Your other problem is you got some of 'em out running around, Lord knows where. One of them is a murderer. Need to find her before she does it again. I've seen a few women killers in my time; not many, though. Hard to believe a woman'd do something like that, ain't it? Now, Pearl's a little demon, but she ain't no killer. Either of the other two got reason to do Charles in?"

I was eager to hear Dr. McFarland's answer. He addressed the sheriff. "Mrs. Packard is quite insane, but she remains a lady. Her violent tendencies are expressed in her verbal accusations against her husband and her treatment. I do not believe she had any cause to resent Charles. As far as I know, they had very little interaction."

He fingered the fringe of the scarf covering the table. I was sure he was choosing his words with care. The inner workings of the hospital's therapies were not widely known. The sheriff was a representative of the Jacksonville community whose residents Dr. McFarland hoped viewed him with respect.

Sheriff Paxson dipped his roll in his coffee and raised the dripping fare to his mouth. "Other one?"

Dr. McFarland considered the sheriff. "Angelique's madness is complicated, requiring rather extreme measures."

The sheriff slurped his coffee. "Extreme measures?"

"Her insanity manifests itself in her refusal to assume the characteristics and role of her sex. Her sexual inversion led to attempts to look and act like a man. Her deportment is entirely male."

"I'll be. I seen some of them women come through Jacksonville. I didn't know they was crazy. Can ya cure 'em?"

"Yes, under certain circumstances."

My breathing was heavy, my palms sweaty. I could no longer let Dr. McFarland obfuscate the truth, no matter what the consequences were for me. I hit my fist on the table. "You know exactly why Angelique would want to kill Charles. You allowed him to rape her repeatedly."

The sheriff's eyebrows rose. "That true, Doc?"

Dr. McFarland's face blanched. He stood and walked to the window with his back to me and the sheriff. "Angelique's lunacy is entrenched. In cases like hers other asylums have used forced coupling successfully. Intimacy with a man exposes such women to one of the joys of womanhood. Sexual intercourse makes them more amenable to the acceptance of their own femininity—"

I jumped from my chair and took a step toward Dr. McFarland. "Is striking her while forcing his manhood on her included in increasing the joy she feels? You knew Charles was beating her. How can you call his actions therapy? Such treatment is vicious and criminal."

Dr. McFarland faced me. His lowered voice quivered with anger. "You dare to challenge me, Adam? You have gone too far."

"Angelique is not the only one who has suffered under your benevolent supervision. The baths, the holding chair, punishments for challenging your treatments. I am sure even more horrors I know nothing about are executed in the name of treatment."

Sheriff Paxson put his thumb in his watch pocket and leaned back in his chair. "Sounds like she had reason to do him in."

I turned to Sheriff Paxson. My voice was shaking. "Charles was often called upon to force our patients to acquiesce to Dr. McFarland's prescribed cures."

I no longer cared if my emotions controlled me. My rage was directed to Dr. McFarland. "What purpose does your instruction to limit food for all the patients fulfill, other than to punish those unfortunates left in your prison? You are Satan himself, disguised as a man of healing. You bastard, you—"

Dr. McFarland's calm voice demonstrated that he had regained control of his emotions, while I had lost control of mine. He had vast experience facing behavior beyond reason. "Adam, I must ask you to leave."

My body trembled with fury. In my rush out the door I knocked my chair over. I did not look back. "With pleasure, sir."

I sprinted up the stairs and entered my room. I packed my few belongings and went out the front door of the administration building, through the stone pillars I had entered a few short weeks before.

A clearness of mind and body emerged from my indignation. My spirit had been released from captivity. I had been discharged from my duties. I had no means of support. I was in a strange western state. I had no idea what lay beyond the asylum's gates for me. I did not care. I was free.

CHAPTER TWELVE

I found myself out of breath walking down the road outside the hospital. My need to flee the odious hospital quickened my pace, not any eagerness to reach a destination. Halfway to town I remembered three ladies and a child needed me. I focused on how I might ensure their safety.

I thought of stopping the carriages and wagons going in the direction of the asylum to warn the drivers of the horrors in that evil place. Instead, I kept my head low. I told myself my hesitation to reveal the hospital's secrets was a result of the cold; I could not expose my body to the delay conversation would bring. Deep in my heart I knew I did not want any interruption from my flight.

Those inmates left behind would continue to be exposed to the cruel realities of the hospital without my help. It was too late for me to relieve their suffering.

My last trip to Maude's was a blur in my memory, but I did not want to ask a passerby for directions when I entered Jacksonville. Association with such a business would certainly mar a young physician's reputation. But I had no professional status to protect. I no longer practiced medicine.

I walked into the open doors of a livery stable near the Jacksonville depot. A stable hand was sweeping out one of the stalls. "What can I do for ya?"

Rubbing my chapped hands together I blew my breath on them. "I am in need of some directions. Are you familiar with Maude's House of Leisure?"

The worker's lanky body leaned over his rake. He looked up at me from under the brim of his hat. "Ever'body knows where Maude's is. You from outta town?"

"You could say that. How do I get to her, uh, home?"

He gave me directions with short gestures and few words. "Tell Maude hey for me, will ya?"

I tipped my hat, shoved my hands into my pockets, and headed down the short blocks to my destination.

In the daylight Maude's house might have been mistaken for a respectable residence in Jacksonville. Only the gas lamp lit in the middle of the day betrayed its true purpose.

The outside stairs were deserted. No belles leaned against the frozen railing. I pushed the big wooden door open and recognized Dicey, the girl who had helped me find Ginny on my previous visit. She directed her practiced smile at me.

"If it ain't Henry's friend. Glad to see ya, Doc."

I felt a rush of heat flow to my head.

"I heard you been a busy boy."

I was not sure how much Dicey knew, but I suspected she could tell me if the ladies had arrived without harm. "Did the women arrive safely?"

"Sure did."

Dicey pulled off my overcoat. She took my hand and led me to one of the small parlors off the hallway. "You look like you could use a drink. Come on in here and I'll git you some whiskey."

Joe sat behind the bar reading a newspaper. He squinted through the smoke of his cigar. "Hey, Doc, what can I git ya?"

"He needs a shot of the good stuff, Joe." Dicey pushed me gently into the horsehair chair and handed the drink to me. She rubbed my shoulders and a wave of release came over me.

As soon as I finished the shot she handed me another glass. "You sit here and let Dicey take care of you. You been worryin' bout them women too much."

The room became dreamlike. No filter remained between my senses and what stimulated them. I was in Dicey's hands.

"Ya got any money, Doc?"

I knew why Dicey was asking about my financial status and I was unconcerned. "Yes, I have enough."

"Let's go on upstairs." She tugged my arm and without effort, my body rose. Joe raised his head from his newspaper and nodded. Dicey's hand guided me out of the room and up the stairs. The steps appeared small, as if I were peering at them through a microscope.

Upstairs we went into a room off the hall. My intellect was dull, but I remember thinking the room was no bigger than a patient's private bedroom in the asylum. Daylight pushing around the edges of a heavy shade provided the only light.

I stood motionless while Dicey removed my jacket and pants. She counted out her money from my pocket and put the bills on the table, before she unbuttoned my shirt and pushed me gently down on the squeaky bed. She removed her gauzy wrap. I noticed her body's sickly thinness, but the sweet odor of her perfume and the softness of her skin aroused me. She straddled my legs. Her breasts touched my chest. Her hair brushed against the side of my head. I moaned as she grabbed me and put me inside her. I no longer knew or cared what I was doing.

My shudders ceased and I wondered if I had held her waifish body too tightly. I lay back on the mattress and watched Dicey gather her robe around her. She put the money in her pocket. "Nice doin' business with ya, Doc. Always 'preciate such a clean customer. Been workin' all night. Mind if I sit here for a spell?"

"No, no, of course not."

"You know when those gals showed up here last night, Maude didn't know what to do with 'em at first. Ended up stowin' them in her room. We was so busy we didn't have an empty room in the place. Good thing Pearl was here. She went right to work."

Dicey's statement about Pearl brought me out of my comfort. "Pearl went to work? What do you mean?"

Her mouth curled into a grin. "What'd you think I mean? She took care a' some of the gents. Said she needed the money to git her and Ginny away from the sheriff."

I sat up and buttoned my shirt. "Did Mrs. Packard and Angelique know about this?"

"Don't know about Angelique. Hard to tell what's goin' on in that head. Mrs. Packard went to sleep as soon as she got here. I don't think she was payin' attention to Pearl."

I picked up my pants. How could Pearl have gone back to the same life that had endangered her and her child? Did she not see the immorality of a mother engaging in the activities of such a den? I had expected Mrs. Packard's influence to inspire Pearl to seek a legitimate life.

My voice was cold. "I need to talk to Pearl."

Dicey watched me out of the corner of her eyes. "She's around here somewhere. Prob'ly in the kitchen with Ginny."

My indignation propelled me down the back stairs. The scent of stew warming in a pot over the fire pit drew me into the kitchen. At the end of a long table in front of the fireplace sat Mrs. Packard, hovering over a bowl of potatoes she was peeling. Pearl and Ginny huddled on the floor behind her.

Mrs. Packard rested her knife on the lumps in the bowl. "Dr. Fletcher, you have arrived. You seem concerned. No need, as you can see; we are all safe. Through the charity of Miss Maude we are even dressed as others of our sex, except for Angelique. She refused to give up the male clothes Henry gave her. She is even going further to attain the appearance of a man. One of Miss Maude's girls is cutting her hair in the room next door."

From her cheery greeting I was reassured that Mrs. Packard did not know of Pearl's transgressions. I sat in the chair next to her, careful not to look in Pearl's direction. "The sheriff is searching for all of you. As we thought, they suspect Angelique of Charles's murder. You cannot stay here for long."

Pearl rose, approached the table, and spoke directly to me. "We can't hide from Sheriff Paxson much longer. We better git."

I maintained eye contact with Mrs. Packard. "I have an idea that may allow you both to begin a new life, if a fresh start is what Pearl wants."

Pearl sat on my other side, her head bent to catch my eye. I refused to look at her. "What'd you mean, if it's what I want?"

Mrs. Packard responded for her. "Of course that's what Pearl wants, for her and Ginny."

"My sister lives in our family home in Seneca Falls, New York. She has many Christian associates who are committed to assisting those who need help."

Pearl kept her eyes on the table. "You think she'd help us?"

"If you can make your way to Seneca Falls I am sure she will. If you want, I will telegraph her and notify her of your impending arrival. The train trip is a long one, perhaps arduous with a small child. Even so, we have no time to prepare for any other option. You must have train tickets. If I had not left my employment abruptly, I would be in a position to purchase the tickets. I am afraid I do not have enough funds to buy them."

A flicker of guilt flew through my mind when I remembered how I had spent the last of my money.

Mrs. Packard sat up straight. "You left the hospital?"

I did not want to describe my final scene with Dr. McFarland. "That is not important now. We need to make plans to get you out of Jacksonville."

Mrs. Packard picked up the knife and began to peel a potato. Pearl stared at Mrs. Packard's lowered head. "We got the money fer tickets fer Angelique, Lizzie, and me. Enough fer our girls, too."

Mrs. Packard kept her eyes focused on the bowl before her, and I realized she knew what Pearl had done. How could she condone the girl's actions? How could she let herself benefit from Pearl's sins? My bewilderment became anger. I pushed my chair away from the table. "I will telegraph my sister."

I had taken great risks to release the women from an unjustified incarceration. Now I found they might deserve society's censure. I could almost excuse Pearl; she had no family, no breeding, but Mrs. Packard had been raised a Christian woman. Were her morals no better than an adolescent whore's? And yet I had seen both of them brutally abused. Perhaps their mistreatment in one of society's institutions did justify their challenges of all civilization's rules.

On my way out, I stopped to observe the scene in the room next door. Angelique sat in a straight-backed chair, still dressed in the garb she had worn when she ran from the hospital. One of Maude's girls held a pair of shears above her head. "You sure you want to do this?" She stroked the dark tresses. "Your hair sure is pretty."

Angelique's steady voice rose. "Hack it off. As near to a man's cut as you can."

The girl placed her lips close to Angelique's ear. I could barely hear her voice. "Either way, you're a beauty." She kissed Angelique's cheek, and cut the first lock.

Angelique spotted me. "Hey, Doc, come on in. Gettin' a trim to go with my outfit."

"How did you fare on your way here? Did you have any trouble?"

"Naw. Pearl knew where she was goin'. When we got here a couple of the girls even tried to do business with us, 'til we took our hats off."

The girl behind Angelique laughed. "Sure looked like boys. We thought they were comin' to Maude's to find their manhood."

The hair fell to the floor and Angelique's face lightened. She already had the manner and gait of a man. Now her smooth face was the only characteristic revealing her female nature. The girl cutting her hair was right; she looked like a male, a pretty one.

Angelique's face glowed. "What do you have up your sleeve, Doc?"

"I am going to make arrangements for you, Mrs. Packard, and Pearl to go to my sister, Sarah, in Seneca Falls. We are headed to Farmington to pick up Mrs. Packard's daughter. Then we will get all of you on the train to New York."

A shadow crossed Angelique's face. "How're we payin' for the tickets?"

My voice sounded much harsher than I intended. "Pearl has enough money for the tickets."

Angelique grunted as a man would. "Don't be too hard on her, Doc. She's just doin' what she gotta to get Ginny outta here. Ain't nothin' she wouldn't do for her child."

I had not thought of Pearl's actions in that way. Her willingness to revert to a sordid way of life was an attempt to rescue her daughter from the same fate. It was all she knew. Nonetheless, Mrs. Packard's acceptance of Pearl's help was incomprehensible to me, until I realized she, too, was desperate to rescue her child. The moorings of my principles shifted. Nothing I believed in was assured.

"Besides, Doc. I hear you and Dicey had a purty good time this morning."

My head jerked sharply to Angelique. Wasn't a man paying to utilize Maude's services different than a woman selling her body?

I stepped outside the room and met Mrs. Packard. Her downcast eyes revealed her hesitation to speak to me. "I feel I owe you an explanation, Dr. Fletcher. As you have suspected, Pearl went back into Miss Maude's employ last night. I did not know what she intended or I would have tried to dissuade her. She informed me this morning of the money she earned. At first, I was furious that my influence meant nothing. When I observed her reintroducing herself to her child, I understood her motives. She would make any sacrifice for Ginny."

"Pearl's acts and your acceptance of them trouble me a great deal, but I am still committed to helping you get your daughter."

Mrs. Packard sighed. "I confess I felt superior to Pearl until this morning, when I found myself agreeing to take her money with little or no hesitation. Both of us will do anything to be with our daughters, even use money that comes from the fruits of immoral acts. I have found I am no better than Pearl."

The hallway felt uncomfortably warm. "I am on my way to telegraph my sister."

She handed me a folded note. "I took the liberty of writing the telegraph for you. Those of us who assist runaways from one depot to the next communicate in certain ways so if the message is intercepted, the uninitiated reader will not be able to understand the content's true meaning."

I opened the paper.

Sarah,

Sending three large and two small packages to you. Pick them up Sunday or Monday on Chicago train. Contain items I wish you to store.

Adam

I was impressed with the simplicity and naturalness of the message. Who would question such a telegraph from brother to sister? "I am not sure my sister will understand this message. I know she has friends who are abolitionists, but I do not know how much she is involved in their activities."

"We must put our faith in God. He will ensure the message is understood."

I was not so certain. "If my sister does not meet you, ask the stationmaster to send a message to Sarah Fletcher on Prophet Road to pick you up." Unlike the escaped slaves the Underground Railroad usually carried, our runaways could walk freely in Seneca Falls, far from Sheriff Paxson or Mrs. Packard's irate husband.

"I will not forget your instructions, but I believe God will bring your sister to the station."

Mrs. Packard continued to pray for God's intervention. I, on the other hand, was not sure what forces controlled events. My beliefs or lack thereof led me to hope Sarah's good sense and trust in me would bring her to the railroad station to pick up the packages as I asked.

I walked to the train depot and handed Mrs. Packard's note to the telegraph operator. He tapped out the message immediately. I was about to leave when I felt the cold wind of an open door behind me. I turned to see Sheriff Paxson filling the doorway. "There ya are, Doc. Left the hospital in kind of a hurry, didn't ya?"

Before I could move away from the window, the sheriff stood next to me. He leaned against the counter, straining to see what was on the operator's desk.

"Sendin' a telegraph? Who's it goin' to?"

I faced the sheriff without fear, even though he was at least six inches taller than I was. "To whom I send a telegraph is none of your business."

"It is if it has something to do with those missin' crazies." The sheriff reached over the counter and seized Mrs. Packard's note out of the hands of the startled telegraph operator. "Who's this Sarah?"

Seeing my private message in his paw inflamed me. My voice filled the waiting room. "For your information, Sarah is my sister. I am sending my things to her. As you know, I have left the employ of the asylum. If I'm shipping something to Timbuktu, it is no concern of yours."

His palm rested on the butt of his pistol. "Where are these packages? I don't see them nowhere."

My anger drove me past intimidation. I stood, legs apart, hands on my waist. "The location of my things is none of your affair."

I maintained my stance. The sheriff spit a brown liquid on the floor. My throat closed at the stink of tobacco coming from his brown teeth. "Those packages wouldn't be three ladies from the madhouse, would they?"

I stared into the sheriff's eyes and hoped my shaking legs were not visible through my pants legs. "I do not know where the ladies are."

"You don't, do ya? Well, I got a pretty good idea they're at Maude's. That's the first place I'm going to. Maude better be careful or she'll find herself run outta town."

The sheriff held his finger in front of my face. "Let me tell you something, Doc. I think you're lyin'. I expect you know exactly where those whores are, and if you ain't already done it you're goin' to try to get them outta Jacksonville."

He shook Mrs. Packard's note in front of me. "I ain't no dummy. I seen messages like this before. Those Underground Railroad people talk like that. They're breaking the law, stealin' slaves from their owners. Those women ain't slaves, but it's illegal helping escapees from the hospital, too. I catch you and you'll be sorry."

I stood up straight, straightened my lapels, and headed to the door. "I have no reason to worry about you."

He started for me, my insolence more than he could take. As quickly as he moved in my direction, he froze. A well-dressed couple entered the waiting room. The man tipped his hat at the sheriff. The woman bowed her head.

Sheriff Paxson doffed his hat. "Good day, Reverend, Mrs. Stone."

"Good day, Sheriff. I am so glad we ran into you. Could you help us set up the nativity scene in front of the church? You did a beautiful job last year. We need—"

I slipped behind the couple. Hesitating in the doorway, I caught the sheriff's eye, tipped my hat, and smirked before I made my exit.

Only after I left the station did I realize how close the sheriff had come to uncovering our plan. His distrusting nature had led him to examine my telegram. Mrs. Packard's precautions had been justified.

I believed Sheriff Paxson's motives were not so much to capture a killer but to catch Pearl. She had defied his authority and he would never forgive her rebellion. As long as she was locked up, she was still under his power. Free, she defied him still.

I hoped I would arrive at Maude's before the sheriff came to search for Pearl. Perhaps the reverend's Christmas preparations would take some time to discuss. We could not wait until nightfall to leave for Farmington. We had to leave immediately.

I ran past the girls waiting on the stairs into the kitchen. Mrs. Packard, Pearl, and Ginny remained in front of the fireplace. "You have to hide until I can get a wagon. The sheriff's on his way to search the house."

My noisy entrance attracted Maude, who came in from her room off the kitchen. "Sheriff Paxson's probably guessin' I'd hide you girls. Don't worry, Doc. Ain't the first time I hid something from the sheriff. I can take care of him for a while. Go git the wagon. Tell the livery hand I'll pay him later."

I ran to the stable near the depot. An unhitched wagon with sides surrounding the bed stood in the center of the barn.

The same stable hand sat on the same bale of hay, eating a biscuit.

He looked up at me and took another bite. "You find Maude's all right?"

I hesitated for a moment to catch my breath.

"Better sit a spell. You look tuckered out."

I shook my head, unable to respond to his kind offer.

"What ya in such a hurry for? One of Maude's girls chasin' you?"

"No, no—I need your help."

"What do you need?"

"I want to hire this wagon. I need to leave right away."

"Well, you're in luck. Nobody's usin' this one. I'll hitch up ole Junior soon as I finish my dinner."

"You do not understand. I need to leave immediately."

The man stood up and stretched. "What's yer hurry?"

"Believe me, my trip will be a matter of life and death."

A sneer covered the man's face as he put on his gloves. "Life and death, huh? That don't happen very often."

The man's refusal to recognize my urgency annoyed me. "Please hurry. I need the wagon now."

He ambled into one of the stalls and led a bay to the wagon. "This here's Junior. He'll do good for you."

After an eternity I was sitting on the seat, reins in hand.

Junior and I sped out of the barn and headed for the brothel's rear door. If the sheriff had not already arrived at Maude's, I did not want him to see me on the main street going in the direction of the brothel. The clouds of grit kicked up under the wheels must have caused passersby to take interest. I took no notice.

I came to an abrupt stop at the sight of Maude standing outside her back door. "The bastard's inside, makin' noises about searching the house. Girls are hidin' in the old summer kitchen. Here, you'll need to cover 'em up." Maude threw a bundle of quilts and coarse woolen blankets in the back of the wagon. She leaned over the side and put a basket on its floor. "Got some food for ya, too. It's a long way to Farmington. Pearl says that's where yer headed."

"Thank—"

Dicey stuck her head out of the door. "You better git in here, Maudie. The sheriff's saying he's goin' upstairs."

Maude turned to me before going inside. "Stay here. I'll send the girls out shortly."

I did not want the sheriff to see me, but my peaked energies refused to let me wait outside. I opened the back door and stepped into the dark hall. I could hear Maude and the sheriff talking in the kitchen. "Now, Sheriff, you know I wouldn't be lyin' to you. I don't know where them gals is. See Pearl's young'un sittin' in front of the fireplace. If Pearl'd come through here, she'd never leave Ginny."

Crackling sounds came from the logs in the fireplace. I pictured the screwed brow of the sheriff as he spit into the flames. "I see yer point. Where else would they be? Pearl's the only one knows anything about Jacksonville."

"She's a hard one to figure. Why don't you let one of the girls get you a drink? You had a bad day, with those maniacs and all. They're probably long gone."

I moved into the shadows of the hallway as footsteps came out of the kitchen. Maude led the sheriff down the corridor, where Dicey swayed her skirts close to him. "Hiya, Sheriff. Want a whiskey?"

The sheriff's voice was lower than its usual bombastic tone. "Sure could use one. Can't stay long, though."

Maude closed the parlor's door and walked down the hallway. I stepped out of the dark corner. "Where are they?"

Maude's stance was full of annoyance. "God-damn, Doc. I told you to stay outside. Lucky for both of us the sheriff didn't see you. Come on."

Maude's determined gait led me to the kitchen. She scooped up Ginny, who barely acknowledged her change in position. I followed her out the back door and into a building I had assumed was a storehouse.

Mrs. Packard, Pearl, and Angelique stood next to a dark fireplace inside the one-room structure. Pearl took the girl from Maude and wrapped the end of her shawl around her. "You all right?" Ginny never took her eyes from the rag doll she held close to her.

Angelique's appearance as a man was complete. The clothes Henry had given her were too big for her small frame, but they suited her, hiding any evidence of her sex. She stood up straight, her hands in her pants pockets. She examined me with a directness I had never seen in females. "How we gettin' outta here, Doc?"

"I have hired a wagon. I left it out back."

"Who's gonna drive it?"

I could not risk finding someone who knew the route to take us. I would have to drive the wagon myself. My knowledge of the roads to Farmington was vague. I hoped Mrs. Packard could guide us. "I am. I have been to Farmington before."

Mrs. Packard approached me. "Parts of the Farmington road are hardly visible. I believe I can guide us, though."

Angelique stepped close to Mrs. Packard and me. "The skies look like snow's comin'. Could cause us some trouble."

"We have no choice. We have to leave now."

Angelique buttoned her woolen coat. "Let me drive. No one'll know who I am. Lots would recognize you, and if the sheriff is out and about he'll want to see what you have in the wagon."

I could not argue with her reasoning. "Do you know how to drive a wagon?"

Angelique headed out the door. "That's one thing my Pa did learn me. Said I could handle a horse better than the boys."

Pearl pulled her attention away from Ginny. "Stop this yakkin'. Let's go."

Angelique untied Junior and climbed up onto the seat. I helped Mrs. Packard and Pearl into the back of the wagon and lifted Ginny up to Pearl. "Do you think you can keep Ginny quiet?"

"She ain't said a word since I been here. I think she'll be good. "

Maude wrapped the ladies with the quilts and after I lay down, she covered us with the canvas tarp lying on the wagon bed.

Angelique yelled over her shoulder. "What'd you say this horse's name was, Doc?"

"Junior" was my muffled reply.

"Yaah, Junior."

The wheels bumped over what I had thought was a smooth street. I was beginning to worry we would not survive the banging and tossing without injury when the wagon slowed to a stop. Angelique's low voice penetrated our covers. "Lots of wagons and carriages waitin' to cross in front of the train depot."

I heard a familiar voice and my stomach clinched. The sheriff had walked up to our wagon to direct traffic. "Hold up, boy." He had not stayed at Maude's long.

Angelique pulled the brake. We had no choice but to wait. I could not see Mrs. Packard's face. I could barely discern Pearl's eyes when she gripped my arm. In spite of the darkness of our hiding place, Ginny's attention to her doll never faltered.

The wagon vibrated slightly and Junior's neighs reached my ears. Angelique held him firmly. "Whoa, Junior."

The sound of a knock against the side of the wagon unnerved me. "Go on, boy. Road's clear."

Angelique slapped Junior's rump with the reins and the rocking of the wagon resumed.

The rays of the sun saturated the blankets. I felt hot and in need of brisk air. I pulled a corner of the blanket from the bed of the wagon. The cold air blasted through the opening. Closing the gap, I knew we would have to wait until Angelique told us we were safe to come out of our wrappings. She was our guide now, our protector. Our lives and our fates were in her hands.

CHAPTER THIRTEEN

I struggled to breathe under the wagon's tarp. The mushy odor of horse dung and cow pies forced me to inhale through my mouth.

Angelique's sharp yells punctuated the muffled clatter of wagons and loud conversations in front of the depot. "Yah, Junior, gid up." After some time, the wagon moved steadily into a reassuring silence.

Though the bumpy road and the hard bed jarred our bodies, Mrs. Packard and Pearl moved little. Even Ginny did not attempt to leave her comfortable spot between the ladies. My bones ached, but most of my discomfort came from my ignorance of our circumstances. I did not know where we were, or if we had aroused the sheriff's suspicion enough for him to follow us.

The only sounds were the creak of the wheels and Junior's occasional whinny.

Farmington was at least thirty-five miles away. I remembered from my trip with Henry the road off Jacksonville Road was little more than a trail. I hoped our meager knowledge of the roadway would be enough to get us through the fields safely.

I could not say how much time passed before I felt the wagon navigate over even rougher terrain. Angelique cried, "Whoa, whoa, Junior," and we came to an uneven stop.

Angelique's voice penetrated our layers of covers. "Safe for you to get some air. We're outta sight of town. I been keepin' a close eye out. Nobody around. No farms in sight, either."

We had stopped in a grove of trees lining a small creek. Although any traveler who passed by the trail's opening could see us, we were much less visible inside the thicket.

Angelique pulled a bucket from under the seat. "Stretch your legs a bit. I'm goin' to get some water for Junior." She disappeared through the trees. A cracking sound came from Angelique's direction. She had broken a thin layer of ice covering the stream.

I climbed over the side of the wagon and lifted the others down. Ginny's slight body stiffened when I hauled her over the side and handed her to Pearl. I could not presume to know what life had been like for Ginny, or how many hands had passed her from person to person.

Mrs. Packard walked to the road to ascertain our location. She stepped back into the trees within seconds. "Silence; a rider is coming."

The sound of hooves hitting the hard dirt drew near. Crouching behind the leafless center of a large, tangled bush, I gestured to Angelique to hide behind one of the trees next to the creek. Hopefully the rider would not discover our little party.

Ginny's voice startled and yet reassured us. "Moo. Moo."

Too late, Pearl put her hand over Ginny's mouth as the intruder came into view. A lone cow ambled into our hideaway. The heifer's languid pose showed no surprise at our presence.

Angelique's coarse laugh punctured our nervousness. "I'll be. Somebody's wandered away. We better git, in case someone comes lookin' for her."

I assisted the ladies into the wagon, while Angelique loosened Junior's bit and held the water bucket under his head. Sitting against the front side of the wagon directly behind Angelique, we wrapped the blankets around ourselves. The wagon tarp lay at our feet, ready to hide us if travelers from Jacksonville came near.

Ginny pulled Pearl's sleeve. "Biscuit."

Pearl's shining smile was directed toward her daughter. "You wanna biscuit?" Ginny took a bite of the biscuit Pearl offered her from Maude's basket. She held the treat up to the black thread that formed her doll's mouth.

"She's startin' to talk, Lizzie. Think she knows I'm her ma?"

Mrs. Packard smoothed Ginny's tangled hair. "I think she knows you love her. I hope my Libby remembers my love as well."

Angelique shouted over her shoulder. "Think it's safe for you to ride up here, Doc. Why don't ya come on up?"

I climbed over the seat and sat next to Angelique.

"Didn't want to scare the ladies. Look at that sky. Could have some snow."

The sky was an uninterrupted expanse of gray. Almost certainly snow was coming.

"Could be rough traveling. The Jacksonville Road we're on is purty good. I heard Lizzie say the Farmington road ain't nothin' but a scratch. Don't want to hurry Junior neither. This is kind of a long haul for him."

I had heard stories of farmers disoriented on their own property during a storm, lost on land they had tilled and harvested many times. How could we, unsure of our direction, find our way on an unknown road covered in snow? I could not allow myself to think about what lay ahead. "We cannot go back. All we can do is hope for the best."

"Whatever you say, Doc."

I turned to the back of the wagon. "Mrs. Packard, have you recognized any signs on the road? Can you tell how much farther until we arrive at the Farmington cutoff?"

"I am afraid I do not recognize anything. The single time I traveled to Jacksonville was when my husband brought me to the hospital. My emotions were in such a state I did not pay attention to the road."

Her answer made me realize we had to rely on Angelique's skill and my limited knowledge from one trip to Farmington. I, too, had not paid much attention to our path, relying on Henry's prowess. "You and I are on our own, Angelique. I do know the crossroad where we turn north is marked by a post with the word Farmington carved on it."

Angelique's eyes were barely visible behind the brim of her lowered hat. "Any idea where that crossroad is?"

I held the ends of my coat collar in front of my chin. "None at all."

Her masculine manner and tone, as well as our common approach to the dangers of the journey, made me forget I was speaking to a woman. We both readily accepted that we were the first line of defense for the women and child in the back of the wagon.

Angelique was right; the wagon ruts were easy to see on the well-traveled path. Once again, the scant edges of the trail between the Jacksonville Road and Farmington came to my mind and my uneasiness grew.

Crows flew into the stands of trees lining the frozen fields. An occasional deer walked to the edge of the woods, peered at us, and went back to the safety of the forest.

I shivered as the temperature lowered. I looked to the back of the wagon. The heads of the two women almost touched, with Ginny sheltered between them.

Angelique removed a handkerchief from her pocket. She folded the bandanna into a triangle, tying it around her face, the point downward. I pulled my hat over my forehead and stuffed my hands in my pockets.

A damp fleck hit my cheek and I knew the snow had come. Angelique's muffled voice stated what we both knew. "Here it comes, Doc. Better tell the ladies to cover up with the wagon tarp. Keep 'em as dry as they can." Our fears had become reality.

Angelique and I bent against the growing swirls of snow and the dropping temperatures as Junior plunged into the opaque space in front of us. The passengers in the back leaned against the side of the wagon bed behind the driver's seat. The tarp formed a loose tent above them.

The gusts were steady, but I could not tell the direction of the wind. The snow, heavy with moisture, did not fall down from the heavens. The wet flurries hit us sideways, from what I thought was the northwest. Very soon the winds changed and I was convinced the flakes originated from the south.

Angelique's black hat and coat had become white. Even the handkerchief covering her face took on the snow's hue. "Looks like we're headin' into a bad one."

Our vision was increasingly limited by the snow. We were unable to see much past Junior's harness. Even though the sun was still above the earth, only traces of the road were visible in the sky's eerie light. I tried to sound confident. "We are making good progress."

As if Providence was determined to mock my observation, Junior strained against his bridle. We came to an abrupt halt, like a giant hand had reached down and pulled the wagon in the opposite direction. Angelique tugged at the brake. "What the hell?" We vaulted down. Our boots penetrated the yielding snow.

Mrs. Packard and Pearl peered over the wagon's side. "What has happened? Pearl banged herself against the seat. Is the wagon damaged?"

Pearl rubbed the back of her head. "Ain't nothin', Doc."

"Let me see." I reached up and removed the shawl covering her hair. A small swelling was beginning to rise. "How do you feel?"

Pearl grabbed her shawl out of my hand and covered her head. "Probably have a knot is all. Go back to getting this thing movin'."

I searched for Angelique on the other side of the wagon. She held up a ripped blanket. "Found the trouble, Doc. This here blanket fell off and wrapped itself around the back wheel. Got all tangled up. Ain't much good now, except you and I could put what's left over our legs. Come on. We best git a move on."

The scrap of blanket on our laps helped little against the cold. Angelique pushed it from her. I wrapped the thin cloth around my freezing hands, until a sweep of wind blew the minuscule cover away.

No matter how many times I stamped my feet against the floor of the wagon seat, I could not stop shivering. The weather and my knowledge of our precarious position made it impossible for me to sit still.

My senses were alert, but we had more and more difficulty seeing the road. I tried to divine the wagon tracks in the middle of thick eddies of flakes. I leaned forward, certain my concentration was necessary for Junior to stay on course.

I raised my head to the sky. Darkness had replaced the gray abyss. The sun had set and we were now headed into a blizzard with no light. The coming of night would have elicited more fright in me if the darkness made much difference. The swirling maelstrom merely assumed a different shade of gloom.

We persevered for hours before Angelique pulled the reins and bound from her seat. "Can't see shit."

The clank of Junior's harness and the groan of the wagon ceased. I was mesmerized by the sound of the wind flying over the prairie and I was unable to move. The power of the vast emptiness we were trying to overcome engulfed me.

Angelique's voice came from Junior's direction. "Come on down here, Doc. Keep close to Junior."

I moved along the horse's flank until I bumped into Angelique crotched down in front of him. "Stand on this wagon track, Doc. I'll see if I can find the other one."

I stood on the rut Angelique had found by brushing away the snow. She crossed in front of Junior's nose and bent down. Angelique had to shout for me to hear her even though we were a mere wagon's width apart. "Found it. Goes a little to the left. Guess we'll do the same."

We made our way back to the wagon. Mrs. Packard was on her knees, leaning over the seat. "What is going on? Are we lost?"

Angelique slapped Junior. "Not yet. At least, I don't think so. You gals warm enough?"

"We are as comfortable as is possible. Pearl and Ginny fell asleep miles ago."

"You better cover up. No sense in you gettin' cold."

Through the night we paused at regular intervals to feel for the road, until one of our stops led us to discover we were not following wagon tracks at all. Angelique bid me to stand as usual to the right of Junior. She had not stepped more than a foot in front of the horse until she came upon another groove in the earth. She moved on and found another rut the same distance apart. Three more evenly spaced crevices led us to the same conclusion. We were not on a road; we were crossing rows where plants had been planted and harvested, the soil plowed under.

Angelique and I stood inside the oasis of warmth created by Junior's breath. "We're lost, Doc. In the middle of a God-damned field. I don't even know when we got off the road and I ain't got no idea how to get us outta here."

I had no more knowledge of where we were than Angelique, but I knew we had to act. "We cannot stand still. We have to go somewhere."

Angelique strained to see in the darkness. The bouncing flurries taunted her eyes. "Only thing I can think of is to go back the way we come. Maybe we'll find the road that way."

Retracing our way, we felt the jolt of every row in the field, something we had not noticed when we left the road. Without warning, the wagon swayed back and forth violently. I grabbed the seat to keep from pitching to the ground. I was sure we were falling deep inside the earth.

A scream came from the wagon bed, followed by a wail that had to have come from Ginny. Pearl's voice quivered. "We're lost, ain't we? We're near froze back here." Ginny buried her sobs in Pearl's chest.

Mrs. Packard stood behind the wagon seat. "What's happened?"

"Sit down, Mrs. Packard. We have hit a deep crevice."

Mrs. Packard ignored my directive. "Is the wagon intact?"

The ladies' panic was more than I could handle and I am afraid my voice was filled with exasperation. "We cannot go on unless you sit down. Do as I say."

"Now, calm yourself, Lizzie." Angelique pulled up the reins and stepped down on Junior's left. She walked in front of him to his right. "Musta hit a ditch at the end of the field. Think we found the road."

Angelique turned to the back of the wagon. A smile erased the lines in her forehead that had deepened since the snow began. "We're all right, girls. Just a little snag."

Our passengers settled onto the floor of the wagon, calmed by one of their own, not their doctor.

Hoping we were headed east, we resumed our periodic stops to find the road. I had no idea how long it was before I noticed the snowfall had lessened. After some time, the storm was over and we traveled under a multitude of stars.

Angelique and I punched each other's arms when the sky brightened in front of us. We were headed east. The colorless landscape stretched for miles. We could see the slight outline of our wagon's tracks behind us.

Angelique handed the reins to me. "I'm gonna follow our tracks back over that hill. See if I can see any signs of the Farmington turnoff."

She disappeared over a hill about half a mile behind us. Mrs. Packard and Pearl stirred in the back of the wagon. "Where are we? Are we in Farmington?"

"We think we are on Jacksonville Road. The sky is lightest in front of us so we are headed east. Angelique went back to see if the road to Farmington is behind us."

I began to worry that Angelique was lost and I would be left to take care of our charges alone, when I saw her wave her hat as she stumbled in our direction. Her voice carried over the silent snow. "I found it."

We traveled back about a mile before we came to the marker. Angelique had scooped away the snow from the top of the sign to see the carved word FARMINGTON.

North of the crossroad, the white expanse of snow covered any sign of the Farmington road. Angelique and I descended from the seat and resumed the same method we had used the night before to find the trail. We now had the advantages of light, no blinding snow, and the observant eyes of Mrs. Packard. She had joined us on the wagon seat in hopes of recognizing landmarks near her home.

Mrs. Packard pointed across the field to a log cabin some distance to our right. "That is the Phillips homestead. We are headed in the right direction. Farmington is just over the next hill."

Angelique glanced at Mrs. Packard. "Maybe we could rest with your neighbors a bit. Junior's purty tired."

"No, I will not be well-received there. They are strong defenders of my husband. My home is not much farther. A mile over the hill is my husband's church and the parsonage. The Wyatts's home is a mile beyond that."

I knew Mrs. Packard was correct. The images of her solemn husband and gloomy daughter came into my mind. "We are not far now."

Before long we were adjacent to the parsonage. Smoke came from a chimney on the back of the building. Someone was astir, likely fixing a lonely breakfast for two. Mrs. Packard stood. "My Libby is held in that house. I must go to her."

I reached up and pulled her to the seat. "Mrs. Packard, wait. If you rush into your husband's home he will not release your daughter to you. He may very well attempt to detain you until he can send for the authorities to take you back to the asylum. I suggest you put your shawl over your head. He will probably observe us passing. You are in danger if he sees you. Remain between Angelique and me so he will not recognize you."

She reluctantly covered her head. "My daughter has been torn from the love only a mother can give."

"You must control your feelings. When we arrive at the Wyatts's we will make a plan to retrieve your daughter."Mrs. Packard's body shriveled between us. She fixed her eyes on the house that had once been her home. "You are right, Doctor."

The lane leading to the Wyatts's farm was covered with unbroken snow. Trees lining the road interrupted the sparkling white of the drive. A colorless orb had replaced the hints of orange and yellow in the early morning sky. Footprints tainted the purity of the snow in front of the barn. The blizzard had not interrupted the daily care of the animals.

Angelique stopped the wagon in front of the barn door. Josiah ran up the hill, his unbuttoned jacket flapping open, to grab Junior's bridle.

Mrs. Packard stood at the sight of Dr. and Mrs. Wyatt rushing through the doorway. "Agnes, I have come home. I have brought others who need your help."

"Of course, of course." Mrs. Wyatt took Mrs. Packard inside.

I saw recognition in Josiah's sharp eyes when I tipped my hat to him, but he did not acknowledge me. His brows rose when Angelique's feminine voice gave instructions for Junior's care. "Better git him some water and oats. Been a long trip."

The Wyatts helped us remove our coats and shoes. We sat close to the parlor's lit fireplace. A cup of tea and a book, entitled *Uncle Tom's Cabin*, lay on a table near the window. My sister had mentioned the title to me, but I had not bothered to read the volume.

While we settled in the parlor, Pearl placed the sleeping Ginny on a day-bed underneath the window and covered her with a quilt.

Mrs. Wyatt hurried to the kitchen. "I'll help Ethel prepare a warm breakfast. The tea kettle is already over the fire. We have plenty of bacon in the larder."

Mrs. Packard took Pearl's hand. "We are safe now. My friends will help me get Libby from my husband and we will be on our way to Dr. Fletcher's sister."

"I was mighty worried about Ginny when we were in the blizzard. I was afraid we were gonna freeze to death."

Mrs. Packard's brittle smile betrayed an uncertainty I had never seen in her before. "God has led us here. We must thank Him."

"If you say so, but I'm gonna thank Angelique." Angelique stood in the corner, away from the fire.

Pearl's eyebrows lifted to me. "Oh, you, too, Doc."

"You are right, Pearl. Without Angelique we would be lost along the road."

"I best be checkin' on Junior." Angelique buttoned her coat and walked out the front door.

Mrs. Wyatt and Ethel carried in trays filled with steaming tea, biscuits sopped in bacon grease, and slabs of bacon.

The little food Pearl ate seemed to make her drowsy. She slipped under the quilt next to Ginny and was soon asleep. I noticed in slumber they could be mistaken for sisters, not mother and daughter.

Mrs. Packard positioned her stocking feet on the foot warmer in front of her. "Agnes, I am so grateful. You have no idea how thoughts of you kept me from losing my sanity in the asylum. Knowing I have friends who support me helped me endure."

"Elizabeth, did you forget our Lord will never desert you?"

"No, but I am sure you are His instrument. You must help me. I cannot let Libby go to her aunt in Manteno. I have already lost my other children. If she leaves now, I will never see her again."

"How do you propose to stop your husband from sending her away?"

"I plan to go to the parsonage and take her."

"Take her? He will never let you have her. He is very bitter. We heard he preached that you are possessed by the devil himself."

"The devil? He is the one who has been led astray by Satan. I have to get her away from him."

"Even if you were to take her, where would you go? You are a fugitive. If the reverend sees you, he will certainly call the authorities. You will find yourself back in the asylum."

"I will take Libby with us to New York."

"New York?"

"Dr. Fletcher's sister lives in Seneca Falls, New York. He has sent a message to her, asking her to receive us. We will start a new life back East."

"How are you going to get to Dr. Fletcher's sister?"

Mrs. Packard's gaze drifted to the day-bed holding Pearl and Ginny. The intense sunshine reflected off the snow, flowed through the window, and rested on them.

"We have enough money to take the train. I was hoping you could get us to the depot in Springfield. After we take Libby, that is."

"Of course; Ethel will prepare food for the journey and Josiah will drive you. Once you are on the train you should be safe. How will you get Libby?"

Dr. Wyatt stood. "I believe Dr. Fletcher and I can help. Reverend Packard, like the worst of masters, has separated his children from their mother, enslaving both in deplorable conditions. Our divine mission is to lead slaves to freedom. God has given us this opportunity to free Elizabeth's child. We cannot desert her. We must emancipate Libby, even if force be necessary."

He scanned the room. "Dr. Fletcher and I will distract the reverend outside the parsonage while you ladies go in the backdoor and spirit Libby into the wagon. Then Josiah will drive you to Springfield. I have instructed Josiah to hitch the horse to the wagon."

I thought the plan weak, but I had no alternative to offer.

I had forgotten about Ethel until I heard her sharp voice behind us. "You have no right to take Libby from her father. She is not a slave. Her father loves her and protects her, even from—" She stood in the doorway, her hands clasped in front of her. Her sharp eyes cut past her brother and landed on Mrs. Packard. "—her insane mother."

For a moment I believed she was going to strike Mrs. Packard. I rose from my chair and grasped her arm. "Ethel, please—"

She shook off my hand and continued her condemnation of Mrs. Packard. "I have kept quiet long enough. Your husband was more than willing to care for you and allow you the privilege of raising your children. It is your fault you lost his marital love and your position as wife and mother in his household. Your public espousal of evil ideas was more than he could bear."

Mrs. Packard gawked at Ethel, her mouth open.

All of us stood silent, except for Ethel. "Your husband provided a Christian home for you. Any woman would be proud and blessed to accept the life he offered you. Yet you challenged his ideas, his authority, his rights as a father and your husband. Our Lord dictates the husband is the head of the family."

Ethel's tirade inspired Mrs. Packard to rise from her chair. She held her clenched fists by her sides. Her firm stare never left her accuser. "My husband does not have the right to dictate my thoughts or my beliefs. I answer to no one but my maker."

Ethel lifted a trembling fist between them. "Pastor Packard is the final authority over you and your children."

Mrs. Packard's countenance turned ominous. "I have the God-given right of a mother. I will take Libby with me."

"Not if the authorities finds out. The law gives a child's custody to her father. Besides, who would allow an insane mother to take her child?"

Mrs. Wyatt stepped between the two women. "Please, please, I am sure we all want the same thing. Ethel, you know Reverend Packard will take Elizabeth back to Jacksonville if we do not help her get away."

"That is where she belongs, with the other maniacs."

"Ethel, enough. She is as sane as you or I."

"She is not. Her husband, with divine guidance, took her where he thinks she should be. He told me himself he prayed intensely before he made the decision to commit her."

Mrs. Packard shook her head. "How could you side with him? Do you not see he is unfit as husband or father?"

Ethel stood straight. "You are not fit to be wife or mother."

Dr. Wyatt clutched Ethel's arm. "Sister, how can you defend him? He does not even support our efforts for abolition."

"I do not support your efforts either, but I have kept my beliefs to myself."

"Then why did you leave his church with us?"

"Do you truly believe I had a choice? If I do not agree with you, I am still unable to leave your household. I have nowhere to go. You are my one living relative."

"Ethel, I had no idea you felt this way."

"How would you know my feelings? Have you ever asked me what I believe? Have I not always accepted your authority as the man, the head of the family? Unlike Elizabeth, I have kept my feelings private, unwilling to disrupt the family." Ethel faced Mrs. Packard. "You'll never get her."

The sound of Ethel's words was more than Mrs. Packard could endure. She grabbed Ethel's arms. "I will get Libby. I will—"

Ethel wrenched her shoulders in an attempt to free herself. She could not break Mrs. Packard's grasp. "Let me go. Let me go." Ethel's body went limp. I was sure Mrs. Packard had overcome her.

I could not have been more shocked when Ethel threw her body against her attacker with such force that Mrs. Packard's hands fell away and she was propelled backward. Her head hit the fireplace mantel and she collapsed to the floor. All of us rushed toward Mrs. Packard. I examined her as best I could and did not detect any injury.

Not until we heard the turning of wheels and a loud "Yah" did any of us realize Ethel had run out the door and taken the wagon Josiah had readied for us.

Dr. Wyatt and I ran outside to see the snow kicked up through the wheels' spokes as Ethel sped down the lane toward the parsonage. We could not catch her. Our plan to emancipate Libby could not succeed.

Angelique and Josiah came out of the barn at the sound of our alarmed voices.

Dr. Wyatt gestured toward Josiah. His voice was without expression. "Go to the parsonage and bring the wagon back, Josiah. Ethel won't need it now. I'm sure she has accomplished her mission."

Josiah grabbed a hat off a peg inside the barn door and trudged along the wagon tracks toward the road.

Dr. Wyatt turned to the front door. "The ladies should be ready to go as soon as he brings the wagon back. I'm guessing Pastor Packard will get the authorities as soon as he can."

We entered the hallway and Mrs. Packard ran to Dr. Wyatt. "I will not leave without Libby."

"What do you think will become of you if you stay behind? Do you think your husband will accept you? After his humiliation?"

"He will have to take me back. I cannot lose my baby."

"Elizabeth, he will take you back to Jacksonville. He believes you are a danger to Libby, that you will lead her to eternal damnation. He will not let you mother her and most certainly he will not let you remain free."

"If I promise to be the mate he wants, maybe—"

"How long will you last as the wife he wants? God made you unable to keep still if you are forced to accept beliefs not your own. You will begin to counter him and he will lock you up again."

Mrs. Packard dropped to her chair. She stared into the fire, her body motionless. "I have no reason to go on."

Ginny and Pearl crossed the carpet to Mrs. Packard. The corners of her lips rose slightly when Ginny raised her arms to be lifted onto her lap.

Once again, Pearl knew how to help Mrs. Packard. "I'd hate me and Ginny to go to New York without you."

"If I can help you with Ginny, I will come with you. I have nowhere else to go."

Pearl wrapped a shawl over Mrs. Packard's shoulders. "Ready when you are, Doc."

Not long after, we heard the crunch of snow under the wagon's wheels. Dr. Wyatt and I went outside to find Josiah sitting on the wagon's seat, holding the reins loosely.

Dr. Wyatt patted the horse's rump. "Any trouble?"

"Naw. Wagon sittin' by iself in front of the barn. Didn't hang round long enough to see a body. Jest pulled out quick."

I watched Josiah with curiosity. The successful execution of our plan depended on a man I knew little about. "How did Josiah come to live on your property?"

"After slave catchers caught him crossing one of our fields they returned him to his owner in Kentucky. His master's will made provisions for Josiah's freedom. He remembered our farm and has been living here ever since. In exchange for use of the shanty and a share of the crops' harvest, he works on our homestead. He takes many risks as a conductor on the Underground Railroad."

While the ladies settled into the wagon I took Angelique aside. "Do not go to the parsonage. Mrs. Packard has agreed to the futility of trying to take her daughter, but she is distraught. I do not know what she may try to do. Do not let her dissuade you from going directly to Springfield. Turn right at the road."

"Sure, Doc. Don't fret none. I'll take care of it."

I offered my hand. "Good-bye Angelique. Take the utmost care."

I saw a glint in Angelique's eyes I did not understand. She grabbed my hand and shook it with vigor. "Mighty nice travelin' with ya, Doc."

The Wyatts and I watched the wagon head over the white lane. My stomach tightened when the horse stopped at the road longer than I thought necessary. I did not speak until Josiah guided the horse right and headed for Springfield. "Time for me to get back to Jacksonville, Doctor. I'll go harness Junior."

"I'll prepare something for you to eat." Mrs. Wyatt squinted in the direction of the road. "Who is that man coming down the lane?"

A man wearing a black coat and hat followed one of the wagon wheel's ruts headed in our direction. I soon recognized his manner and then his face. "Angelique, what are you doing here?"

Her face was pink with cold, her movements full of energy. "Josiah don't need no help getting' them to Springfield. Never wanted to go to New York, anyway. 'Sides, I ain't sure you can get back to Jacksonville by yourself. Took two of us to get here. Prob'ly take two of us to get back."

CHAPTER FOURTEEN

Angelique and I did not mind Junior's easy pace on our way home. The windless day was cold and bright. The trail we had left when we arrived at the Wyatt homestead was clearly visible. We were confident our way to Jacksonville would be free of obstacles.

The heat of the sun in the cloudless sky and the rocking of the wagon created a sense of quiet peace. Only the sound of Angelique's voice interrupted my contemplation. "That Ethel's no Christian, if you ask me. She spouts the words all right. Keepin' a ma from her baby—that just ain't right."

"I don't think any of us expected her to act the way she did."

"Bein' the way I am, I run into a lot of her kind, talking about Christian love and all. Whenever I'd say I weren't gonna marry, they'd really start prayin'. I heard a lot about how God meant for a woman to take care of her husband, stay behind him. Didn't sound like God's will to me. Sounds like some man wantin' a woman to do all the grunt work. If you don't do it they talk about the devil being in you. Treat you right hurtful."

"What would make Ethel betray Mrs. Packard?"

"Don't make no sense unless she's moonin' over that reverend. Why else would she take his side? Mighty hard for her to stay with Doc and Mrs. Wyatt now. Losin' her home over some man. Whoooeee!"

"Their family will never be the same."

"Doc and the Mrs. is good people. Didn't bat an eye at my clothes."

"What do you mean?"

"I can pass for a fella all right, except for one thing. Ain't nothin' manly about my voice. Been tryin' to stay quiet this trip. Finally had to talk to them about Junior and all. Even so, they acted the same as they did before I said a word."

"Maybe they thought you were a boy who had not reached his manhood."

"Could be. Maybe I can get away with speakin' until I start to get wrinkles."

"People will wonder if you drank from the fountain of youth."

"Joke's on them, huh?"

"Do you intend to live as a boy?"

Angelique watched the scant trail. "Can't say. All I know is it feels right good to wear these clothes and not have to do up my hair."

"You surely look and act like a boy."

"After what we been through on this here trip, I feel like I can measure up to any man."

"Anyone, male or female, should be proud to have done what you did. You rescued all of us."

I sensed Angelique felt as I did—settled in our accomplishment, proud in our success. We had delivered the ladies to Farmington through the most difficult of circumstances.

The sun moved steadily across the sky. Angelique turned her head toward me. "Something I been wonderin', Doc. How'd you come to be in Jacksonville? I lived around here all my life and I ain't never heard of ya."

My arrival in Illinois had been a short time ago, yet I felt years away from the beginning of my journey to the West. The young man I had been on the train from New York no longer existed. "I lived with my sister, Sarah, in Seneca Falls. I had a medical practice I wasn't very happy in, but never thought of doing much else. The doctor I apprenticed with learned of the need for a medical doctor in the asylum and asked me if I was interested. I agreed to take the position and came by train to the hospital."

"So you came out here and took the job sight unseen?"

"I did. I had no idea what I was getting into."

"Just like the rest of us."

"I could not begin to claim my situation was the same as yours and the other patients'."

"Naw, you weren't no patient, but you did yer best to help us. Whole lot more than Dr. McFarland and Matron Ritter. Talk about devils."

"I never guessed what they were capable of. Dr. McFarland can be very convincing when he speaks of the mission of the hospital and the effectiveness of his cures. When I observed the results of his practices I started to question the asylum's treatment of patients. I was unsure what to do about my doubts until circumstances led me to action."

"You mean when you saw what they were doin' to that little Georgia? Hiding her with Judd and helpin' her go home with Mrs. Jenkins?"

I jerked my head in Angelique's direction. "How did you know about that?"

"You're forgetting us patients know ever'thing about that place. We got nothing else to do except keep an eye out. I can't believe how people that work in the hospital miss things right in front of 'em."

"What do you mean?"

"Well, take Pearl. She moved outta Ward Three purty fast. Before you knew it she was up in Ward One. Doc McFarland even bragged about how she wasn't crazy no more. Didn't you think it was kinda funny she was cured so fast?"

"I did notice Pearl made tremendous progress. I saw her when she was admitted. She was quite out of control."

"Pearl's a smart one. She learned right away who was really runnin' the place so she saw her opportunity and took it."

"What are you talking about?"

"She knew if she let Charles have his way with her, she'd move up in no time. Like I said, she's a smart one."

My stomach tightened at the thought of Pearl using her body to get what she wanted.

Pearl's actions did not trouble Angelique. "Don't blame her none. She did what she had to do."

The chaos of the storm was past. A lone hawk glided over the fields seeking prey. Only the crunch of the wagon's wheels on the frozen snow broke the silence until Angelique spoke. "What ya gonna do now, Doc?"

A slight laugh escaped me. "No idea, Angelique. All I am sure of is that I must take Junior and this wagon back to the stable."

I did not know what lay ahead of me, except that I had no desire to go back East. I loved my sister, but our paths were diverging. She did not need me, nor I her. To return to the asylum for any reason was a risk to my freedom. I was sure Dr. McFarland and Matron Ritter saw my challenge of their practices as a symptom of insanity. The sheriff would not hesitate to assist them in committing me. Their attempts to cure me would undoubtedly take years.

In spite of my uncertain future, my soul was light. The asylum was one small space in a vast land where no one had heard of Dr. Adam Fletcher. I had nowhere to go. No one expected me. The rocking of the wagon, my pleasant companion, and the clear landscape was all I was sure of, and I was content.

Angelique leaned against the back of the seat. "You need to get outta Jacksonville. The sheriff's gonna want to question you 'bout how you left the same time three maniac women busted out."

"I am sure Sheriff Paxson knew I lied to him. I have no doubt he would put me in jail for helping our friends get out."

"Why is he so hell-bent on catchin' Pearl? I heard he set her up in a little house for himself on the outside. Can't he get another one of those girls?"

"His anger was a matter of manly pride. She decided to work at Maude's to earn money to run away from him. He wanted her for himself."

"Is Ginny his kin?"

"Pearl says he is her father. She is fiercely loyal to that little girl. He does not care about the child at all, except as a means to punish Pearl."

Angelique shook her head. "I ain't missing anything, keepin' away from men, present company excepted."

"What about you? What are you going to do?"

"Don't rightly know. Sure like to find some land I can farm. Workin' the fields makes me peaceful. One thing's sure, though: I ain't taking these clothes off." Angelique's jaw tightened. "Ever since I can remember, I hated them stupid dresses. Ma couldn't git me to pick up a needle. Couldn't stand to be around my sisters and their foolishness. Happiest when I worked outside with my brothers and Pa. I could clear brush, fell trees, and harvest crops better than any of 'em."

"How did you come to be committed to the asylum?"

A trace of sadness skimmed across Angelique's face. "Coulda been like Ethel, if I'd acted like a lady. After my sisters and brothers left home to get married, I stayed and took care of Ma and Pa. Then they passed, and my brothers split up the homestead. Seeing as it was rightfully left to them, they began to farm it. Didn't want me livin' with them. Said I didn't act like a woman should. As far as they was concerned I ain't never been right. Thought somebody actin' like me gotta be a lunatic. Doc McFarland agreed with them."

I recalled the careful attention Sarah and I had given to each other after the death of each of our parents. The deep loss we felt brought us closer. Because Angelique was an embarrassment to them, her siblings disregarded her grief at the loss of their parents, and forced her from the only home she had ever known into a residence of suffering. "Many patients are put in the hospital because their families don't want them, not because they are insane."

"Never thought most of us in Jacksonville was crazy. Take Lizzie. She's a bit feistier than ladies like her. Most of 'em don't speak up against their husbands, or any man for that matter. Speaking yer mind ain't no reason to get locked up, man or woman." Angelique grinned. "She sure let Dr. McFarland have it a few times. His face blew up and got right red when she'd keep at him about goin' home. Tried to sweet-talk her into agreeing with him. He thought she was a weakling like his wife, prob'ly."

I smiled at the trouble Mrs. Packard had brought to Dr. McFarland. Her challenge of his authority had interrupted the smooth operation of his institution, as well as his reputation as a well-intentioned healer. "Mrs. Packard did infuriate him."

"She's a true Christian lady. Saw being in Ward Three as a chance to help those poor souls. None of the patients listened to nobody else but her."

"I have the utmost respect for her."

"Ward Three can do things to you. Purty near convinced me I was loony."

"You are perfectly sane, Angelique."

"I thank ya for that, Doc."

The image of Angelique holding the bloody knife she had used to stab Charles came to mind. The painful rejection she had experienced on the outside did not compare to the violence she had endured on the inside.

"You are especially strong to have withstood such cruelty from Charles."

Angelique flipped the reins on Junior's rump. "Don't think I ever thanked you proper for carrying me outta Jacksonville. If it wasn't for you and Lizzie, I'd still be locked up or worse. Hate to think what they woulda done to me for killing Charles. Some might say I'm evil to kill a man. I can't say I regret it."

"You saved yourself and countless others who suffered from Charles's actions."

"Ain't had time to think about it much. Been kinda busy."

We stared lazily at the setting sun. The necessity of rescuing the ladies had kept at bay whatever demons we both faced.

We came into Jacksonville several hours past sunset. The stable's door was wide open, the lone business open. The man who had rented the wagon to me looked up as Angelique pulled up to the door. "Found yourself a boy to drive you, huh?"

Angelique and I jumped to the ground while the stable hand took the reins. "Sure did. I wouldn't have gotten through the storm last night without him."

"Where'd you go?"

"I had to deliver some goods to Farmington. The weather made the trip pretty rough."

"Heard that. How'd Junior do for ya?"

"He did his job well. I believe he's ready for a good long rest."

"He'll git it. Maude sent one of the girls down this evenin' to pay for it. Thanks for yer business."

I tipped my hat to him and turned to Angelique, assuming she was standing behind me. She was gone. My eyes searched up and down the street, but the darkness limited my vision. I did not see anyone in the road. The wagon creaked as the stable hand pulled it inside the barn and unhitched Junior. I had no idea why Angelique had left so abruptly or where she was headed. She had disappeared.

The night chill reminded me I could not stand outside much longer. I remembered I had left my carpet-bag at Maude's. More from having nowhere else to go than for the need to retrieve my paltry belongings, I walked down the empty street behind Maude's.

Maude answered my knock. "Doc, how'd it go? Worried about you in that storm. Get in here and sit by the fire. Josie'll get you some stew."

The aroma of simmering meat and the warmth of the kitchen made me light-headed. I remembered I had not slept the night before and had eaten little.

Josie dipped a ladle into the iron pot hanging over the coals. Her eyes remained downcast as she filled my wooden bowl.

The embers in Maude's kitchen resembled those in the Wyatts's hearth. Josie maintained a household, albeit a different kind than the pious abode of an abolitionist family. If Ethel had not had family she might have been forced to take employment in a place like Maude's. Or, like Angelique, found herself in the asylum.

Maude stared at me as if assessing my condition. After some time she stood and pulled a bottle of whiskey from the larder.

"Here, this'll bring your strength back."

The whiskey felt hot inside my chest.

Maude continued her interrogation. "What happened on your way to Farmington? The sheriff's been in here a couple of times, askin' if I seen Pearl and why Ginny wasn't around. Told him those temperance ladies took her to the orphanage in St. Louis. He ain't no friend of those ladies, so I don't think he'll be asking them any questions."

"We got out of town easily, thanks to Angelique. She was right; everyone who saw her thought she was a young boy. The hardest part was getting through the blizzard. We got lost, but Angelique pulled us through."

"She's somethin' all right."

"She has vanished. I do not know where she is and I am concerned about her survival. She has no family to welcome her."

"Wouldn't worry none about her if I was you. Angelique can take care of herself. What happened to the other two?"

"One of Mrs. Packard's acquaintances betrayed her to Reverend Packard. Since he knew of her intent to take her daughter, any attempts to get her would have been hopeless. We feared he would try to detain her and send for the authorities to bring her back to the asylum. She reluctantly agreed to go with Pearl and Ginny to the train depot in Springfield."

"Sorry to hear that. She was sure set on gettin' her girl."

Maude poured more whiskey into my glass and I gulped it down. My vision narrowed and the light from the fireplace became hazy. I was barely able to hold my head up.

"The sheriff's not the only one lookin' for you. Henry's been here. Said I should let him know if you showed up."

My words blurred. "Henry, all for one, one fo—"

"Why don't you grab some sleep? Your bag's in the corner next to the cot. You can bunk in here tonight. I'll send somebody out in the morning to tell Henry you're here."

I walked unsteadily to the dark corner where the small bed sat. My eyes were half-closed as I lay down. Before consciousness left me, I felt the weight of a cover fall on me.

Vigorous shaking of my shoulder woke me too soon. "Well, if it ain't one of the three musketeers—a little worse for wear, I'd say. If I didn't know better I'd say you been on some toot."

I sat up on one elbow to see Henry leaning over me. "When did you get here?"

"Few minutes ago. Maude filled me in about the ladies. Said you had a bumpy ride to Farmington." Henry pulled a chair up to the edge of the cot. "Gettin' pretty tough for an easterner, ain't ya?"

I did not know if my sore head was a result of the whiskey or his sharp rousing. "If you had told me what was in store for me a few months ago I would not have believed you."

"You sure got a way of bein' in the middle of things. What you gonna to do now?"

I shifted my legs over the side of the bed. "I have no idea. I do not want to go home to New York. Yet, given the sheriff's interest in me, I best not remain in Jacksonville."

Henry pulled a folded paper from his pocket. "Kinda figured you wouldn't want to go back East. Saw this at the train station. Thought you might find it interestin'."

I opened a circular telling of a wagon train leaving for California from St. Louis. The flyer stated that after they were outfitted, settlers interested in going west would leave St. Louis after the first thaw. In addition to further details, small print at the bottom said the trail boss was hiring people to organize the trip.

"I have never been on a wagon train."

Henry sat up straight. "Always thought I'd go someday. To tell ya the truth, I'm pretty well set at the farm. Kinda call my own shots and all. Besides, I'd hate to leave some of those fine girls in the kitchen. A young fella like you could use a little adventure. What ya got to lose?"

"I don't even have enough money for a train ticket to St. Louis, and certainly not enough to outfit myself to travel such a long distance."

"Maybe you could sign on to work for the trail boss."

"What would I do? I don't know anything about driving wagons across the plains."

Henry bent to the floor and reached behind him. He twisted around with my medical bag in his hand. I had not thought to retrieve it from the asylum during my hasty exit.

"Heard they always need doctors on those trips."

"But—"

Henry set the bag next to me. "I got to get back. If you decide to go, you got ever'thing you need in that bag."

We shook hands and said our good-byes.

I slumped down on the cot. Josie was serving biscuits to a girl hunched over the table. I smelled bacon, but I was not hungry. Go on a wagon train as a doctor? I wondered if the trail boss would hire me, and if I had the endurance for such a trip.

I had voyaged into the unknown before. I had left everything familiar in New York to seek a promising professional opportunity in Illinois. I accepted a position I believed secure, only to find unforeseen challenges that forced me to conquer hazards I never dreamed of. Traveling farther west without purpose or destination would be full of uncertainty.

An emptiness rose within me, but the vacuum contained no dread or fear. Instead, glimmers of anticipation seeped into the void.

I raised my unfocused eyes and opened the black bag. On top of my medical instruments sat a silver dollar, and underneath it, a train ticket to St. Louis.

Henry was right. I had everything I needed.

CHAPTER FIFTEEN

February 27, 1858
My Dearest Brother,

I was so pleased to receive your letter, Adam. I hope this response will reach you in St. Louis before you leave for parts unknown. I understand primitive travel over the vast plains is unpredictable. Even so, I hope you will not forget your devoted sister and write frequently.

Your telegram instructing me to pick up packages at the train depot was most confusing until I discussed it with my friends who are dedicated abolitionists. They assured me your message contained code telling of the arrival of fugitive slaves. On the days you instructed I went to the station and awaited the Chicago train most anxiously.

My first trip to the depot I was sorely disappointed to see all disembarking passengers met by those waiting on the platform. On the following day I returned to see all passengers, black and white, picked up immediately except for two unaccompanied women and a small child. They waited after the train departed, their eyes searching up and down the platform.

When it became apparent they were the only ones left, I approached the small party.

The older woman spoke to me first. "Are you Miss Fletcher?

When I nodded, she said, "Your brother Adam has sent us."

I was startled to find your "packages" were not slaves escaping to freedom. I wondered why such ladies traveled in secrecy, but I sensed they were in need of assistance. I was happy to welcome them into our home.

In our conversations over many evenings, Elizabeth and Pearl revealed the horrors they had endured in the asylum. Elizabeth has told me much about her vile husband. His attempt to take her freedom was surpassed by his success at keeping her family from her. It is hard to believe a so-called man of God would perpetuate such horrors on the mother of his offspring. Her heart is broken. She will never stop grieving for her children.

Elizabeth's unfortunate plight is not unknown to my acquaintances who are working to improve the lot of women. Many abolitionists are committed to women's rights as well. I have taken Elizabeth to hear Susan B. Anthony speak. We were both quite taken with her and the ideas she proposes.

Pearl is not as forthcoming about her past and the reason she was in the hospital. I gather she did not have the protection of family or home. Although not well-bred, Pearl is a sincere girl and devoted to Ginny. The child is blossoming, I believe, due to the constant attention we three ladies give her. She is speaking very clearly and does not hesitate to make her wants known. I do not know how she will help but be spoiled with so much attention thrust on her.

Both Elizabeth and Pearl speak of you with the utmost respect. They consider you their savior, rescuing them from the hell of that hospital. I have always thought you had wonderful intentions, Adam. I had no idea you were capable of such bravery. I am proud of you.

Elizabeth has obtained a teaching position in a community nearby and with our two salaries we live in reasonable comfort. For her contribution, Pearl insists on taking care of the household. After many culinary disasters, she has become a passable cook, keeping our home in wonderful order. Given the opportunity and the encouragement of her housemates, she is learning to read. Almost every night, after Ginny is in bed, I find her sitting near the fire deciphering another reader.

All of us are devoted to the women's rights movement. Elizabeth has even been asked to speak to sympathetic gatherings about her experiences in Illinois. Our struggle is a difficult one, fraught with criticism from others and discouragement. Whenever we think of abandoning the cause, we think of dear Ginny. It is she who gives us reason to persevere.

So, little brother, your plan to bring Elizabeth and Pearl to me has succeeded. They are now our sisters and are safe.

I must thank you, as well. You have rescued me from the loneliness I felt at your departure. Your "packages" have become my family and we are utterly at ease living together.

I am sorry your position in Jacksonville ended badly. Who would have surmised the true nature of the asylum or its superintendent? The tone of your letter was optimistic and I hope you find God's blessing on your new journey.

I send my love and deep affection from Elizabeth and Pearl.

Your loving sister,

Sarah

March 3, 1858
Dear Doc,

I knowd you didn't 'spect me to answer yer letter, but here it is.

You didn't need to send money fer that train ticket. It was nothin' but one musketeer helping another.

Big changes here in the house. So far Judd and me's kept the farm workin' the same. Doc McFarland and the matron have skedaddled.

Seems one of the former patients has an uncle on the hospital's Board of Trustees. She told him how patients were treated around here. It was Ada Jenkins who sicced the board on Doc and the matron. I never picked her to be the kind to get even. They shoulda been nicer to Georgia.

After the first of the year the trustees and the governor hisself came waltzin' right through the front door. Brought some Pinkertons in to study ever'thing. They didn't like the looks of Ward Three. Lotta people in the holdin' chairs, chained to the walls. Patients still not gettin' full rations. Lots of 'em pretty skinny.

Guess the doc's bank account was pretty hefty. One of the girls on the inside overheard a detective askin' how he was able to live so fancy when the patients were gettin' nothin' but soup and bread. They was pretty sure he was paid off to take some patients off their rich kin's hands. Trustees fired him and the matron on the spot.

McFarlands left town that day, 'cept for Hayes and Lucy, that is. Hayes's workin' for a lawyer in Jacksonville. I was glad to hear that. Ya never know when you might need one of them fellas. Lucy refused to go with her ma and pa. She's stayin' with Hayes.

Ran into Hayes at Maude's the other night. Had a coupla whiskeys so his tongue was pretty loose. Told me his ma and pa moved in with her folks in Bloomington. Didn't take long for the doc to start drinkin' pretty heavy. Appears her people never did like him much. Decided they didn't want no unemployed drunk on their hands. Hayes went up to git him and took him to a place for lunatics in Indiana. I had to laugh when he called it a rest home.

Stable hand in town heard Matron Ritter was dealin' cards on a riverboat until one of the sharks caught her cheatin'. Kicked her off in St.

Louis and put her in jail. She didn't have nowhere else to go when her time was up, so they let her stay in one of the empty cells. Scrubbin' floors for the jailer.

The new superintendent's purty good. I noticed the patients are roamin' the grounds more often. Hard to know what's really goin' on in there. One of the kitchen girls told me they upped the food for the inmates right away. She's a sweet gal. Been spendin' some time with her behind the barn.

Better close now. My fingers are gettin' right sore with all this writin'.

Oh yeah, one more thing you might be wonderin' 'bout. The day I got back from seein' you at Maude's I was puttin' Juanita in the barn when I noticed smoke comin' outta that deserted cabin the other side of the corn-field. I showed it to ya once. Been there as long as anybody can remember. As far as I knowd just squirrels lived in it, so I was surprised to see a sign of human life. I walked over and around to the back of the shack. You coulda blown me over with a feather when I seen Angelique splittin' fire wood. She looked up at me with those dark eyes and said just as purty as you please, "Evenin', Henry." Dressed in the clothes I gave her and the other gals the night they took off.

Turns out she knew how it was abandoned and all. Said she planned to stay in it and asked if I could use some help now and then. I ain't never had nothin' against Angelique, so I went along with it. 'Course I gotta keep her whereabouts to myself since she's officially wanted as an escapee. I take her supplies sometimes. Always pays me back with firewood or somethin' from her garden. She can work harder than any man I know. Content just bein' left alone.

My hand's really startin' to cramp up so I'll say good-bye. Don't you forget, if you need somebody in these parts, I'm yer man. As they say, one for all and all for one.

Your friend,
Henry

The End

Acknowledgments

Appreciation goes to everyone who read and commented on *For Their Own Good* along the way, especially the Attic Girls for their critiques and friendship, to family and friends who encouraged me, to Curtis Veach and Lori Sanchez-Vera who traveled miles with me, and to my husband who is always in my corner. Thanks Mike.

More books from Harvard Square Editions

People and Peppers, Kelvin Christopher James
Gates of Eden, Charles Degelman
Living Treasures, Yang Huang
Close, Erika Raskin
Anomie, Jeff Lockwood
Transoceanic Lights, S. Li
Nature's Confession, J.L. Morin
A Little Something, Richard Haddaway
Dark Lady of Hollywood, Diane Haithman
Fugue for the Right Hand, Michele Tolela Myers
Growing Up White, James P. Stobaugh
Calling the Dead, R.K. Marfurt
Parallel, Sharon Erby